The Preacher's Daughter

Kendra Dunn

www.lafemmefataleproductions.com

Published by La' Femme Fatale' Productions

Library of Congress Catalog Card No: In publication data
ISBN: 978-0-9792656-7-9
        0-9792656-7-3
Copyright: @2010 by La' Femme Fatale' Productions
The Preachers' Daugher:
Written by: Kendra Dunn
Cover Design: www.oddballdsgn.com
Model: Candace Christian: Cchristian06@yahoo.com
Edited by: Michelle West: Miamorjeans@yahoo.com
Publicist: Alicia Brown
Text Formation: Ni'cola Mitchell

Published by
La' Femme Fatale' Productions
9900 Greeenbelt Road
Suite E-333
Lanham, Maryland 20706
www.lafemmefataleproductions.com

Acknowledgments

First and foremost, I must thank God for making everyday a blessing and receiving day, for arranging things in my favor and for helping me to understand that on the other side of every set back is an opportunity. Each day I thank Him for the seen and the unseen—knowing that my biggest dream isn't as vast as the plan He has for my life.

To my Uncle Rick (I feel the tears coming), God placed you in my life to be the father that I never had. Your love, support and guidance have shaped me into the woman I am today and I am eternally grateful. I love you more than you could ever imagine. To my Aunt Diane, please know that I love and appreciate you equally. You two raised me as your own and I will forever be indebted to your selflessness. You all may not agree with my every endeavor, but your love and support never wavers. There's comfort in knowing that at anytime I can always come back home. Thank you and I love you both will all of my heart.

To my little brothers, Lil' Rick and Dalton, thanks for all of your love and support also. Lil' Rick, I am so proud of you. You have grown into a responsible young man (if you and Brooke could just stop breaking up every other day…lol). Also, Lil' Rick, attending college is a dream that many young men have but don't ever see come true. I hope that you realize the sacrifice your parents are making for you to receive a college education. Continue to make us proud! Dalton, I did it! You were my biggest supporter—always inquiring about my progress on the book. You can be anything that you want to be from the next Iron Chef to a star running back in the NFL. Just be all that you can be!

To my mother, Rita, thank you for realizing what was best for me and allowing me to hop on that plane when I was just fifteen-years-old. If it was not for your foresight and courage to make such a decision, this work of fiction could have easily been my reality. I love you with all of my heart too...don't ever doubt it.

Brandy, my sister, life has so much to offer than what you're settling for. I love you and my bad (but cute) nephew, Bubba.

To my big bro', Dr. Terrance Hughes, thanks for all of the great advice and for listening to me go on and on...sometimes about nothing at all. Still, you laugh and you listen. Thanks for your support and I love you more than you will ever know. To my advisor and strong-willed Aunt Lolethia Chapman, JD/MBA, in the past few years you have played an instrumental role in shaping my future as a business woman. Your wisdom and insight are invaluable. Thank you and Aunt Shirley for your guidance, love and support. I love you both.

Special thanks to my God sister, mentor, friend and attorney, Phillis Rambsy, Esq. Thanks for all that you have done for me—from the legal aspect to being an example of the ultimate Don Diva to letting me crash at your place for months at a time...love ya!

Camille, we're both on our way. Me the writer; you the director. It's on! Dawn...chick, no more black Fridays! Where there is a road blocked...there's a detour. Your name will be suffixed with Esq. sooner than later. Tiffany, on any given day your life is as action packed as an...urban fiction novel! Your courage to live your life under your own terms is inspiring. Love you and Chip.

To Michele Fletcher and the La` Femme Fatale` family, I am truly excited and grateful for this opportunity. Michele, in this day in age, you don't find too many publishers willing to take the time to develop a writer and also teach him or her more about the business side of publishing. In such a short time with La` Femme I have learned a lot. Thank you and I appreciate your willingness.

To all of my family and friends unnamed, you know who you are and all of you have had an impact on my life in one way or another. Thank you and I love you all.

Thank you in advance to my fans in the making. Stick with me and I'll try never ever to let you down! Also, hit me up on Facebook and MySpace. Check me out on You Tube and follow me on Twitter. And don't forget to write your review of the book!

Finally, to those who judge a book by its' genre…don't miss the message! Enjoy.

From My Heart to Yours,
Kendra Dunn

Dedication

This book is dedicated to my late Uncle DL—the king of swag. You are greatly missed.

The Preacher's Daughter

Chapter 1

Part One

TEENAGE LOVE AFFAIR

"Babygirl, you're gonna be a heartbreaker."

Those were the very first words Slay had ever spoken to me. I was twelve then, just a little girl with two braided ponytails, one on each side of my head that stretched down my back. My great grandmother's genes had skipped everyone in my family except for me. She was Black and Native American and my great-grandfather was Nigerian. His blood was strong and as generations passed, the percentage of red blood running through the veins of my maternal bloodline decreased significantly. There wasn't another sighting of a female in our family with my great-grandmother's physical traits until the day I was born—with a head full of jet-Black hair and clay-colored skin.

Growing up, other females always called me lucky. I was exempt from a lifetime of getting a perm every six to eight weeks to straighten my hair but I didn't like to think of myself as lucky, just blessed I suppose.

My mother, out of fear that some jealous broad would take a pair of scissors and cut off my crown and glory, never let me wear my hair down. At fourteen, I talked her into letting me wear one braid instead of two; I was tired of walking around looking like Pippi Longstocking. At sixteen, I just started leaving the house with my hair down. My mother never said a word. I was growing up—my body faster than my mind and niggas were starting to stare holes in my jeans, including Slay.

My father's church was on one end of the block and Slay conducted his business on the other. It was a street that, depending on which direction you were going, led you to heaven or to hell.

"Don't ever let me catch you down on that corner." My father forbid me to travel to hell. "They're up to no good down there. I don't want any of those thugs bothering my little girl."

At the time, I didn't have the fortitude to tell my father that as a disciple of the Lord, down on the corner is exactly where he needed to be—slinging scriptures as the dope boys slung rocks.

Slay had waited until I was seventeen, about to round the corner to eighteen, before officially inviting me into his world. I was a senior in high school and the year was sailing smoothly. Although, I was exhausted from fielding questions about my future from classmates, teachers and my parents. My grades and ACT score guaranteed me a scholarship into any college or university I applied to. Staying home, close to home or moving away was a tug of war for me. I'd never been away from my parents or little sister for longer than a week at a time, only when I attended summer camp or traveled for a school-related trip. The other part of me wanted to get away from them as far as gravity would allow. I should've been more careful for what I wished for.

Outside, after school one day—amongst the sea of yellow buses—was a candy-apple red 1968 Cadillac Deville Convertible sitting on solid gold twenty-four inch rims. A crowd of wide-eyed teenagers, boys and girls, stared at the machine in amazement as loud thunderous beats blared from the car's speakers. Of course, everyone who lived in the hood knew who the driver was. My father's church was in the hood so I knew too. I walked into the crowd, disobeying my father's commandment—no fraternizing with "thugs."

"Get in." Slay was talking to me. He reached over and opened the passenger side door. I obeyed him and got in the Deville.

We sped off in silence, driving blocks before a word was said.

"What took you so long?" I asked.

"Was waitin," he said, leaning back in his seat and steering the car with one hand.

"For what?"

"For you to grow up."

"I'm not grown."

Slay took his eyes off the road and looked at me with wanting eyes. I was seventeen, but my body was in its' twenties. I kept his stare. He read my mind.

"If that's all I wanted…I would have took it a long time ago," he said.

"You would have violated me?"

"Wouldn't have needed to. You would have easily given it up."

Slay was aware of his power—in the streets and over me. He was right. I would have taken my own panties off and served myself to him on an all-you-can-eat platter. I had been thinking about it since that moment when I was twelve.

"I have a boyfriend."

"You talkin' 'bout Mike…that fake ass, high school, wanna-be-baller nigga? You sleepin' with him?"

"You have a girlfriend."

I wasn't asking a question, I was making a statement. Aleesha was Slay's older, live-in steady. She was thirty-seven, ten years older than him. He treated her like shit, from what I could see, and there was no real reason to believe that he would treat me any different.

"You sleepin' with him?" Slay asked again. This time with fury in his tone, as if our future depended on the answer.

I told the truth. "No."

"You lyin' to me, Shar?" He addressed me by my first name—a sign that I would learn indicated that he was upset with me.

"No…" I hesitated, not knowing if he would haul off and blacken my eye for questioning him. "But, what does it matter what I'm doin' when you're givin' Aleesha the business every night? I don't know how naïve you think I am, but…" He cut me off.

"I don't love her. It's just a temporary arrangement and I know you're not naïve. You're more mature than Aleesha and all of those other hood-rat-project chicks out there. You're special, Babygirl. That's why I waited for you. I need someone by my side that I can trust with my money and my life. You hear me talkin' Shar?"

"I hear you talkin'."

Slay didn't fear my father as I did. He pulled in my parents' driveway, music still blaring, and dropped me off just a few feet from the front door. There was no need for discretion on his part. He had decided that I would eventually be his with or without my parents' blessing. All that was needed was my cooperation.

Over the next few months, Slay picked me up every Wednesday after school and gave me a ride home—the only day that I allowed him to because I knew my father would be at church preparing for Bible study while my mother would still be at work. On those days, there weren't any detours to any nearby hotels, abandoned roads or rides to the country. Slay proved himself to be the perfect gentleman. Those short drives to my house lent themselves to minutes of me interrogating Slay about his life. He answered all of my questions without hesitation—even those that would have landed him in jail if a tape recorder was anywhere around. Drugs, money, sex and power—those were the things he lived for.

"Here." He handed me a Nokia flip phone. My parents paid *my* cell phone bill and therefore *my* cell phone records were subject to their scrutiny. Slay knew what he was doing. He'd thought it out.

"Just seeing and speaking to you one day out of the week isn't working for me anymore. Answer when I call."

And if I don't? I wanted to ask, but I knew better than to play with Slay.

He phoned late one Saturday night, requesting that I sneak out of my bedroom window and meet him. He was parked down the street, awaiting my arrival. He was in a canary yellow Cutlass, one of his many treasures on four wheels. I tapped on the window, letting my presence be known before I hopped in the passenger seat.

"If my father catches me out here, he's goin' to kill me."

"He won't."

My shorts left nothing to the imagination. Slay slid his right hand up and down each of my inner thighs. Each stroke landing closer and closer to Ms. Kitty, as I appropriately named my seventeen-year-old vagina. I had talked the talked but never walked the walked. I was a virgin. Ms. Kitty purred. She had never been touched by a man before. I moaned. I was moist down there.

"Did I pee on myself?"

Slay laughed. "Nah, Babygirl, you're just wet. Take your shorts off."

"Right now...here...in the car?"

"I just want to feel you...we don't have to do anything else."

I slid my jean shorts down to my ankles and spread my legs wide open. Slay pushed my panties to the side and entered me with one finger and then two—never removing the .45 caliber from his lap. He penetrated me slow at first and then faster. I couldn't stop what was happening to me. My body jerked and suddenly I was wetter than before. Slay gently removed his fingers from my insides and licked them dry. That shit turned me on.

"You taste like a peach...my favorite fruit."

My silence let him know that I was still savoring the sensation between my legs. He kissed me on the forehead.

"Babygirl, I gotta go...you should get back."

Ms. Kitty wanted more. She was ready for the real deal. Slay saw the desire in my eyes.

"Soon and not like this. I want to make that moment special for you, Babygirl."

Slay was making me feel, in ways both physically and emotionally, like I had never felt before. To soothe my animosity about his and Aleesha's arrangement, I minimized her to being his maid with benefits. She was playing house with my man and I was falling for hers. She did everything for him. She cooked, cleaned, did his laundry, paid his bills and sucked his dick. Slay going home to her had never bothered me before, but to say that I was pissed that he had pleasured me and was now leaving to get that pleasure in return from another woman was an understatement.

Neurotically, I'd rather he be in the line of danger checking on his workers and collecting his day's pay than going home to her. He didn't love her. I believed that. But, he wasn't in a hurry to leave her. She was a woman. I was still a girl.

Pissed, I pulled my shorts up and exited the Cutlass. Slay didn't pull off until I was back in front of my bedroom window. Giving him an ultimatum, Aleesha or me, wasn't an option. No one told Slay what to do, not even me. Besides, I had made a decision; I was going away to college. This time next year, he would be a memory of my past.

I lifted up my bedroom window and climbed in, hitting my elbow on the corner of my dresser drawer. "Fuck."

At the sight and sound of my father's frame swaying back and forth in the same rocking chair my mother rocked me in as a baby located in the corner of my room, I hushed myself.

"Where you been?"

I was unprepared—no lie conjured, no excuse ready.

"Shar, I'm going to ask you one more time. Where…have…you been?"

"Just out…gettin' some fresh air."

"At one o'clock in the morning?"

"Yes, sir, I…I…" I was a terrible liar.

"Don't let this happen again. You're a young lady and I'd like to think that your mother and I raised you to be a respectable one. Climbing in and out of windows in the middle of the night is unacceptable and I won't tolerate it. Do you understand me?"

"Yes, Daddy. I understand."

* * *

Love is powerful and complicated. It is the architect of both peace and war—more war than peace in the streets. The love of money, territory, personal possessions, pussy or dick can corrupt the most virtuous man or woman—no matter the amount of values instilled in him or her since birth. Love can dumb down an educated broad, force her to settle for less than she deserves and manipulate her into risking her freedom and even her life for it. In essence, it can lead a broad to live her life with her heart instead of her mind and that shit's dangerous. Love is so powerful that it can curve a straight path and camouflage wrong as right. I was in love and if loving Slay was wrong...I didn't want to be right. But, I tried to flush him out of my system. At least, I liked to think I did.

Chapter 2

GROWN & SEXY

The Wednesday after my first intimate encounter with Slay, I gave him back the Nokia and told him that I didn't see a future for us—a square and a hustler. I wasn't a DAC, a down ass chick that is. That wasn't me. Risking my freedom for a nigga wasn't in my cards. Love for a hood nigga had a way of destroying a broad's future. I wanted to keep mine intact.

Everything that I wasn't was the reason why he wanted me. I wasn't a hood rat or a project chick. My gear didn't consist of an array of rainbow colored weave or a collection of gold grills—not that anything was wrong with that. It just wasn't my thing. The homely-dressing- preacher's-kid look wasn't me either. My style was a collaboration of the girl-next-door meets the streets meets the boardroom: tailored jackets, fitted tees, skinny jeans, stilettos and always a pair of big-hoop earrings. Occasionally, I would rock a pair of Air Force Ones or some Timbs. I wasn't a gold digger either. There was no need for me to ever scheme to be one. I was raised in a household where a man was the provider and the protector. My nigga, whoever he turned out to be, would take care of me simply because he loved me. Call it naivety, but it was what I believed.

Slay asked if my father had anything to do with my decision not to move forward in lust or love with him. I lied and told him that it was my decision. He leaned over me, opened the passenger side door of the vintage Impala he was driving—another one of his toys on four wheels—and kindly told me to get the fuck out. I did and after that, communication between us ceased. We'd see each other around town and he'd ignore me. I did the same. But, other than Aleesha, he never let me see another broad on his arm.

Graduation rolled around quickly. The day after was my birthday and the following week, I was scheduled to leave early. I had planned on taking some summer classes to get a head start on my peers arriving in the fall. My girls—TaNaysha, Khalilah and me were at the mall shopping for new gear for the big weekend. The three of us had known each other since the second grade. We had been grouped together for a classroom activity and while the other kids were busy playing in paint—making kiddy art for their parents to display on their refrigerators—TaNaysha, Khalilah and I had our lips poked out and our arms folded, pouting. None of us wanted to get our hands dirty or clothes stained. We'd been friends ever since. TaNaysha was straight hood. Khalilah was prissy and I was a little bit of both.

Graduation night, we were all staying over TaNaysha's house, which meant we didn't have a curfew. Her mother, Ms. Trina, was cool as hell. She and TaNaysha were more like sisters than mother and daughter. We planned on partying like it was 2099.

"Don't look now," Khalilah said, pretending to admire a Baby Phat jumpsuit on a nearby mannequin.

I looked. Slay was the color of burnt cinnamon. He was Black and Other. His mother didn't know exactly who his father was, but she had narrowed it down to two Johns—one Cuban and the other Black and Asian. His eyes were slightly slanted but not enough to confirm his ethnicity.

No matter a preacher, drug dealer or the president, broads were attracted to power and money. Both oozed out of Slay. His swagger was intoxicating and his affect on me was that of a foreign substance. *Damn.* Just looking at him got me high. He was looking fresh-to-death—dressed in a plain white tee, wife-beater underneath, Rocawear jean shorts, two-carat diamond studs in each ear, a single platinum chain with a cross dangling in the middle of his chest and a brand new pair of kicks—the Footlocker bag in his hand told me so. He was headed in our direction.

"Shar, I don't know why you playin'. If I had a Nas-lookin' nigga like that tryin' to holla at me…I wouldn't be at the mall with y'all asses now. I'd be somewhere laid up gettin' my shit beat."

"Why you gotta be so foul?"

"Shar, remind me one more time how this bitch became our friend?" TaNaysha asked me, referring to Khalilah.

TaNaysha and Khalilah's bickering didn't faze me. I ignored Slay, pretending to be interested in a pair of skintight jeans. I grabbed a pair—two sizes larger than I normally wore since the brand ran small—and hightailed it to an open dressing room, hoping that when I came out Slay would be gone. He was what I wanted but not what I needed.

There were several items abandoned in the dressing room: a couple of shirts, jeans and dresses. The jeans weren't my size, but I decided to try on the dresses along with the jeans I had. I stripped down to my bra and panties. Slay banged on the dressing room door.

"Babygirl?" He whispered through the hinges of the door.

I didn't answer.

"Babygirl, I know you're in there. Let me in. Please. I miss you. I just want to say hi."

I backed up into the corner of the dressing room like a scared ass white girl about to get killed in a horror flick.

Slay's whisper turned into a loud-and-clear demand.

"Babygirl, open the got damn door or I'll break this shit in two."

Slay didn't wait for me to turn the knob. He didn't break the door down but crawled through the space left open at the bottom of the dressing room door instead.

"What the fuck are you doin'?"

"Babygirl, don't curse at me. Please don't do that. Bitches swear. Babygirl, you're a lady…my lady. My lady doesn't swear."

Funny, I thought when he said that. Before spending time with him, I swore but not as much. My use of profanity had increased since becoming his lady—from listening to him conduct his business, chastise his workers or simply greeting one of his homeboys. It was an unlady like and foul habit but shit, he was my teacher.

Slay grabbed me by my waist and showered my neck with kisses. As hard as it was, I pushed him back and grabbed my shirt and jeans.

"Why you treatin' me like I mean nothin' to you?" He asked.

"Don't you have some drugs to sell or somethin'?"

Slay's hands were around my neck faster than I could let out another breath.

"Don't ever say that shit out loud again. You hear me?"

He wasn't hurting me but letting me know that he could…if pushed. I got the message.

"Babygirl, I love you. Don't you see that? I haven't even hit it yet and I love you. I could care less about the pussy. I just need you to be mine."

He reached in his front right pocket and pulled out a folded wad of hundreds. He handed me ten of them.

"Buy what you want. Get your girls an outfit too." He said, replacing the Nokia I had returned to him with a pink Razor and shoving it in my purse. "Answer when I call."

He left me wanting him more than before. If that was his plan, it had worked.

* * *

TaNaysha, Khalilah and I each left the mall with cash to spare and several outfits to choose from for the club on Saturday night. Receiving our high school diplomas should have been the moment we had anticipated most, but our minds were on the post graduation celebration.

After dinner with my mother, father and little sister I drove my graduation present from my parents—a silver two-door Honda Accord—over to TaNaysha's house for what my parents believed to be a slumber party. Khalilah was already there.

"Hey, Ms. Trina."

"Hey, Arabian Bombshell. Your two partners in crime are in the back."

I quit reminding Ms. Trina a long time ago that I wasn't from anywhere in the Middle East, but all she saw was the tint of orange in my skin and long hair. I thought about getting some Made-In-America stickers and sticking them on my forehead. She wasn't the only one to make the assumption. Everyone thought I was an import.

"Hey, ladies," I said, dropping my overnight bag on the floor by TaNaysha's closet door.

"Hey," they said in unison.

Khalilah, who was known for her promptness, was already dressed in a metallic gold, tube top dress and matching open-toed stilettos. Her shoulder length hair was straightened with a part down the middle. TaNaysha was putting the finishing touches on her ponytail. She had added in some tracks to make it appear fuller. She slipped into a black dress with a plunging neckline, red accessories and shoes. My outfit of choice was a backless, leopard-print cat suit that hugged every curve of my body. It wasn't Halloween but for the night, I was cat woman—unrestrained and dangerously sexy. With summer just a month away, I forwent the patent leather boots normally worn with such an outfit and settled for a pair of black, peep-toe stilettos. I let my natural waves flow, untamed, down my back.

In the car, we debated on going to Club Pulse or The Tap Room. Club Pulse was a hole-in-the-wall club where you had a pulse going in but was lucky to have one coming out. Every other month, somebody's father, son, brother, uncle or cousin was guaranteed to get gun down. The owner, named Greedy, would shut down for a few weeks after a murder and then reopen—not out of respect for the families but to keep the police from sniffing around. He had his mind on his money and his money on his mind. There really wasn't a choice. We were going to The Tap Room, a hip joint for the grown and sexy, owned by two Jewish niggas named Carlo and Frankie. Carlo loved black pussy but wouldn't dare marry it into the family and Frankie was into White broads. Regardless, they were both paid.

The club was packed. The age limit was suppose to be twenty-one and up but smoking aces like me, TaNaysha and Khalilah got in and for free. Plus, Carlo had a little crush on Khalilah and had let us in a time or two before.

As we sashayed through the crowd, niggas were reaching, grabbing and slapping TaNaysha and Khalilah's asses but no one dared to touch me. I wasn't envious of the attention they were receiving. It was just strange not getting any myself. But then, as we walked further into the crowd, niggas were whispering.

"Ain't that Slay's girl?"

The honor evidently came with an invisible, electric collar. Anybody who tried to touch me would get stunned or worse, their throat slashed. Slay didn't garner his nickname without earning it. At fifteen, he was arrested for almost killing one of his mother's Johns. He dissected the man's neck from ear to ear. Niggas on the streets penned him Slay. It stuck.

Miraculously, the man survived and the prosecutor was having a good day when he decided not to try Slay as an adult or charge him with attempted murder. Instead he was sentenced to juvenile detention until he turned eighteen.

We landed at the bar. Khalilah told the bartender that she knew Carlo and he served us without question. TaNaysha ordered a Blue Hurricane, Khalilah a Sex on the Beach and me a Sprite.

"A Sprite. What the hell?" TaNaysha asked. "We came here to have some damn fun. We're grown now."

"Okay, okay." I didn't put up much of a fight, knowing that just a sip of any alcoholic beverage would have my head spinning. I wasn't a drinker and when I did drink, I could never hold my liquor. That's why I seldom drank—that and I hated being out of control. Risking being caught on tape doing some Girls-Gone-Wild shit wasn't worth it, but I had just graduated and my birthday was minutes away. "I'll take a glass of Chardonnay."

My mother drank a glass of white wine every now and then when her First-Lady duties became too much for her to bear and when she needed to relax.

"Chardonnay?" TaNaysha put her hands on her hips. "Give us all a shot of Tequila. Hell, we gettin' drunk tonight…make it two shots each," TaNaysha yelled to the bartender over the music.

We downed the shots. I gulped down the glass of Chardonnay, ordered another and we continued our stroll around the club. The alcohol had niggas feeling good, a few brave souls brushed up on me. I wasn't feeling any of them but directly in my path was Mike, my parents-approved boyfriend. I'd broken up with him when Slay started hitting on me. He and I had never been intimate. We kissed a few times and I allowed him to slip his hand underneath my shirt and feel me up a few times. But, he never made me jerk, twitch or gush like Slay had done.

"You lookin' fly, Mami."

Mike wasn't Puerto Rican or hood. His practiced street lingo humored me.

"Thanks, Papi." I played along, hugging him.

"You wanna dance?"

Mike was oblivious to Slay's existence in my life. We hit the dance floor and we danced to two fast songs before the deejay slowed it down and took it back a few years. He played Usher's *Nice and Slow*. The alcohol was getting to me. It rendered me uninhibited and I gave my best amateur strip show right there on the dance floor. I grinded on Mike so hard that his dick was standing at attention. Anyone who was looking could see Ms. Kitty's print pulsating through my cat suit. I dropped to my knees, my face stopping at Mike's crotch. Before my show could go on, somebody wrapped my hair around their hand, jerked my ass up and drug me off of the dance floor. The last thing I remembered was hurling all over a fresh pair of all-white kicks.

Chapter 3

HAPPY BIRTHDAY

I woke up in Slay's bed and to his wrath. He was awake, sitting across the room in a chair like a king on his throne ready to dethrone one of his many servants and sentence him or her to death. He had been watching me sleep or waiting for me to wake up.

"Don't ever do no shit like that again. You hear me, Shar? Don't think that just because you got a nigga fallin' in love and shit that I won't kill your ass. Understood?"

I nodded. My head was throbbing. "What time is it?"

"Four?"

I sprang up in the bed. "In the mornin'? I'm suppose to be at TaNaysha's. If my father…"

"Don't worry about it. TaNaysha knows the deal."

Slay handed me a bottle of water. "Here. Drink it. It will sober you up." He left the room.

I looked around. Mounted to the wall in front of me was the biggest television I had ever seen and one my father only dreamed of having. He pastored a church but it wasn't a mega church. We weren't rolling in the church's dough.

The bed I was in had to have been custom made. It was larger than a king and fit for a queen. The mattress was so soft and plush that I felt like I was floating on feathers. To my right was a door that opened to Slay's closet. It was the size of my bedroom. To my left was a door that opened to his bathroom. It, too, was the size of my bedroom. Painted on the bedroom ceiling was a larger-than-life portrait of Al Pacino as Tony Montana. I shook my head. Niggas worshipped the fictional-iconic Montana like he was God and treated God like he was fictional.

Every inch of the room, from the nails in the baseboards to the décor was all top of the line. Slay's crib was nice and then it hit me, if I was at Slay's house then where the hell was Aleesha. I jumped up and out of the bed—a little too fast. Dizzy, I stumbled to the floor. The bedroom door opened.

"I know you don't have me up in here with that trick. What y'all doin'…tryin' to kidnap me…traffic me to East Asia or some shit?"

Slay laughed. "First of all…calm the hell down. You're to damn old for those perverts who travel across continents for some ass. Second…stop cussin'…it's not attractive. Third, we're at my condo. Fourth, don't worry about where Aleesha is."

He lifted me off of the floor and laid me back on the bed. He must have undressed me in my drunken stupor. I had on an oversized Sean John t-shirt, panties and no bra. Standing on the side of the bed, Slay reached down and opened the top drawer of the adjacent nightstand. He pulled out a small, blue box wrapped in a white ribbon.

"Happy Birthday, Babygirl."

He didn't go to Jared's…he went to Tiffany's. Like the child I was on Christmas morning, I feverously unwrapped the gift. In between each diamond of the tennis bracelet, was my birthstone. Slay fastened the clasp and I admired the bling on my wrist as he climbed on top of me. The pressure from his body was enough to get Ms. Kitty excited. I put my arms around his neck.

"Thank you."

"Anything for you, Babygirl."

Our lips touched for the first time and I tasted the mouthwash on Slay's tongue. He broke our liplock and bestowed my neck with sweet kisses while sliding one of his hands underneath my shirt to massage my breasts. My nipples stood erect. He stripped me down to my birthday suit and ran his tongue up and down my stomach, stopping to circle my navel before burying his head between my thighs—only emerging for air when my legs trembled and the job was complete.

"Babygirl, I want you so bad."

"I want you too."

"You sure?"

"I'm sure."

Slay reached into the nightstand dresser drawer again, this time pulling out a condom. His boxers fell onto the floor along with the wife beater he had on. Amazed, I took his dick in my hand. Thick, long and stiff, it was worthy of a guest-starring role in a porn flick. Slay removed my hand, rolled the condom over his dick and rubbed it against Ms. Kitty. He entered the tip. I moaned. I was losing my mind and my virginity.

"You okay, Babygirl. Am I hurtin' you?"

"No…don't stop. Please Slay…don't stop. I'm ready."

Gently, Slay worked all of himself inside of me. Five hours later, the sun shining through Slay's bedroom blinds woke me up. The clock on the nightstand said 10:17 am. I had missed Sunday school and was on the verge of missing church. I couldn't ever recall missing one of my father's sermons. I turned to face Slay. His side of the bed was empty. My first thought was that he had gone to smooth things over with Aleesha since he didn't go home last night. Anyone looking at the situation from the outside in would think that Aleesha was Slay's number one, but I knew better. I had had Slay's heart since I was twelve. She was his default.

Juggling a tray with a glass of orange juice and a plate of eggs, pancakes and turkey bacon, Slay brought me breakfast in bed—the money, the phones, the tennis bracelet…none of it meant more to me than him remembering that I didn't eat pork. The latter, coupled with knowing that he hadn't left to go console Aleesha but was busy catering to me, was the icing on my birthday cake.

Missing church was a done deal. Slay and I ate breakfast, talked and fooled around some more before I got up to shower. When I returned from the bathroom, spread out on the bed was a pink, Baby Phat, velour sweat suit along with a pink panty and bra set from Victoria Secret, socks and a pair of pink and gray Air Force Ones. The thought that Slay had given me some of Aleesha's shit to wear was laid to rest when I spotted the price tags dangling from each item.

"Thanks, Baby." I hugged and kissed him.

"Like I said, Babygirl, anything for you. Just give a nigga a chance."

On our way over to TaNaysha's, I remembered that I had forgot to scoop up my cat suit. That bad boy fit me like a glove. I wasn't planning on wearing it again anytime soon, but I needed to add it to the collection of *that-ass-is-fine-in-that-outfit* arsenal in my closet.

"I forgot my cat suit."

"I burned it."

"You burned it! What for? Do you know how much that thing cost?"

"I paid for it."

There was no rebuttal on my end. Without the extra cash Slay had given me, I wouldn't have been able to cop it.

Slay continued. "I was just thinkin' that every time I saw you in it…that it would only remind me of you grindin' all up on another nigga. I could've killed that nigga."

"So, you burned it?"

"Ashes to ashes…dust to dust."

Slay was crazy and so was I for thinking that he did what he did because he loved me. Slay demanded a kiss before he let me out in front of Ms. Trina's and I didn't deny him. TaNaysha and Khalilah raced outside when they heard Slay and I pull up.

"That's that thang," Khalilah said about Slay's Cadillac Escalade. It was fresh off the conveyor belt.

"If you ask me…it's a stupid move. You would think a nigga tryin' to avoid the law would try hard not to look suspect and live simple. That nigga, Slay, be in a different car every day."

At the time, I boiled TaNaysha's remark down to hating but as life went on, I discovered that she was right. Slay's need to showcase how deep his pockets were was a telltale sign that he thought he was above the law. With street notoriety and stacks on deck came the challenge—trying to stay below the radar.

Before we all headed back to TaNaysha's room, Ms. Trina stopped me. "Shar, baby," she said. "Let me talk to you for a minute."

TaNaysha and Khalilah proceeded to the back of the house while Ms. Trina and I walked towards the kitchen.

"You hungry? She asked. "I cooked breakfast."

"No, Mam, I already ate."

"Shar, I know you're not my child and I know you're holier-than-thou ass parents think that I'm a terrible person and mother because of my past. But, baby, I've always kept it real with TaNaysha because the streets don't have a conscience. The streets don't care about your beauty or your future…they'll have you lookin', walkin' and talkin' like a crackhead and you ain't smoked shit. They'll have you doin' anything for the next dollar. And you probably thinkin' that you ain't got shit to do with it cause you just the trophy...the arm candy on a niggas arm. But, Shar, I know firsthand what I'm talkin' about. Once you attach yourself to the game, it's hard to get out. Once you start livin' that life there's no turnin' back. Shit happens that can't be erased. Don't take your freedom or peace of mind for granted."

Throughout our friendship, TaNaysha had shared bits and pieces about her mother's history on the streets. Ms. Trina had dropped out of high school when she was fourteen and started making runs for a smalltime drug dealer named Dino. One day, Dino made her his guinea pig. He polluted her veins with his latest investment, some potent shit, and she became addicted—devoting her life to chasing that first high. She ended up in prison for five years. By that time, TaNaysha was already living with her grandmother. While incarcerated, Ms. Trina got clean and changed her life around. When she was released, she found a job, got on her feet, took TaNaysha back under her care and never looked back. Besides Newports, she hadn't smoked anything since. She was schooled in the streets the hard way. Her life was meant to be my lesson. Guess I should have listened.

Church wasn't over, so I knew my parents weren't on the hunt for me yet. After dishing a few details about my night with Slay to TaNaysha and Khalilah, I headed home—all the way, bracing myself for the lecture that I was sure to get and the punishment that followed for not making it to church. *Shit!* My heart accelerated into overdrive when I saw my parents' car in the driveway. When I walked in the front door, both my mother and father were in the living room. My father got up and walked right past me. I didn't see him for the rest of the night. He didn't even bother to officially wish me a happy birthday. My mother followed me to my room.

"Happy eighteenth, baby."

"Thanks, Ma."

"I'm not going to ask you where you've been or who you've been with," she said—almost sure that I hadn't stayed at TaNaysha's last night. "But, I will tell you that you have a bright future ahead of you. You're leaving for college next weekend…try not to ruin your life in the next week and don't worry about your father. He'll be fine. His little girl is growing up. He's just having trouble adjusting."

My little sister, Shanelle, came knocking on my door next. She was only seven. My parents weren't trying to have another child, but she had come as a welcomed surprise. Creating a footpath that she could follow in was the job my parents had charged me with and up until I hooked up with Slay, I had thrived in the position.

"Daddy's mad at you."

"I know."

"Are you still going to college?"

"Yeah, why wouldn't I?"

She shrugged her shoulders. The innocent always had a way of knowing.

Chapter 4

UNAVOIDABLE

Niggas lie on their dicks and broads lie on their pussy—about how good their shit is. Slay had called me over twenty times in the span of three days demanding to see me, confirming that I had that fire. He had me feeling the same way about him, which is why I was avoiding answering his calls. The more time I spent with him, the less enthused I became about attending college and the more I fantasized about being his wifey. He was offering me what all broads wanted in life—from the uneducated to the educated—good dick on a daily basis and the glamorous life. My plan was to avoid him all together. I was leaving on Saturday, college bound.

The pink Razor vibrated. It was Slay, again. I rearranged the pillow stuffed between my legs and stared up at my bedroom ceiling, wishing that I were laying in his bed looking up at Tony Montana and his little friend.

While Slay was leaving another message on the pink Razor he had given me, TaNaysha was calling on the cell phone my parents were paying for.

"Bitch!" She screamed. I held the phone away from my ear. "Slay is lookin' for you!"

Damn. He was unavoidable.

"Look, bitch. He's givin me a c-note to deliver you to him ASAP."

"What the fuck? You pimpin' me."

"Just bring your ass on. You know you want to see him too."

"Where's he at?"

"Ernie Pain's"

"You know I can't be seen drivin' around in the hood in my car. You know my daddy will trip."

"Look out the window."

I peeked through the blinds. A silver Range Rover with black tinted windows was parked in front of my house. The passenger side window rolled down and TaNaysha stuck her head out.

"Come on, bitch!"

It was eleven o'clock on a Wednesday morning. I was suppose to spend the day packing. Both of my parents were at work and since school was officially out for summer break, Shanelle was spending her days down at the local community center. I slipped on some gray sweat pants, a wife beater, the pink and gray Air Force Ones that Slay had copped for me, swooped my hair up in a ponytail, grabbed my purse and big silver hoop earrings.

Khalilah was driving.

"Whose ride?" I asked, hopping into the back of the Range Rover.

"Bitch, Carlo's," TaNaysha answered before Khalilah could.

"Carlo's!"

"You must've given him the business if he let you push this," I said.

"Nope. He just likes me."

"Bitch, nothin' in life is free," said TaNaysha. "You must've sucked his dick or somethin'."

"Nope…well, I did let him eat me out."

"Bitch, you must got that platinum-p!"

TaNaysha and I hi-fived each other.

* * *

Ernie Pain was an old nigga in the hood. The rumor that had trickled down throughout the generations in the streets was that his dick was bigger than a boa constrictor. According to Ms. Trina, the rumor was true.

"I needed some cash and his ass needed some pussy. So, we made a deal. But, when that old ass nigga pulled down his pants," she said, the day she rehashed the story to me, TaNaysha and Khalilah. "I got the fuck up out of there. His shit filled the whole got damn hotel room. I wasn't plannin' on havin' any mo' kids but damn, a bitch still needed her ovaries."

And thus, that's how Ernie earned his last name, Pain. He'd given a ton of old broads and probably some young, homemade hysterectomies.

Ernie Pain also sold bootleg liquor. Niggas could be seen coming and going from his house all day and all night. As time passed, he eventually started selling bootleg everything: CD's, DVD's, tennis shoes, purses—all kinds of shit. Whatever you needed, Ernie Pain had it. He was the classic example of a hood entrepreneur.

In the summer, he also hosted a domino tournament. He had that shit set up like the NBA playoffs. Niggas in the hood rushed to sign up and pay the $99.99 fee that he charged to enter the tournament. The winner received a cash prize and a trophy, which wasn't shit to most of the niggas who signed up. It was about the competition—one nigga trying to prove he was better than the next.

Ernie Pain held practice rounds at his house during the week. That's where Slay's ass was. but, before stopping at Ernie Pain's, Khalilah busted a few blocks.

Whether a nigga or a broad owned a hoopty or a pimped-out ride, when the sun shined, the streets were crowded—even at eleven o'clock in the morning on a weekday. The tint on the Range Rover kept our identities a secret. We could see out, but no one could see in. We read niggas, lips.

"Who the fuck is that?"

The broads were even funnier. "Ooooohhh, whoever's drivin' that can get it."

"Bitch, we don't want it. We don't swing that way," TaNaysha said, like the broad outside of the car could hear her. "Go somewhere and get the fuck out of yesterday's clothes. Bitch ain't even washed her coochie today."

Shit, neither had I. They had come and scooped me up before I had a chance to.

Old broads, grandmothers of niggas on the block, were sitting outside on their front porches in lawn chairs with aprons on and fly swatters in their hands. Some even had couches they had picked up from the Salvation Army in their yards, charging niggas a dollar to sit. Everyone in the hood had a hustle—no matter how small.

The neon light above the hood never said CLOSED. Business on the corner never stopped. When the day shift was over, in came the second shift workers and then the third. A nigga's status and power in the streets could be measured by how many followers he had. Any nigga who could persuade other niggas and broads to risk their lives and freedom to work for him had serious clout. Slay was that Jim Jones nigga in the hood. Niggas and broads alike lined up to sip the Kool-Aid he was serving. Like the United States of America had three branches of government, he had three levels of operation: niggas and broads working on the corner, niggas and broads catering to his White-collar clientele and niggas and broads moving major weight across state lines—by land and air. Slay kept his hands clean, except when inspecting his product and counting his money. So, I thought.

"Ain't that Slay's droptop Deville?" TaNaysha pointed.

Sure enough, Aleesha was pushing his whip like it was hers, I stared right into her face as the two vehicles glided past each other. She couldn't see me, though. Her hair was finger waved into a 1990's French Roll and she had a front tooth outlined in gold with a small diamond stud adhered in the middle. Her skin was bare and flawless and her eyebrows were arched to a tee and her nails were done—like she enjoyed weekly facials and spa days and shit. She was rocking diamond hoop earrings and a big ass rock on her ring finger. Apparently, she was sending out a memo to all broads—including me—that Slay was her nigga and she was his main bitch.

"Who wears a French Roll these days...and fingerwaves?" Khalilah turned up her nose.

"If I were you I'd get out and whoop her ass right now in the middle of the got damn street." TaNaysha turned and looked at me in the backseat.

"Take me the fuck home. Right now."

Broads fought. I was a lady, back then. I had never been in a fight in my life and I sure wasn't about to get my shit scratched up listening to TaNaysha's hood ass.

"Bitch, I need my money. I'm takin' you to Slay and then if he wants us to take you home. We will."

"Oh, you workin' for Slay now?" I asked.

TaNaysha didn't answer.

* * *

The front part of Ernie Pain's house, for obvious reasons, looked normal. It was arranged in the average living room set up: a couch, loveseat, end tables and a black-and-white, floor model television with a 19" color one on top. A gold-framed portrait of the Lord's Last Super hung above the television and both black and White angel figurines were scattered around the house—for spiritual protection, I guess. To my knowledge Ernie Pain had never been robbed. The angels must have been doing their job or maybe it was the gun cabinet in the corner of his living room. Ernie Pain was packing and it wasn't light. He had grenades and shit.

The back part of his house looked like a liquor store in the middle of a flea market. Slay was in a room with three other niggas holding down a game of dominos. All four of them were packing—each had a gun resting on their lap. Two 42" LCD flatscreen televisions were mounted on the wall adjacent to the table where they played. They were watching ESPN on one and Scarface on the other. TaNaysha, Khalilah and I stood in the doorway.

"Where the fuck y'all been?" Slay asked, never looking up from his hand.

"We just busted a few blocks," TaNaysha said.

"What the fuck did I tell you to do?"

"Nigga, what-the-fuck-ever. Where's my money?"

"You better be glad she's your fuckin' friend," Slay said to me. He handed TaNaysha eighty dollars.

"Nigga, where the fuck is my other twenty?"

"I told you to go get Shar and come straight back. It don't take an hour to go across town and back. Next time, do what the fuck I ask you to do."

"What-the-fuck-ever. Khalilah, let's dip." TaNaysha was pissed.

I turned to follow them.

"Babygirl, you goin' with me." It wasn't a question. It was a command.

Slay laid his hand down, grabbed his heat and said goodbye to his niggas. Knowing better than to confront him in front of company, I waited until I got outside to question him about Aleesha's ass.

"What the fuck? You're married? Huh? I saw that big ass rock on Aleesha's finger. I can't believe this shit."

"Where did you see Aleesha?"

"She's rollin' around in the hood in your droptop."

Slay grabbed my wrist and reached down in his pocket with his loose hand. He pulled out his cell phone and dialed Aleesha.

"Get the fuck home," was all he said before stuffing me into his Cutlass.

Khalilah and TaNaysha had pulled off by then.

"Take me home. I gotta finish packin'."

The Cutlass jerked. Slay had made an abrupt stop.

"Packin'. Where the fuck you goin'?"

I crossed my arms, poked my lips out and stared out the window. Slay had never asked me about my plans after high school. He assumed—like TaNaysha and Khalilah—that I would be attending the local community college.

"Where the fuck you goin'?" He asked again.

"Are you and Aleesha married?"

We sat in silence. He gave up first.

"No. Aleesha and I are not married. Did I buy her the ring? Yes. Everything she has belongs to me from the shoes on her feet to the weave in her hair. She ain't got shit."

Tears streamed down my face. "You say that you don't love her and yet you take care of her...buyin' her diamonds and shit...lettin' her drive your cars. I can't take this shit. I can't be the other woman. When I saw her in your droptop...my heart started hurtin'. I've never felt like that before and I don't ever want to feel like how I'm feelin' right now. Take me home."

"Babygirl." Slay uncrossed my arms and grabbed my hand. "It's difficult to explain. I got love for Aleesha but I don't love her. She was there for me when I didn't have shit...when I was locked up. It's just too much to go into right now. I can't just kick her ass to the curb that easy. I'll end it. I promise. Just give a nigga some time. I love you."

Slay brought his lips to my tears and kissed them away. Instead of taking me home, we rode over to his condo. He carried me up the stairs and laid me in his bed. I looked up at Tony Montana. I was right where I had wished to be.

Slay removed my shoes and slid my sweats down.

"Let me take a quick shower. TaNaysha and Khaliah..."

Slay had already removed my panties and had his head buried in Ms. Kitty.

"I've never eaten Aleesha's pussy. You're the first, the only and the last," he raised his head to say. "That should tell you somethin'."

Chapter 5

CAUGHT UP

After draft day, professional athlete niggas had a tendency to trade in the broads who had been by their sides when they didn't have shit—before the fame and fortune—for the beach fun Barbie types. They made niggas in the hood like Slay look like saints. They might not have been faithful, but they remained loyal to the broads who stuck by them during hard times and those who fed their egos when they were no-name-up-and-comer's on the block or while they were locked up. The real hood niggas did anyways. Slay's loyalty to Aleesha was double the reason for me to distance myself from him. Instead, it only made me respect and want him more. My mind was telling me no, but my heart and body were screaming yes. I was caught up.

Still, I planned on squeezing into my car that was packed full with all of my belongings—with my parents and little sister following me—to head up the interstate to obtain a higher education and procure a bright future for myself. But, I was torn. Leaving meant that Slay would never see me as he saw Aleesha. In his eyes, I would always be the broad who left him and she would always be the one who stayed. My pillow was tear-soaked.

There was a light tapping on my bedroom window and then whispering.

"Shar...it's me."

"Mike?"

"Yeah."

Fucking with Slay, I had learned to think twice about the shit I did. Like, giving strip teases and letting other niggas climb through my bedroom window. Mike, showing up at my house out of the blue, was suspicious. It smelled of some shit Slay would put in motion to test my own loyalty and faithfulness to him.

"Ummm…I'm kind of sleep."

"You sound wide awake to me."

Damn. I lifted up the window and let him in. If it was a test, I had just failed.

Mike and I had dated from the second semester of our junior year up until Slay made his loud and thunderous grand entrance into my life. We went on dates, mostly to the movies. We would always stop at the corner store and stuff my purse with sodas, chips and candy—trying to cut movie expenses. And, we went dutch since Mike never had enough money to pay for him and me too—just the weekly allowance his parents gave him. We had fun together. But with Slay, I never had to pay for shit.

Mike sat on the floor with his back against my bed railing and crossed his legs. I took a seat next to him. He was in his usual gear: t-shirt, two pair of basketball shorts and Jordans—nothing fancy. He was boyishly handsome, pecan colored with a natural curly 'fro, tall, lean and athletic with a big-screen smile—straight-A schoolboy. At times, in front of his boys, he pretended to be gangster using outdated slang and embellishing the story of the one time he almost shot somebody. His parents were out of town and he was home alone when someone tried to break into their house.

Mike said that he grabbed his father's shotgun and chased the would-be-robber down the street. There were no witnesses. Guess he was just trying to fit in with the young hood niggas, swapping and comparing stories.

"Did Slay send you here?"

"Slay? Why would he send me over here?"

"Never mind."

"Shar, I can't believe you're messin' with him. Women who get caught up with men like that…in the end, they end up with the raw deal. Look at what happened to TaNaysha's mama. She got strung out, started…"

"I know the story. Why did you come over here?"

"Is it the money?"

"What?"

"The money…that's why you like Slay. That's why you dumped me to be with him."

"No…"

"Shar, I know I don't have it yet." Mike turned to face me. "But, I got a full basketball scholarship to Duke. If things work out, I'll get drafted by my junior year…maybe even my sophomore year. I'll be able to give you anything you want and everything you need…legally."

One moment in my life had changed the course of my life forever—the very first time Slay had approached me, when I was twelve. I suppose, it was all part of his master plan. Since then, he had been the only man on my mind. Mike and the other middle school and high school boys who I may have let walk me to my locker, carry my books or feel me up never had a fighting chance. No one did—not even my own will power was enough to tear myself away from Slay.

"Look, Mike, my heart just wasn't in it…in us…you and me. I'm sorry."

"I see," Mike said, as he stood to leave. "I never wanted to break up."

I sat silent.

"Well, good luck," he said, climbing back out my window. "Look out for me. I'mma be a star one day."

Slay was the nigga to be on the block. Mike was the brother to be on the court. In his Toyota Corolla, he looked like a giant in a clown car. I waved goodbye. There was no doubt in my mind that he would go pro. Neither was there a guarantee that if he did he wouldn't trade me in for a big-breasted, long-legged, model-thin blonde broad if we had stayed together. It didn't matter. I had made my choice.

Sleep that night didn't come easy. Shit, it never came. Right after Mike left, Khalilah and TaNaysha swung by. My father stood firm in his decision when I repeatedly begged him to allow me to spend my last night in town over TaNaysha's house. The answer was no.

"You're eighteen. Hell, you're grown. Bring your ass on," TaNaysha gassed me up.

Khalilah was still driving Carlo's Range Rover.

"What the fuck is goin' on with you and Carlo?" I asked.

Not only had she been pushing Carlo's ride, she had been rocking new outfits from head to toe and I noticed the new tennis bracelet on her wrist. It was almost as nice as the one Slay had given me for my birthday.

"We're just friends."

"Friends my ass," said TaNaysha.

"I mean...I like him and he likes me but his parent's aren't havin' it."

"I told you not to get involved with that Jewish nigga. You know their families don't play about keeping their bloodline pure. Just like them Arabian and Indian niggas. Don't end up like that Black girl in Atlanta."

"What are you talkin' about? What girl?"

"I saw the story on Dateline."

"Since when does your ass watch Dateline." I laughed at TaNaysha's admission.

"I watch all that shit...20/20, 48 Hours Mystery, Cold Case Files. Shit, you never know when a nigga is tryin' to kill you. I gotta stay ahead of the game. Anyways, she met and married this Indian nigga. Next thing you know she's dead. His father had her killed."

Khalilah looked slightly disturbed as she whipped the Range Rover across town.

"I hope you didn't give him the goods," TaNaysha added.

"Not yet. Carlo isn't pressurin' me. He says that he just wants me to experience the finer things in life."

"Oh, so, he's playin' you like a hood charity case or somethin'?"

"I don't know. I'm just havin' a little fun right now. He's so cute, don't y'all think so?"

"Hell, nah," said TaNaysha, clearly hating.

Carlo was attractive. He resembled a younger version of that actor who played Sonny on General Hospital. He and his brother Frankie were running the real estate game, buying up shit left and right and stacking their paper. I was happy for Khalilah. Although a different game, Carlo like Slay, was a made man.

We rolled around in the hood for a while. Niggas and broads were posted up on their respective corners, chasing and racing up to the cars they recognized and being leery of the ones they didn't.

"Look at that shit," TaNaysha pointed.

Down the alley was a discarded box spring being used by either a prostitute serving a John or a crackhead tricking for her next high. Shit done in the hood couldn't be made up by the wildest of imaginations.

"That shit's crazy," I said.

"That shit's nasty," said TaNaysha. "They need to take that inside a cardboard box or somethin'. Don't nobody want to see that shit."

"Guess you're not thinkin' when you're that far gone," Khalilah made sense of the scene.

She had to stop by The Tap Room to check in with Carlo. None of us were dressed for the club but we could pull niggas wearing garbage bags. We sauntered in, swaying our hips and following a beefed up bodyguard to the back of the club. He knocked three times on a closed door.

"Lilah's here."

"Lilah?" TaNaysha and I both said and looked at each other. "Who the fuck is Lilah?"

"Carlo calls me Lilah," Khalilah blushed. "I like it."

"See. His ass is de-hoodin' you already." TaNaysha shook her head.

Slay called me Babygirl. That shit was endearing and I loved it. It looked like both Khalilah and I were in love.

The door opened. Carlo and Frankie were surrounded by an army of bodyguards. They were all staring up at a wall of computer screens, displaying every square foot of the club—not an inch of the venue was left undetected. Every move made in and outside of the club was caught on camera, from broads giving head in the corner to niggas sniffing lines of powder. Slay had niggas watching his back on the streets but never in tow. Carlo and Frankie were big time. Their operations were elaborate and even though illegal shit was going down in their club, their business was legit—incorporated with a federal ID number.

Khalilah wrapped her arms around Carlo's neck. They didn't kiss, just looked into each other's eyes and smiled. Frankie turned his head. The expression on his and TaNaysha's face was the same, one of disapproval.

"Y'all got some CIA-FBI shit goin' in here." TaNaysha looked up at the digital wall. "I bet they got your strip show on camera." Obviously, she was talking to me. "Better hope that shit don't pop up on You Tube." '

"You don't have to worry about that," Frankie turned to me and said, breaking his silence. "The recordings are stored away and never looked at again unless necessary. Only a select few have access to them," he assured me and smiled slyly, letting me know that my show on the dance floor was a hit amongst the niggas in the security room. Embarrassment washed over me.

We all watched as a fight between two broads was brewing. Their necks were rolling, mouths moving and fingers pointing. One broad apparently spilled some of her drink on the other broad's shoes.

"These are Manolos."

"You mean Ma-no-no's."

I read their lips.

Before the girlfight could pop off, two bodyguards swarmed in and calmed the chaos.

"Y'all should have let them fight."

Frankie looked at TaNaysha like he was ready for her to go. Carlo got the message. He whispered something into Khalilah's ear and we bounced.

On our way back to my house, we heard sirens. Khalilah pulled over to the side. An ambulance and fire truck zoomed past us. They were headed into the hood, towards Club Pulse. We suspected that someone must have gotten shot again. Maybe even killed. We followed the first responders and parked down the street from the club. The crime scene had already been taped off.

Bystanders, some club goers and others from around the block, peered on. Greedy, the club owner, was in a deep conversation with two police officers. The officers took notes but looked like they had heard it all before, too many times to count—same story, new victim.

Khalilah and I stayed back while TaNaysha inched her way through the crowd, in search of details. She came back with devastating news.

"Somebody got killed. They said is was Slay."

"What?" My heart stopped. "TaNaysha, say it ain't so. Say it!" I started screaming and the crowd of bystanders turned their attention to me. Khalilah and TaNaysha guided me to the truck where I ransacked my purse looking for the pink Razor. There were no missed calls or messages. Slay usually called me three or four times before I went to bed. I dialed the number he always called me from. There was no answer. My hands were shaking and my breaths were getting shorter. Then and there I knew, that if Slay was alive, my future was with him—right by his side.

"Go back up there…make sure it's Slay. Please," I begged TaNaysha.

"I'm sorry, Shar," Khalilah tried to console me.

Ten minutes later, TaNaysha came back. "It wasn't Slay. Just a nigga that worked for him."

The pink Razor vibrated, Slay was calling.

"Babygirl, I'm okay." Slay had also heard the rumor that he was the one who had gotten shot and killed. Aleesha too, she was in the background crying and sniffling.

"Slay, I don't ever want to lose you. I love you."

"Babygirl, I love you too. Have Khalilah drop you off at the condo. I'll meet you there in twenty minutes."

* * *

Slay and I laid in bed. The final decision had been made. I was staying in town, enrolling in school at the local community college and moving into the condo. Now, we just had to tell my parents—news that would be devastating to them as Slay's rumored death was to me.

Chapter 6

NO LONGER DADDY'S LITTLE GIRL

When I was younger, in elementary school, we use to live in the hood—before the neighborhood became the "hood". My father moved us across town even though our church remained on the block it was built. Guess my father didn't want to appear to be a complete sell out.

Back then, the hood was occupied with working class Black families. Mothers and fathers worked throughout the week, barbequed on Saturday and greased themselves and their children's faces down with Vaseline before heading to church on Sunday mornings. Folks back then weren't scared to slept with their doors unlocked and didn't think twice about whooping their neighbor's child's ass if he or she was caught in the wrong. It was a time when people actually believed that it took a village to raise a child and niggas just weren't in it for themselves—before the infestation of drugs, violence, sexual degradation and material idolism. Those were the good ol' days I suppose you can say—when shit was more peaceful and less complicated. It seemed that way at least.

My favorite holiday back then was Juneteenth, historically the oldest celebration of the end of slavery. The block party consisted of fishfrys, music blasting from boom boxes and niggas chasing broads and each other with water balloons instead of bullets. Me, TaNaysha and Khalilah would be in the middle of it all—having fun without a care in the world way before we knew what being "fast" meant.

Slavery was over but now, niggas and broads were chained to the hustle and bustle of the hood. Unlike me, most broads in the hood had a reason or an excuse for living the street life. Those who were fatherless sought out niggas like Slay to take care of them— to be the provider and protector their fathers weren't. Some of them were so starved for attention that they would do anything to feel wanted and loved from selling drugs to sucking niggas' dicks for sport. Broads in the hood were simply trapped in a cycle—a generational curse—learning from their grandmothers how to scheme for disability checks, use and abuse the welfare system and have babies for tax credits. Others just needed to do what the fuck they needed to do whether it was moving weight or selling pussy to pay the bills and feed their children. Me, I had neither—a reason nor an excuse for the life I chose to live—just the fact that I was in love with a certified hood nigga and willing to follow him all the way to hell.

Slay knocked on my parents' door. I could have used my house key but clearly, I wasn't thinking. My father came to the door with disappointment in his eyes. He knew that I had snuck out of the house but suspected that I was over TaNaysha's, not laid up. If he could have stopped time, I would still be ten-years-old in pigtails and wearing ruffled socks. But, he wasn't God. And, I was no longer his little girl.

I stood behind Slay like my father was a stranger. I'm sure he thought the same of me. Slay spoke up. He was respectful but not intimidated by my father's sternness. It was a face off between a sinner and a saint.

"Rev. Reid, I'm here to talk to you about me and Shar."

My father didn't race for his shotgun, curse or scream. He simply opened the screen door and let us in. Shanelle, who was standing close to my mother, was sent to her room. She waved and smiled at me. I waved and smiled back.

I took in the last memories I would have of my childhood home. Like Ernie Pain, my mother had her own religious décor strung across the house and hung on the salmon colored walls. A Bible, open to Psalm 91, rested in the middle of the oak table in the living room. A portrait of the Lord himself that once belonged to my grandmother hung above the sofa table that my mother had leaned up against the wall closest to the front door. The portrait was surrounded by family photos, some of my sister and I and others of all of us together. Each of the end tables in the living room displayed a religious artifact—on one, a ceramic set of gold painted praying hands and on the other a statue of a wooden cross.

An interior design picture of a Black angel was hung on the wall above the couch where my parents sat across from Slay and I, who were seated on the matching loveseat.

"Well, Sir, Shar and I are in love and with all due respect, she's a grown woman and has the right to make her own decisions. With that, she's decided to stay in town and go to school at the community college here."

"Son, I know who you are and what you do. My daughter may love you but your first love is the streets."

"Sir..."

My father held up his hand, signaling to Slay that he wasn't finished.

"Apparently, you're not here to ask me for my permission. Nor, am I prepared to give anyone my blessing that chooses to live in sin. Shar's a smart girl but not a wise woman...not yet." My father spoke about me as if I weren't in the room. "Son, when your world comes crashing down and it will, what's going to happen to Shar?"

"Sir, Shar will always be taken care of."

Around the same time that my father had moved us across town, more and more young broads in the hood were dropping out of school and having babies. My father never blamed them for their situation but felt nothing but ill will towards the niggas who knocked them up and sold them false hope.

My preacher-father looked me in the eyes and told me that if I left with Slay, I would never be welcome back into his home.

"Do you understand the consequences of your decision?" He asked me.

I didn't, but I shook my head yes anyway. I left my father's house with nothing but the clothes on my back. He didn't beg or plead with me to stay. He let me go, forever. And my mother stood by his decision. Slay was all I had.

* * *

Slay had three residences that I knew of: the house, the condo and the streets. The first couple of nights at the condo, he stayed and held me as I cried myself to sleep. I was missing my parents and little sister. The fourth day we had our first argument because he hadn't come home the third night—he said he had been out collecting his money from his first-level operation employees or the niggas and broads working on the corner, chasing cars and selling rocks out of Advil and Tylenol bottles.

"All night?" I asked, with my hands on my hip with major attitude.

"Yes, all night and don't ever question me about where the fuck I been as long as you're bein' taken care of."

Like my father essentially said, I was book smart and street stupid—but not that stupid. Slay was smelling and looking fresh in a different outfit other than the one he left the condo in the night he didn't come home. I didn't recall seeing him leave with a duffle bag. I knew his ass had at least stopped by the house to see Aleesha where he apparently had a second wardrobe and more than likely, fucked her.

"Come here." He gestured for me to come over and sit on his lap.

I didn't bulge but stood in my panties and tank top with my lips poked out and my arms crossed. He reached inside his jean pocket and pulled out a single car key. I could see the Mercedes Benz emblem engraved in the leather key chain it was attached to. He dangled the key in the air like a zoo trainer parading a steak in front of a tiger.

"If you want'em, you gotta come get'em."

Gingerly, I made my way over to him and eventually cracked a smile. I sat in his lap, facing him with my legs straddling the sides of the dinette chair he was sitting in. He popped my breasts out of my tank top and nibbled and sucked me wet. I unbuckled his belt and unzipped his jeans. He slid out of them and his boxers. I eased on top of his dick. It was the first time we had fucked without a condom. Insanely, I believed that he would never put my life in danger. Surely, he stayed strapped when fucking Aleesha. And shit, if I got pregnant, a child would just be an added blessing to our life together. We pleased each other and all was forgiven.

After we kissed and made up, he handed me $500 and the car key. It was to a black, CLK 430 Mercedes Benz. It wasn't pimped out like Slay's other vehicles. It was simple: factory rims, stereo and tint. I loved it. He left to handle some business but promised to be home for dinner. I planned on cooking my first meal—ever—and looking scantly divine while doing it. I had two stops to make, the grocery store and Frederick's of Hollywood. I scooped up TaNaysha. We were meeting Khalilah at the mall.

"Bitch, this shit is fire," TaNaysha said as she hopped into my gift from Slay. "I'mma get me a dope boy or a sugar daddy one."

"It's not all about that. Shit, Slay could be homeless and I'd still love his ass."

"Umm-hmm. What-ever-the-fuck you say. I'm not buyin' it."

"I do love him."

"That, I don't doubt. I'm talkin' about the still-love-him-if-he-was homeless shit. Anyway...you gonna get a job or somethin'? School don't start until August. My mama got me filling out applications every damn where."

Honestly, I hadn't thought about getting a job and Slay hadn't mentioned me getting one.

"I don't know."

"Bitch, you better. Usually, I would tell a bitch to get what she can get from a nigga...use'em like they be usin' bitches. But, you don't have a gold-digger mentality. Shar, you're a fuckin' romantic and ain't shit romantic about livin' the street life. You need to get your ass a job so you can have your own money and you need to open up a checkin' account. And don't fuck off all of the money Slay gives you. Save some of that shit. Just in case you need it for a rainy day...just in case some shit pops off."

Ms. Trina had schooled TaNaysha about the streets. In turn, TaNaysha was schooling me. I was thankful for the lesson, but Slay was my nigga. I believed him when he promised to take care of me forever.

The mall was swarmed with teenagers out of school for the summer. We met Khalilah in the food court. She was sporting another new outfit, but it wasn't her usual choice of gear. She rocked a pair of loosely fit, white shorts that came to her knees with a pink, polo t-shirt and a long-sleeved, lime green shirt wrapped around her neck and shoulders. Instead of her usual choice of tennis shoes, a pair of high top Air Force Ones, she had on some Keds.

"What the fuck? You 'bout to go play tennis or somethin'?" TaNaysha looked her up and down, confused.

"You look like you are about to go sailin' on a yacht or somethin'," I added with my nose scrunched up.

"Or, maybe lunch at the Country Club," TaNaysha said, pompously.

"None of the above. Carlo picked this outfit out for me. I don't know. At first, I didn't like it but now I do. It's more comfortable than those tight jean shorts I be wearin'."

"Sounds like you like whatever Carlo likes," TaNaysha said and I seconded.

But shit, the truth was if Slay had wanted me to dress like I belonged in an episode of Little House on the Prairie, I would. I was the skillet calling the kettle Black.

We walked the distance of the mall to Frederick's of Hollywood. Their lingerie was sexier than what Victoria Secret offered. I copped a red and White, see-through lingerie set. Since Slay had already played Santa, buying me a Benz, I thought I'd surprise him by being a sexy Mrs. Claus.

TaNaysha and I parted ways with Khalilah and headed to the grocery store. TaNaysha could cook like somebody's grandmother. Occasionally, when I was growing up, I would watch my mother work her magic in the kitchen but cooking never interested me. For me it was an option to learn how to cook. For TaNaysha it was a necessity. A lot of shit she just had to learn to do-being that her mother was locked up most of her childhood and her grandparents were aging. She helped me put together a menu of fried chicken, garlic mashed potatoes, macaroni, sweet potatoes and biscuits. She even took the time to write down all of the cooking instructions for me.

The first few pieces of chicken that I had fried were a perfect shade of golden brown. They looked done but like TaNaysha had instructed me to do, I slit one of the larger pieces open to find it still raw on the inside. *They're not done until they've floated to the top.* I re-read the directions she had written down.

Despite the rough start, I had prepared my first meal. Besides the biscuits, all of the food was done. I turned the eyes on the stove down to low, tossed the biscuits in the oven and went to take a shower. While relishing in my domestic accomplishment in the kitchen and imagining how good I was going to look for Slay in the lingerie I had copped, I totally forgot about the biscuits. The fire alarm sounded. *Shit!* I hopped out of the shower to find Slay in the kitchen fanning the smoke away from the smoke detector and a pan of burnt biscuits on the counter.

"Oh my God! Slay, I am so sorry." I rushed over and cut the fan above the stove on. Both Slay and I were coughing up smoke out of our lungs.

"Shar, shit!" He continued to fan the smoke. "You can't be doin' shit like this. The last thing I need is for the white and blues to show up over here."

I took it that the white and blues meant the police.

"Just 'cause you don't see shit out in the open don't mean it ain't here," Slay continued his rant. He was mad but at least he had came home.

* * *

Slay's only complaint about the meal I had prepared—other than I had almost burned down his condo along with the money and dope he had stashed in the walls and laid down the welcome mat for the police to come over—was that he didn't see anything green on his plate. He wasn't talking about money or marijuana. He was referring to vegetables.

"Everybody should have somethin' green with each meal," he said, sounding like a nutritionist instead of a street pharmacist. I knew better than to comment on Slay's business, but I was thinking: *How the hell does a nigga who sells shit detrimental to people's mental and physical health care about other niggas eatin' their vegetables?* It didn't make sense. But, a lot of shit in life didn't—a lot of unexplainable shit. Like how a young girl raised in a loving, two-parent home turned out to be a drug-addicted prostitute or a young man—raised under the same circumstances— turned into a weight-moving murderer, hustler or pimp. It was a risk all parents took when making the decision to have children. Their seeds would either blossom into a beautiful flower or sprout into an unwanted weed. I'm sure Jeffery Dahmer's mother and father weren't expecting their blonde-headed, blue-eyed baby boy to grow up into a serial-killing-flesh-eating monster. And my religious parents surely weren't expecting my life to end up how it did.

Over dinner, thinking back to TaNaysha and my conversation, I asked Slay if I should get a job. He laughed like I had just told him a joke.

"Babygirl," he said, smothering his chicken in Louisiana hot sauce. "What the fuck you need a job for? What is it that you need that I can't get for you?"

"Nothin'…I guess." I swirled my fork around in the mashed potatoes on my plate.

"Babygirl, you my woman and my woman doesn't have to work. But, if you're bored just sittin' around here all day...go ahead...get a job," he said between bites. Bored. No, I wasn't bored. Spa days, shopping, eating out, driving around in my Benz and not having to worry about paying for shit—I was living the life most broads only dreamed of. I was living la vida-fucking-loca but little did I know that nothing in life was for free, especially for those caught up in the game. Even if a broad, like me, was just benefiting from a nigga's street wealth, eventually she would have to pay up, whether it was with her freedom or her life.

Chapter 7

AT THE PARK

Waking up on a Sunday morning and not attending church was strange, for lack of a better word. I was glad to be free—not of God—but from my father's dominion. Being a preacher's kid and a preacher's wife was as grueling as being a preacher. Granted, my mother, my sister nor me had to stand in the pulpit and preach up to three sermons a day. But, we had to be present at each and every service my father presided over: Sunday school, morning and afternoon service, Wednesday night Bible study and revival services at our church and the ones my father was invited to be the guest pastor. The shit was just tiring.

To me, if a person believed that the only way to the road of salvation was by attending church alone then they were doomed from the beginning. God is omnipresent and therefore can't be boxed into four walls, but my father believed that hearing the Word was important. I believed that studying the Word was as essential and that a lot of people who faithfully attended church would hear those dreadful words from the Lord come judgment day, "I never knew you, depart from me." There were a lot of hypocrites in the church—my father, being one of them. He had preached numerous sermons on forgiveness. Yet, he never forgave me.

I, myself, had strayed from the Word and just as I believed that when praises went up, blessings came down, I also believed that curses fell when the Word was ignored. I had taken refuge in

Slay and learned the hard way that no one could indeed serve two Gods.

* * *

At the park on Sunday evening was the place to be or not be when niggas started shooting and broads started fighting over those same niggas. But before the bullets started flying, broads showed up to flaunt their bodily assets and niggas posted up fresh-to-deaf in the latest kicks next to their pimped out rides—flashing gold grills, platinum chains and rubber-banded rolls of money, trying to attract new pussy.

TaNaysha, Khalilah and I circled the park in my Benz before we got out and walked the park's strip. Khalilah was back in her normal gear: a fitted Baby Phat tee, some tight-ass jean capris and a pair of all white low top Air Force Ones—probably because she didn't have plans with Carlo. Her hair was up in a ponytail. TaNaysha had on a jean tube-top dress with a pair of chocolate-and-caramel colored hightop Air Force Ones and she rocked a strawberry blonde quickweave that was cut into a chin-length bob. I felt like dressing up and wore a short, red, spaghetti-strapped sundress with gold wedge sandals and accessories. My hair hung close to my ass. It had taken all morning to flat iron every strand. Niggas were calling me Pocahontas.

From one end to the next, the park was congested with niggas like ants on an ant farm. They were everywhere and all eyes were on us as we strolled the strip. We swayed our hips with the wind and niggas were hissing at us, trying to get our attention.

"Hey, Shawty," they all greeted us the same.

"Hey is for motherfuckin' horses," TaNaysha spat back. "Approach a bitch correctly."

One nigga grabbed my wrist. I jerked it back. "Nigga, you don't know me or who I belong to," I said. At the time, I was unaware that I had begun to minimize myself to simply being a possession of Slay's.

"Fuck you then, bitch."

"We'll see who the bitch is when my nigga slits your fuckin' throat."

We kept it moving. Slay was over at Ernie Pain's playing dominos but he had eyes everywhere, watching me. The last thing I needed was to be embarrassed by him jerking me up like he had done at The Tap Room. Plus, receiving attention from other niggas was all in fun and games to me. Slay was the only one who could get it and *was* getting it: morning, noon and night on the days and nights his ass makes it home.

A crowd of onlookers surrounded the basketball courts. Some wanna-be-AND-1 niggas had started a pick-up game, dunking and passing the ball like they were the Harlem Globetrotters. They were hyping the crowd up. I'm sure Mike would have been out there if he hadn't left for college already.

Kids were running wild all over the park from the monkey bars to the swings to the slides while their mothers and grandmothers yelled for them not to get their Sean John, Rocawear and Baby Phat outfits dirty.

The smell of marijuana, Black-N-Milds and alcohol was in the air. Shit, I received a contact high just by breathing. My head started spinning and I was feeling lightheaded. Occasionally, yes, I drank but I had never smoked anything in my life.

"Let's sit down for a minute," I said, motioning towards an empty park bench that faced the strip.

"Damn, don't tell me you got a contact high just by walkin' past motherfuckers smokin'. You just need to go ahead and smoke a joint and get that shit over with. Then you won't get fucked up so easily. I'm sure Slay has plenty of weed for you to test," TaNaysha said.

"I'll be alright in a minute."

We chilled on the bench for a while, peeping everybody's game—niggas trying to holla at various broads and vice versa. Broads were looking for fathers for themselves and their kids. Niggas were looking for ONS's or one-night-stands.

"Who…the…fuck…is…that?" TaNaysha pointed to a jet-black nigga leaned up against a yellow and black Ducati motorcycle. "He is fine as hell."

Shit, I only had eyes for Slay but the nigga was a showstopper. He was tall, about six feet. He was lean but muscular and his skin looked like it had been kissed by Africa's sun. But from the looks of it, he wasn't African—just black as hell. If he was from Africa, he had been Americanized. His style was simple but sexy. Unlike the rest of the niggas in the hood, including Slay, his clothes weren't two sizes too big. They weren't snug either. They simply fit. He rocked a black tee, black jeans and black Timberlands. That's it. No bling in his ears. No ice on his wrist. No cross on his chest. His swagger was natural, not counterfeit.

"Shit, he might be from Africa with all that black on. It's hotter than hell out here. You know them African niggas don't get hot." TaNaysha observed.

"He is fine." Khalilah bit her bottom lip.

"He must be new on the block," I said.

"Must be and we need to introduce ourselves. Come on." TaNaysha hopped up and sashayed towards him. Khalilah and I followed.

TaNaysha wasn't the only broad vying for his attention. Broads were swarming to his left and right and he was swatting them away like flies. We were next. If he treated us the same, my feelings weren't going to be hurt. I had a man.

"You new around here?" TaNaysha asked. Khalilah and I kept our distance.

"Sort of." He kept it short.

"You in school?" She asked, trying to extend the conversation.

"No."

"You work?"

"I do me."

"What's your name?"

He hesitated. "Tyrell."

"I'm TaNaysha."

He said nothing.

"Okay, well, maybe I'll see you again…soon."

"Maybe."

Tyrell. He wasn't from Africa and his voice didn't give away his lineage. I couldn't decipher where he was from: the North, South, West or East. We turned and walked away. I looked back and we locked eyes. He smiled and there was the bling—the brightest, whitest set of perfectly straight teeth I had ever seen on a nigga. Quickly, I averted my eyes but not before TaNaysha witnessed the exchange. *Damn.*

Walking back to my Benz, I spotted Aleesha. She was walking towards us in an orange, strapless terrycloth dress and the same got-damn gold wedge sandals I had on.

"Guess yall got the same taste in shoes as you do men," TaNaysha couldn't resist.

Aleesha glanced at me with knowing eyes as I with her, but we didn't say shit to each other.

"Y'all some stupid ass broads."

I ignored TaNaysha, arguing with her wasn't worth wasting my breath. She'd go on and on until she won the fight and the battle. The only thing on my mind was dropping off my sandals at the Goodwill.

* * *

The domino tournament had officially kicked off. Slay, of course, had entered along with every other nigga in the hood and a couple of broads too. Big Steph, short for Big Stephanie, was one of the broads. She didn't pose a threat to Slay and my relationship. She was a lesbian, the aggressive type, who resembled Cleo from the movie *Set It Off.* She was one of the few women pimps in the hood. Her hoes serviced anybody who paid in cash and if you asked any of them they would tell you that they liked working for Big Steph. She treated them fair and was like the mother many of them never had. She was cool. If you didn't fuck with her, she didn't fuck with you and there was no drama.

After dropping off TaNaysha and Khalilah, I called Slay. He was still at Ernie Pain's. Him and Big Steph were playing in the same domino game with two other niggas. She was whooping all of their asses. He said that he'd be home soon, which meant he wouldn't be home for a few hours. Going home to an empty house wasn't appealing. I headed to the bookstore.

Like I was raised in the church, I grew up surrounded by books. My mother was a librarian and when I was younger, sometimes I'd tag along with her to work—engrossing myself in the fantasies of fiction. Back then I read for fun. Now, I found myself wandering the aisles of Barnes & Noble, searching for a book to be my companion in the wee hours of the morning on the nights Slay didn't come home.

I wasn't looking for a particular author or genre, just an entertaining read and ended up with two books—both urban fiction. The heroines in each reminded me of myself and were struggling with the same problem I was, loving and living with a hustler.

On the way to the register, I took a detour down the Money & Finance aisle and flipped through a couple of self-help books on money matters: stocks and bonds, money markets, investing and other shit that was foreign to me.

"This shit is like reading Spanish," I said out loud and to no one in particular, which is why I was startled when I received a response.

"It's not that difficult to understand."

I didn't have to look up from the book I was attempting to read to know who was talking to me. I recognized the black Timberlands. Tyrell was standing right next to me with a book in his hand.

"I can teach you all you need to know…about investing that is," he said.

My heart was racing but it wasn't because of Tyrell. I was scared that Slay was watching.

"Thanks, but no thanks. I'll figure it out." I walked away, never looking up at him.

* * *

Slay's Escalade was in the driveway. He was home. I turned the key and opened the door to him staring directly at me. He was sitting on the loveseat that faced the front door with a glass of Coke and Crown in his hand.

"Where the fuck you been?"

"At the bookstore."

"Didn't I fuckin' tell you that I would be home soon? I've been sittin' here for two hours waitin' on your ass."

"Well, now you know how the fuck I feel when you don't come home some nights. When you're out fuckin' Aleesha and God knows who." Cursing had become second nature to me and Slay had stopped calling me on it.

He threw the glass against the front door, inches from my face. It shattered into a million little pieces. Slay was in my face.

"Shar, don't make me kill you. I'm gonna ask you one more time. Where the fuck you been?"

"I told you that I was at the bookstore." I held up the green Barnes & Noble shopping bag for him to see and ran past him, crying.

"Babygirl." he followed behind me. "Babygirl, I'm sorry. I just can't imagine you being with another nigga. That shit drives me crazy. I'm sorry."

"Just leave me alone."

"Babygirl, please don't be mad at me. I love you...not Aleesha or any other fuckin' broad out there. And for the record, I haven't fucked Aleesha or anybody else since you moved into the condo. I've been over to the house to check on my shit but that's it. Babygirl, you gotta believe me. When I'm out...I'm out handlin' my fuckin' business...tryin' to keep an eye on these niggas I got workin' for me. You believe me...don't you?"

I nodded my head yes.

Chapter 8

LIKE CRACK

The nigga who got shot and killed at Club Pulse was one of Slay's major-weight-moving workers. He was known in the hood as Yo—given the nickname because he was from New York and began every sentence with "Yo, Son."

Slay showed no emotion over Yo's death. His only concern was the upcoming drop Yo was scheduled to make in Ohio before he was gunned down.

"That's just how shit goes down sometimes, Babygirl," Slay told me as he lined several duffle bags with baby pampers to mask the smell of the blocks of cocaine he had stuffed them full with. I'm sure it wasn't the first time he had made a drop himself, but it was the first one I had ever known him to make. He and another young nigga he had promoted from slanging on the corner were going to make the delivery.

"Slay, please don't go," I begged. "I just got a funny feelin'."

"Babygirl." Slay palmed my face. "The world don't stop spinnin' just cause one nigga gets killed. These niggas in Ohio are expectin' their shit to be delivered on time and I'm expectin' them to have my motherfuckin' money. Your Benz, this condo, the clothes on your back...how you livin'...this is how I get it and unless you fine with a nigga workin' at McDonald's bringin' you home chicken nuggets instead of caviar then you got to dry them tears up. I miss you already, Babygirl. I'll be back...don't worry."

Slay kissed me on the forehead and loaded the duffle bags in the trunk of the bite-size Ford Focus he had rented. In the hood, he drove around in luxury but transporting illegal drugs on the interstate called for him to travel inconspicuously he reasoned. But, thinking back, how two gangsta-ass niggas cooped up in a Ford Focus wasn't conspicuous was beyond me.

The three days Slay was out of town, I was on pins and needles—scared that he wouldn't return and petrified of a future without him. He was my provider and protector. He was the man I loved. He was my everything.

The first day, I stayed in bed, only getting up to pee. The second day, TaNaysha came knocking on the condo door.

"Damnnnnn...you look a hot-ass mess. I know you ain't smokin' that shit."

"Hell nah. Slay had to go out of town and I've just worried myself sick."

"Bitch, you need to get it together...cut out all that damn cryin' and shit. You might not be dealin' but you livin' with a nigga who is. That means you in the street life too and pretty soon there'll be no turnin' back. You need to start thinkin' about the what-if's in life. Shit, nothin' in the streets is guaranteed and that includes the fairytale endin' you think you and Slay gonna fuckin' have."

TaNaysha was one of those people you either loved or hated. Like her mother, she was a tell-it-like-it-is type of person. She lacked tact, but she didn't give a fuck. She spoke her mind and held nothing back. She was the queen of keeping shit real. Some days I wondered how our friendship had weathered her trash-talking ways, but then I remembered that there wasn't anyone else who I trusted more to tell me the truth—even when it hurt. But some times, most times, I just wanted to tell her to shut the fuck up.

"Why are you so damn negative all the time?"

"Bitch, I'm just tryin' to help you out."

"Where's Khalilah?" I asked, changing the subject.

"Somewhere stuck up under Carlo's ass. I told her that shit ain't gonna ever work."

"I think they make a cute couple," I argued on Khalilah and Carlo's behalf.

"If you say so. I bet he won't ever take her ass home to meet his mama. Anyways, bitch, put some clothes on."

"Why? Where we goin'?"

"Where my mama use to take me."

* * *

The chamber was full. TaNaysha had loaded the .40 caliber pistol with thirteen bullets and fired them all without hesitation.

"Damn, GI Jane," I said, ducking out of the way of the flying shell casings.

TaNaysha retrieved her results—five bullets to the head, five to the chest and the remaining three landed in the neck of the human figure outlined on the paper target.

My mother and Ms. Trina were like night and day, each of their ideas of motherhood shaped by their life experiences. Ms. Trina's life was tragic, an urban tale about the loss of her innocence, freedom and sadly herself. My mother enjoyed a privileged childhood and lived a straight-laced life—college, career, boy, love, marriage, mortgage and then came the baby carriages. She raised me how her mother had raised her and wasn't to blame for her inability to predict the road I would take in life.

Upon her release from prison, Ms. Trina began taking TaNaysha on field trips to the gun range while other mothers were taking their daughters shopping for training bras—mothers like my own who never dreamed that their daughters would ever get caught up living the street life. But, all it took was one glance from a hood nigga to derail the course of their lives and Ms. Trina was all too aware of that. She wasn't grooming TaNaysha for the streets but preparing her for the life making wrong decisions could lead her to live.

It was my turn. My hands were shaking.

"What the fuck you scared of? It's not the gun that can kill you. It's the nigga pullin' the trigger. Here." TaNaysha loaded a .22 and handed it to me. It was the first time I had ever held a gun. "You gotta crawl before you walk," she said, her reasoning for teaching me to shoot the much smaller pistol than the .40 she had used.

Like a dance instructor, TaNaysha positioned my feet in an aim-ready-shoot stance and showed me how to grip the gun. She told me to drop and relax my shoulders. I felt like a new police recruit. I pulled the trigger, unconsciously closing my eyes.

"Bitch, you can't be closin' your eyes and shit. You be done killed an innocent bystander. Go, again."

I fired the two remaining bullets in the chamber. None of the bullets I fired hit the target.

"Damn, you suck," TaNaysha said.

"Well, forgive me if my mama isn't a damn trained assassin or some shit like that."

After a few more rounds, my fear of guns had eased up and I had even hit the target a few times. It was a fear I wished I had never conquered—the feeling of being afraid to take a life.

* * *

Watching daytime television was getting old. There should have been a limit on the number of paternity tests the Maury

Povich Show was allowed to conduct; the number of tears Oprah shed and the number of times the Price Is Right allowed a contestant to bid just $1. I clicked the television off and threw the remote down on the other end of the couch. It didn't take me long to discover that maybe, just maybe, there *was* one thing that Slay couldn't give me—the feeling of accomplishing something other than padding my wardrobe and collecting designer handbags. I wanted a job, a temporary gig, just to pass the time until I started school in the fall.

With only a high school diploma, I didn't expect to find a job making more than minimum wage. I headed to the mall to round up some applications. Retail seemed more my speed than working myself to exhaustion in an unairconditioned factory everyday.

There were several retailers in the mall hiring summer help: Macy's, Express, Banana Republic, Aldo's, Baker's, Yankee Candle, Bath & Bodyworks and some others. I picked up an application from each and there was one more place I had remembered seeing a We're-Hiring sign, the bookstore.

The aroma of coffee beans and intellectually focused conversations filled the air. Students with their books open, laptops up and headphones on were scattered all over the bookstore. For the first time since moving in with Slay, I regretted choosing him over going away to college. And for a moment, I resented falling in love with him. But, the animosity was short lived. Slay was my nigga and more than not, I loved being his Babygirl. There was no greater feeling. Like a crackhead gone off crack, I was gone off Slay.

Before asking for an application, I couldn't resist roaming the aisles of the bookstore. Slay wasn't due back until tomorrow and I was in for another lonely night. I had finished the two books that I had purchased previously and settled on two more—romances this time. Not completely sold on the books I had chose based on the short synopsis's found on the back covers, I found an unoccupied sitting area in the back of the store. Reading the first few paragraphs of each book would encourage or discourage my decision to buy or not to buy.

"You must live here."

"I can say the same about you," I said, looking up at Tyrell. He was rocking a plain white tee, some dark denim jeans and some tan, untied Timberlands.

"May, I?" Tyrell gestured to the empty chair next to me.

"What if I said no?"

"Then I wouldn't sit there. I never want to be anywhere I'm not welcome."

"I can't stop you from sittin' where you want to sit. It's a free country."

Tyrell took a seat. He had a book in his hand, a collection of poems by Sonya Sanchez.

"Danielle Steel?" He laughed, looking at the book I had in my hand.

"What's wrong with Danielle Steel?"

"Nothin'. I just didn't figure you for a Danielle Steel fan."

"I didn't figure you for a nigga who read poetry," I said, flipping my hair out of my face.

"You have beautiful hair."

"Thanks…I guess."

Tyrell leaned in closer to me. The smell of his cologne seeped up my nose. *Gucci.* Slay's favorite too. Before I allowed another nigga to get my panties wet, I quickly gathered up my shit and left.

* * *

My nightgown was soaked. Slay had poured a pitcher of ice-cold water down my back, waking me up out of my sleep. The water seeping into my pores felt like a thousand needles pricking my skin. Until then, I hadn't known such physical pain.

"What-the-fuck?" Startled, I jumped up. Ice cubes slid down my back into the crack of my ass. "Fuck!" I ran to the bathroom, shivering and covered with chill bumps.

"I'm gone for three motherfuckin' days...makin' this money...tryna take care of your ass and you disrespect me by bein' all up in another nigga's face...flirtin' and fuckin' flippin' your hair and shit."

"I don't know what the fuck you're talkin' about." I locked the bathroom door.

The me a few weeks earlier would have been down on her knees crying but living with Slay had hardened me. My softer side was dissipating. It was one of the many side effects of living with a nigga like Slay. I didn't shed a tear—guess I was becoming immune to his outbursts.

"I'm talkin' 'bout the nigga at the bookstore. Don't play with me, Shar."

"Fuck you!" I said. "I've given up a lot of shit for you...my family...my education. Why the fuck would I go out and fuck with another nigga? Your ass is crazy."

"Don't let me find out who the nigga is."

"Whatever," I said, thinking: *This shit is for the birds.* Even though I didn't think once about flying the coop.

Chapter 9

JEALOUS ASS NIGGAS

By the middle of the summer, my jewelry box was overflowing with tennis bracelets—Slay's way of apologizing for his rage-filled outburst. After each argument, he'd leave the house, stay out all night and come home the next day with a Tiffany's box. Then we'd fuck. A week never went by without the dramatics. If Slay wasn't accusing me of cheating on him, he was accusing me of contemplating to—forgetting that he was the one not only fucking another broad but also taking care of her.

In the beginning, I nagged him constantly about cutting his ties with Aleesha. But, after one broken-promise-to-do-so too many, I stopped—resigned to the fact that until she was six feet under, I would be sharing Slay with her forever. I don't know who was the dumber broad, her or me.

Slay had made it to the finals of the domino tournament, beating out Big Steph and a handful of other niggas. He was over at Ernie Pain's, fighting for the title of being the hood's best domino player. Being the hood kingpin wasn't enough.

From front to back, I had finished reading the two Danielle Steel books that I had copped, but I had been forced to keep my distance from the bookstore. Another run-in with Tyrell and Slay's hands would be around my neck. He was worse than an incompetent jury at presuming the innocent guilty. Not only had he forbid me from going back to the bookstore, he had shredded all of the applications I had picked up from the mall. Needless to say, I was still unemployed. Slay had changed his mind about me getting a job. "Save your energy for school," was all he said.

Mohammed, an Arab-nigga who owned the Shell station in the hood, had hired TaNaysha. They were like oil and water. They didn't mesh and were constantly bickering. But, he welcomed her take-no-bullshit attitude to deal with the young hood thieves who stuffed their pockets full of his merchandise. Since she'd been working for him, the number of theft incidents at his gas station had declined.

TaNaysha was behind the glass-encased counter, slipping some lottery tickets to an elderly Black woman whose knees were swollen and bruised from being on her knees, praying to hit the jackpot when I walked into the shell station. Even a small sum would have eased her burden, I guessed—maybe helping her pay a utility bill here or fill a prescription there.

A group of young niggas, jeans sagging and underwear showing, waltzed up and down the aisles. Mohammed watched them closely from behind the counter with a baseball bat in his hands.

"What the fuck you gonna do with a baseball bat? If them niggas were thuggin' forreal they would gun your Arabian ass down. You need a gun up in here." TaNaysha shook her head.

"You shut up. This is a Louisville slugger…best bat in America," Mohammed said in his thick Middle Eastern accent. He raised the bat up in the air.

"Mohammed, you got one more time to tell me to shut up. Don't make me snatch that damn turban off your head."

"Hey, Mohammed," I said, leaning up against the counter. "You ready." Between my trips to the mall and Regina's Nails, I was TaNaysha's chauffer for the summer—taking her to and picking her up from work. I truly didn't mind.

"Yeah, let me get my shit." TaNaysha reached for her purse.

"Where do you think you're going?" Mohammed asked her.

"Nigga, I'm goin' home. My shift is over."

"You came in eight minutes late," he stressed.

"And, I came in thirty minutes early the other day. Don't act like you don't remember that shit, Mohammed."

He waved TaNaysha off.

"He gets on my damn nerves," she said as we were heading out of the door.

"Bye, Mohammed," I yelled back.

TaNaysha and I circled a few blocks before I took her home to change out of her work gear. We were meeting Khalilah at Red Lobster. She said that she had something to tell us. Supposedly, she had been gone for two weeks at church camp— that's the lie she told her grandparents. We guessed that her ass was somewhere off with Carlo.

We rode past Ernie Pain's. Cars were parked outside of his house, in his front and back yards, like he owned a used car lot. One nigga had the nerve to put some rims on a Fiesta. It was parked in the front yard.

"That's some dumb shit," TaNaysha laughed.

Slay's new ride, a pimped out Caprice Classic, was parked in the back. It was sitting high on some twenty-six inch rims and was two-toned in color, red and gray. I was just glad that he was where he said he'd be.

Ms. Trina and her friend Louise, who everybody in the hood called LuLu, were in the kitchen. LuLu was doing Ms. Trina's hair, gluing in some tracks with a Newport hanging from her lips. Ms. Trina had one in her hand.

LuLu was puff-puffing and gluing away. She was short and big breasted and wore house shoes during the winter, spring and fall—the same ones. She had two sons, Tremaine and Jermaine, both of them were locked up for selling drugs. Additional time was added to their sentence because they were conducting their business within the vicinity of an elementary school. They were new to the game and apparently, hadn't been schooled on the do's and dont's. Her only daughter, Porsha, had three kids and another one on the way. But, all of her kids were by the same nigga and in the hood that was impressive.

"Girl, I heard you was pregnant," LuLu said.

"Who, me?" I pointed to myself.

"Yeah, you. Heard that's why yo' mama and daddy kicked you out of their house."

Rumors spread rampant in the hood. If niggas didn't know the truth, they would come up with some shit from off the top of their heads. Jealous broads were the same way. They would say anything to ruin another broad's reputation. Shit, it wasn't the first time I had been rumored pregnant. Me, TaNaysha or Khalilah. Broads were forever hating on us.

"That's news to me," I said, recalling my last period. It had ended just days ago.

"Your fast-ass daughter is the only one around here havin' babies every other day," Ms. Trina said to LuLu.

TaNaysha was dressed and ready. "Bye, Ma. Bye, LuLu."

"Bye," I waved.

"Don't pay any attention to LuLu. Half the shit she says she heard she made up her damn self," TaNaysha said when we were in the car on our way to Red Lobster.

I pulled into the parking lot and parked next to Carlo's Range Rover. Khalilah was still whipping it. We spotted her sitting in a corner booth of the restaurant.

"Is that bitch glowin'?" TaNaysha asked under her breath as we followed the waiter. "I bet she's pregnant?"

"There you go makin' up shit like LuLu," I said.

Khalilah was beaming. Her usual manila-file-folder colored skin was tanned a golden brown. Her once black shoulder length hair was fuller and longer with added extensions and dyed brown with subtle blonde highlights. Her make up was applied naturally. Shades of earth tones covered her eyelids, cheeks and lips. She was wearing a strapless black dress. It was fitting and hung inches above her knees, very classy. She matched the dress with a simple pair of black stilettos. TaNaysha and I looked at each other and then down at ourselves. Shit, compared to Khalilah I felt like I needed an extreme makeover. We rushed past the waiter to the booth where she was sitting.

"Bitch, where the fuck have you been and don't lie?" TaNaysha demanded to know the details.

"It sure as hell wasn't church camp," I said with my hands on my hip.

"Hawaii."

"Hawaii!" Both TaNaysha and I screamed, sliding into the booth.

"Yes! Carlo just called me out of the blue and told me to pack my bags. Next thing I know we're on a plane on our way to Maui. I had the time of my life. Carlo had already made an appointment for me at the hotel's salon before we even touched down. We went to the spa everyday and got massages. We shopped, ate and Carlo even taught me how to play golf. Y'all...I think I'm in love. No one has ever treated me better."

TaNaysha and I were so caught up in Khalilah's fairytale love affair that we didn't even notice the rock on her ring finger. "Carlo asked me to marry him." She excitedly waved her left hand in the air.

TaNaysha choked—on air. "Bi...bi...," she couldn't even get her favorite word out.

My mouth was paused wide open.

"I met his family. His father is very nice. His mother...well, she wasn't thrilled about us but she said all that mattered to her was Carlo's happiness and if he loved me...she'd just have to deal with it."

"When...when are y'all gettin' married?" I asked.

"I don't know but he wants me to move in with him by the end of the summer. Frankie's moving out. I'm still goin' to school in the fall, though."

"Okay...when his mother wakes up and realizes that your ass is Black and not Jewish and your ass ends up missin' don't say shit," TaNaysha had gathered her thoughts.

"I guess it's a risk I'm willin' to take for love." Khalilah shrugged her shoulders.

I sat stunned, admittedly jealous and enlightened. There was a big difference in a nigga saying that he loved you as opposed to him treating you like he did.

* * *

Slay wasn't a scary nigga. At least, he didn't appear to be on the surface. He was aware of the consequences and repercussions of being a player in the game. He acted like he didn't fear them—prison or death and maybe both. Oddly, he came home from Ernie Pain's nervous and more lovey dovey than normal.

I was lying on the couch when he came over and rested his head in the pit of my stomach, clutching my hips. I ran my hand over his thick waves. Out of fear of my own, I remained silent, afraid that I'd ruin the moment and awaken the Dr. Jekyll in him. He pulled my panties down and stretched his left hand up my chest while the fingers on his right hand tickled Ms. Kitty. I arched my back and moaned, lifting my pelvis to his mouth. He nuzzled his chin in Ms. Kitty's hair and then his tongue took over for his fingers. In seconds, the levee inside of me had broken. I had never come so quick or so hard.

Slay slid his jeans and boxers off. I got down on my knees and returned the favor, taking all of him in my mouth—bopping my head up and down, stroking, sucking and slobbering him all the way to ecstasy.

"Damn, Babygirl, you talented," Slay said, catching his breath.

The morning after, I learned that some niggas who worked for a nigga name Cheez had been busted for serving an undercover cop. Cheez was a fat ass nigga, from eating too many damn ninety-nine cent cheese hamburgers from McDonald's. He left a paper trail from the drive-thru window throughout the hood, discarding cheeseburger wrappers out the window as he devoured them. The urban legend in the hood was that he bought fifty cheeseburgers at one time and visited Micky D's three times a day. He would ride through the hood taking up both the driver and passenger sides of his car and was grossly disgusting but not because he was obese. He was a dirty nigga, always walking around with ketchup and mustard stains on his white tee and dirt under his fingernails. He was just one of those niggas that looked like he preferred taking wash-ups instead of baths, reserving bathing for the holidays. But, he was paid and could afford both gastric bypass surgery and plastic surgery. The nigga just didn't care about nothing but his loot.

Cheez operated out of a house that looked abandoned on the outside but resembled a research lab on the inside. He was the next nigga in line, after Slay, who ruled the streets. They, along with the small time hustlers had been able to cohabitate in the same hood, divvying up corners—Slay presiding over the majority of them. But, it didn't take a psychic to predict that sooner or later niggas would start to feel the need to scratch their itch to be the big fish in the pond.

Slay was convinced that Cheez would encourage one of his prison-bound, ex-employees to snitch—giving up the name of the big boss in the hood.

"Baby, them niggas are more scared of you than they are Cheez," I said, trying to offer Slay some comfort.

Snitches received no respect and if they weren't in the witness protection program, more than likely they tiptoed along with a mark on their lives—target practice for some young nigga without a conscience who would kill for a pair of kicks or simply to impress another nigga. I personally wasn't worried about a nigga snitching. But Slay, for the first time, looked like he was. Another encounter with the "white and blues" would be strike three for him and land him behind bars for the long haul.

"Niggas are startin' to smell themselves, Babygirl. Jealous ass niggas...I'mma lay low for a while."

Chapter 10

YO'S REPLACEMENT

The gut feeling that death or incarceration was on the horizon had its' way of changing a hood nigga or broad—forcing them to temporarily live right until the feeling materialized into reality or subsided. Slay's road to redemption was short lived. He had parked the Escalade, Caprice, Deville and Cutlass and didn't leave the condo for a week, not even to go check on Aleesha. Which, I had no qualms about. Shit, I didn't care if her ass starved to damn death. As long as Slay was by my side, I didn't have to worry about him fucking with her. We laid up the entire time: fucking, watching movies, eating, talking about our future together and fucking some more. From time to time, he would take a phone call and cuss the fuck out of one of his workers. Although he stayed out of sight, business went on as usual.

The week was on track to being the first that we hadn't argued about something whether it was him staying out all night or accusing me of some false shit until I made the mistake of mentioning all of the shit Carlo had done for Khalilah—whisking her to Hawaii, catering to her every need and proposing. Slay went ballistic while I balled up like a roly-poly in the corner of the living room, shielding myself from the flying debris—picture frames, coasters, remotes and anything else that was within his reach. He restrained himself from hitting me, but I was sure my time was coming—guess it was just a gut feeling. After Slay calmed down, he left, told me to clean up the mess he had made and to be dressed when he returned.

An hour later, he pulled up in the driveway in the Cutlass, honking the horn. I didn't keep him waiting. I grabbed my purse and ran out of the condo faster than a Jamaican sprinter. By the time I made it to the Cutlass, I was out of breath.

"What the fuck you runnin' for?"

"I didn't want to upset you again," I said with my head hung low.

Slay lifted my chin. "Babygirl, I'm sorry. You know I love you, don't you."

"I know."

He didn't spring for a trip to Hawaii or any other romantic island. Instead, he took me on a shopping spree—told me to get whatever I wanted but all I really wanted was him to myself, not having to share him with the streets or Aleesha. Still, I racked up at the mall, buying unnecessary shit—more of what I already had: shoes, clothes, purses and jewelry. The trunk of the Cutlass was packed full with shopping bags.

On our way back home, Slay noticed the police or as he referred to them, the "white and blues" behind us. He trailed us for a few blocks before flashing his lights and demanding that we pull over.

"This is some bullshit," Slay said, pulling over to the side of the street. He must have noticed my nervous energy. "Just be calm, Babygirl. Ain't nothin' in here," he said, indicating that he didn't have any illegal substances on him or in the car. I breathed a sigh of relief.

The middle-aged, White police officer slowly approached the car. He had his right hand on his gun and a flashlight in the other, shining it in the backseat of the Cutlass and then into Slay's face.

"How may I help you officer?" Slay asked, making an attempt to respect the law.

"Your license and registration please."

Slay retrieved his license from his wallet and the registration from the glove compartment. "What seems to be the problem, officer?" he asked.

"You work?" The officer asked.

The look in Slay's eyes said it all. *What the fuck does that have to do with anything?* Reluclantly, he answered. "Yes, Sir. I'm employed down at the Y, doing janitorial work. I saved a little money from my last paycheck and was just comin' back from takin' my girl out to eat."

Slay wasn't exactly lying. He was on the payroll down at the YMCA. The Vice President of Human Resources for the organization was one of his white-collar clients. He agreed to hire Slay on paper, giving him a cover for a valid source of income, in exchange for Slay keeping his dirty little secret. He was a major cokehead.

The officer handed Slay back his information. "I pulled you over because you have a broken tail light. I'm going to assume that you weren't aware of it and let you go on a warning... this time."

"Thank you, officer. I'll get it fixed right away."

Slay dropped me off at the condo, because he had some business to take care of. His days of laying low were over and it was back to business as usual. He switched vehicles and sped off before I could attempt to ask him what time he thought he'd be back home; although, I wasn't expecting to see him again until in the morning. As I did every time he left the house, I said a silent prayer that God would protect Slay even if he were a solider in the opposing army.

Not even a full two hours later, I heard the condo door unlock. *That was quick,* I thought, peeking out the living room blinds. Slay came in and went straight to the kitchen. He reached for a dish towel and some ice to make a makeshift icepack. His knuckles on both hands were bruised and swollen. Right away, I knew who was at the receiving end of the blows Slay had thrown—Aleesha. She had wrecked the Cutlass and forgot to tell him. He made her his human punching bag. True, she was the other woman. Shit, maybe I was the other woman. Regardless, in that moment, my sympathy ran deep for her.

* * *

"Bitch, you know my mama can't breath from smokin' all them damn Newports. Shit, my lungs are probably as black as hers from the second hand smoke. Anyway, she was over at LuLu's playin' cards last night and started coughin' and shit. LuLu had to rush her to the emergency room."

"She alright?" I asked TaNaysha.

"Yeah, she's cool. Anyway, bitch, guess who they saw up in there?"

"Who?"

"Aleesha…said her face and shit was all fucked up and that her arm was broke. You know nosy ass LuLu asked her what happened."

"What she say?"

"Said she slipped and fell. Bitch, please. Everybody knows Slay gave her a WWE beat down. Shit, he whooped her ass like she was another nigga. He ain't hittin' you. Is he?"

"Nah," I said. *Not yet,* I thought.

"You need a gun and to stop with that non-violence-Martin-Luther-King shit. You gotta go Farrakhan on these niggas."

"You think havin' a gun is the answer to everything."

"Damn right it is...will stop a nigga dead in his tracks. You can get beat the fuck up if you want too. I wish a nigga would."

I swerved into the Shell station. "What time you get off?"

"Mohammed got my ass workin' late tonight. Don't worry about pickin' me up. Porsha gonna come pick me up."

"LuLu's Porsha?"

"Yeah. She needs some gas money. Her babies' daddy ain't worth shit."

"Alright, cool. Call me in the mornin'."

Since Slay was slacking on the romantic tip. I went home to romance my damn self. I ran a bubble bath, lit some candles and put on some Etta James. She was my mother's favorite artist and one of mine too. In the delivery room, when my mother was giving birth to me, she demanded that my father sing an Etta James tune to calm her nerves. He sung *My Funny Valentine*. I'm surprised they didn't name me Etta or Valentina. I leaned back in the Jacuzzi tub, listening to Etta sing.

Fool that I am for falling in love with you
Fool that I am for thinking you loved me too
You took my heart than played the part of little go get
And all of my dreams just disappeared like smoke from a cigarette

Fool That I Am was the name of the song playing. It was the theme song of my life. I was just too stubborn to admit it. I clicked the CD player off and sat in silence with my thoughts about how unpredictable life could be. Months before, my life was on another track, much like my mother's—college, career, boy, love, marriage, mortgage and babies. Now I found myself, technically, in a three-way relationship—sharing the man I loved and feeling sorry for the broad he was sleeping with. *What kind of shit is that?*

I asked myself. And then there was the abuse and all of the rest of the bullshit that came with living with a nigga in the game. Yet, I wasn't unhappy. Maybe having all of the material shit I wanted at my disposal made the difference or being known as the biggest-dope-dealer-in-the-hood's broad. Or, maybe I was just a fool in love—overpowered by Slay's swagger.

My grandmother had a saying that she use to say, "Can't help nobody that don't want to be helped." For me, there was no escaping Slay because I didn't want to be free. The same stronghold that Slay had on Aleesha—the one that led her to stay with him beating after beating—he had on me.

* * *

Slay was looking for a nigga to replace Yo. He had been promoting and demoting niggas and broads within his operation—rearranging their positions and sticking them where he thought best. Most of the broads he had working for him remained in place. A broad flying with a suitcase full of cocaine looked less suspicious than a nigga doing the same. He didn't fire anyone, making enemies was the last thing he wanted to do. He called me on the pink Razor, excited like a kid in a candy shop.

"Hey, Babygirl."

"Hey, Big Poppa."

Slay laughed. "I love it when you call me Big Poppa."

We were having a good day. Slay started going on and on about the nigga who had won Ernie Pain's domino tournament—about how clever and unselfish the nigga was. The two qualifications Slay required for a nigga to work for him. "Dumb niggas make mistakes and selfish niggas get greedy," Slay liked to say.

"That nigga black as hell but he's smart...a genius. The nigga was tellin' everybody at the domino table exactly...domino for domino…what they had in their hand. He read mine's like a fuckin' pychic. After that nigga won, he offered to spilt his winnings with everybody at the table."

I had never heard Slay speak highly of another nigga, not Yo or anyone else. "Sounds like you found Yo's replacement."

"This nigga gonna turn out to be better than Yo. I'll be home in a few."

I stayed in the tub for a few minutes longer before getting out and lathering my body with lotion. I was in the mood and put on one of the many Frederick's of Hollywood get-ups I owned. I heard the alarm sound. Slay was home and I assumed he clicked on the television since I heard another voice in the background. Half naked and looking like a Playboy Bunny, I seductively strutted down the stairs into the living room.

"Surprise!"

My eyes darted from Slay and then to Tyrell and then back to Slay. I was the one surprised and Tyrell seemed to genuinely be also—to find out that I was Slay's girl. Apparently, he was the last nigga in the hood to know.

"Didn't I fuckin' tell you that I would be home in a few? Get the fuck upstairs and put on a robe."

I turned to head back upstairs. Out of respect for Slay, Tyrell looked the other way.

Chapter 11

Part Two

ALWAYS AROUND

Tyrell was always around. He wasn't just Yo's replacement; he was Slay's protégé. They were the hood's Batman and Robin, attached at the hip. Slay taught him all about the logistics of every level of his operation. Shit that I didn't even know—where Slay manufactured his products from the ten to twenty dollar rocks and bags of weed slung on the corner to the brick-shaped blocks of cocaine he copped wholesale and trafficked over the interstates and airways to be distributed at the retail level. Tyrell, in turn, used his contacts and brilliance to make Slay's operation more efficient. He convinced Slay to start a small moving company called Makin' Moves Truckin' Company. *We Deliver Anywhere!* was their slogan. The company was legit but packed amongst the furniture belonging to unsuspecting clients was major weight. And, by chance the moving trucks were ever pulled over, the client was the party responsible for all of the property in tow—not the truck driver or company owner. Tyrell guaranteed Slay's hands would remain clean. He also tried but failed to convince Slay to wave goodbye to the corner hustle. The ten and twenty dollar rocks and bags of weed added up but the money was nothing compared to the loot the price of cocaine brought in. But, Slay wasn't ready to retire from the block or downsize his workforce—also suggested by Tyrell. He thought that Slay had too many cooks in the kitchen. Slay thought otherwise. Guess he was getting greedy. But, other than a few small disagreements, Slay trusted Tyrell with his business, his life and with me. The moment Tyrell found out who I was he turned cold towards me—nothing like the warm, poetry-reading nigga he appeared to be at the bookstore. He never looked my way or acknowledged me in or out of Slay's presence.

Once again, Slay was out of town, dealing with them Ohio niggas. Tyrell had stayed to keep an eye out on the other niggas and broads working for Slay, to collect Slay's loot from them and to run Makin' Moves. He was leaned up against a wall in the club with a drink in his hand; rocking an all black New York Yankees fitted cap, a long-sleeved black button down, jeans and a pair of fresh black hightop Air Force Ones. *Black must be that nigga's favorite color.* He had his jeans tucked behind the tongue of his right shoe and out and over the left. He bopped his head to the music and I watched his lips part, rapping the lyrics to Jay Z's classic *99 Problems.* The deejay had remixed the joint and included bars from a newer Jay Z hit. He had niggas in The Tap Room hype.

A broad with tangled weave, triple D-sized breasts popping out of her too little spandex dress and crusty ass heels hanging over the back of her shoes walked up on Tyrell. Wesley Snipes in drag looked better than her ass. She danced in front of him like a Magic City stripper. He took a sip of his drink, paying her ass no attention at all. She turned around, revealing nothing but a flatter-than-a-pancake ass, and backed in closer to him.

"Who the fuck let the air out of that tire?" TaNaysha laughed.

We were in Carlo and Frankie's security room watching all of the shit taking place in the club on the security monitors. The broad did everything she could to spark Tyrell's interest, but he wasn't biting. His dick didn't budge. Pissed, she stormed off.

"Let me show this bitch how it's done." TaNaysha stood up, smoothed out the wrinkles in her own too-little-ass dress, retouched her lip gloss and switched her ass out into the club. She didn't make any pit stops. She walked right up to Tyrell and put her hands on her hips.

"What's up?" I read her lips.

"The sky," Tyrell said.

"You're funny...real funny."

Tyrell shrugged his shoulders. "If you say so."

"You wanna dance?" TaNaysha asked.

"I got two left feet?" He turned her down easy.

She stepped in closer to him and whispered something into his ear.

"No, thanks." He mouthed.

Knowing she was being watched, TaNaysha gracefully walked away and came back into the office.

"That nigga gay."

"Why you say that?" I asked.

"Don't no straight nigga turn down that much free pussy. Broads been tryin' to get up on him all night. I'm tellin' you...that nigga gay."

"I gotta pee."

I got up, readjusted the lace bustier top I was wearing and ironed out my hip-hugging jeans with my hands. My Farrah Fawcett-curled hair hung past my bare shoulders and my French pedicured toes peeped out of the open-toed, electric-blue, snakeskin stilettos that I was rocking. I tucked my matching clutch under my left arm and waded through the crowd of drunk niggas and horny broads.

"Back the fuck up." I had to hold my own against a braided-up broad trying to holla. There was no shame in her game. *What the fuck she doin' at the straight club anyway?* There was a line to use the restroom. *Shit.* I maneuvered my way to the bar and ordered a Sprite. There was no damn way I was going to get mopped the fuck up off the dance floor again. Slay was like a magician, always popping the fuck up out of nowhere. I reached into my purse to pay.

"Don't worry about it," the bartender said. "The gentleman put you specifically on his tab."

"Who, Carlo?"

"No, not Carlo. My man T."

I looked over in the direction where Tyrell had been standing. He was gone.

* * *

The after party was at Carlo and Frankie's crib. TaNaysha and I followed behind Carlo and Khalilah. Ahead of them was Frankie in his Expedition with some White broads and some niggas who worked as their bodyguards.

"Damn!" TaNaysha and I said at once.

Carlo and Frankie's crib was like some celebrity shit off of MTV Cribs.

"That bitch done hit the motherfuckin' jackpot. You...you just won a scratch off," TaNaysha turned and said to me, comparing Carlo to Slay in lottery terms.

"What-the-fuck-ever...Carlo ain't got shit on Slay. My nigga got swagger."

"Who the fuck needs swagger when they're livin' like this?"

The condo was worth a quarter of a million dollars. Shit, I had no idea about the house Aleesa was living in. But, Carlo and

Frankie owned a million-dollar mansion: brick, three levels, four-car garage, six bedrooms, nine bathrooms, formal living room, family room, dining room, theater room, media room, laundry room, library, swimming pool, basketball and tennis courts and guest quarters. The foyer alone was larger than the condo's living room. Khalilah gave us the grand tour. She hadn't officially moved in yet because she and Carlo were waiting for Frankie to move out.

"Why Carlo kickin' Frankie out? There're enough rooms to house a thousand motherfuckers up in here?" TaNaysha asked.

"Carlo's not kickin' Frankie out. Frankie's the one who wants to move," Khalilah said, flicking on the lights to show us the master bathroom.

The bathroom was constructed with his and her vanities, his and her showers, a Jacuzzi tub big enough for three Cheez-size niggas and a 50" inch flat screen television built into the wall. I was living like a princess. Khalilah was about to be living like a queen.

"Oh, I get it," TaNaysha said. "How the fuck Frankie gonna hate Black people when his ass is constantly surrounded by them. Hell, we the ones makin' his ass rich…payin' twenty dollars to get in the club."

Khalilah and I looked at TaNaysha.

"Since when did you ever have to pay to get up in The Tap Room?" Khalilah asked, a little agitated that TaNaysha had brought up the race issue again.

"I'm talkin' 'bout all the other motherfuckers who have."

"Carlo got to be involved in some other shit," I said, ignoring their conversation.

"Their father owns a few Burger King franchises."

"See, I told you them Jewish niggas be buyin' up shit," TaNaysha nagged on.

Partied out, everybody ended up in the theater room. *Deja Vu*, with Denzel Washington and Paula Patton, was playing on the wall-sized screen.

"She's fine," Frankie blurted out.

"She's Black," TaNaysha reminded him. "Your ass don't fuck with Black bitches. That's Carlo."

"Khalilah's not Black."

Me, TaNaysha, Frankie, the White broads and the other niggas in the room all turned and stared at Carlo like he was speaking fucking Chinese.

"You talkin' out the side of your head," TaNaysha said.

"I'm not sayin' she doesn't have Black in her. She's White too. Who says she has to pick one or the other?" Carlo argued.

"Motherfucker, she doesn't get to pick. Society picks for her." TaNaysha was heated and about to cuss Carlo's ass out.

We were all waiting for Khalilah's response.

"Carlo's just saying that I should embrace my White side as I do the Black in me."

"Bitch, you Black. When you go on a job interview...you Black. When you try to hail a taxi cab...you Black. When you get pulled over by the police...you Black."

Khalilah was almost in tears, pissed that TaNaysha had reminded her of who she was. Both she and I were prime examples of broads who would go to uncertain lengths for a nigga—even a Jewish one.

"That nigga Carlo done brainwashed you...got you on some *Imitation of Life* shit."

Too tired to drive us home and knowing Slay was out of town, I talked TaNaysha into staying the night over Carlo and

Frankie's. It was our first and last visit. Shit—like our friendship with Khalilah—was starting to change.

* * *

As soon as I opened the front door to the condo, Slay was in my face.

"Where the fuck you been and who the fuck told you that you could go to The Tap Room? Huh?"

"When the fuck did I start needin' your permission to…"

Slay slapped me with the force of two trains colliding into each other at full speed. His handprint was bruised into my face. Before his fist could make contact with one of my eyes, Tyrell intervened.

"Slay, my nigga, calm down. I was at the club…she wasn't doin' shit…just there with her girls. Forreal…if I would have seen her disrespectin' you in anyway I would have snatched her up my damn self."

I cried a river. My eyes were swollen and my jaw was fucked up. If Tyrell hadn't been around, there's no telling how many bruised and broken bones I would have endured. Shit, Aleesha's ass was walking around with a permanent scar above her right eye from the beating she received for wrecking the Cutlass.

The first day of fall classes at the community college were to begin that Monday. Slay fucked my face up on a Sunday. I couldn't go to class looking like I just escaped from being tortured at Guantanamo Bay. And thank goodness TaNaysha had saved up enough money over the summer to cop a ride to get her back and forth from school and work. I was sure I would have run out of excuses to feed her before my face healed.

As expected, Slay left and came back apologizing. He ran me a bath, undressed me, carried me into the bathroom and gently lowered me in the tub. He washed my hair and shaved my legs.

Afterwards, he lotioned my entire body and handed me a silk robe that he had bought while he was out. He asked that I go downstairs until he called me back up. I didn't dare object.

"Okay, Babygirl." Slay came down the stairs in a pair of red, silk boxers that matched my robe—exposing his six pack. Even the muscles in his calves were sexy. *Damn.* I hated myself for loving him so much. He told me to close my eyes and carried me up the stairs to the master bedroom we shared when he was home. "Okay, open."

Rose pedals were scattered everywhere, covering the floor and bed. Candles were lit all around the room and mellow music was playing in the background. Slay was trying hard to compensate for his shortcoming—his temper.

"Babygirl." Slay couldn't look me in the face. He knelt before me with his head hung low. "I'm sorry. There's no excuse for me hittin' you. After I did it…I just felt like killin' myself. I never want to see you hurt or sad…especially by my doin'. I love you and…"

Slay reached into the nightstand.

Another tennis bracelet.

"I want you to be my wife. Shar Reid, will you marry me?"

Slay opened the little black box. Shining in the candlelight was a platinum, three-carat, emerald-cut center diamond complete with three rows of round diamonds set in the band.

"Oh my God! Oh my God! I jumped up and down. Yes! Yes!" I answered without hesitation.

Slay slid the ring on my finger and for the rest of the night, I forgot how fucked up my face looked.

Chapter 12

TOO FAR GONE

It took a couple of weeks for the bruise on my cheek to heal. There was no way I could keep from falling behind in all of my classes since I had enrolled as a full-time student. My assigned guidance counselor advised me to sit out the fall semester and try again in the spring. I suppose I could have dropped to part-time status instead of dropping out completely, but I made the decision thinking that I had all the time in the world to get an education.

TaNaysha was attending school part time and working full-time at the Shell station, which made avoiding her until my face healed much easier. We both hadn't really spoke to Khalilah since that night at Carlo and Frankie's. She and TaNaysha had a class together but sat on opposite sides of the classroom. The love was still there. We were all just headed for different fates: a happy ending for one of us, hell on earth for another and death for the unluckiest of us all.

I became obsessed with everything wedding related. Although Slay and I hadn't set a date, I started to plan the entire ceremony. They knew my name at David's Bridal. I tried on every dress that they had in stock, even the ones that were designer disasters. Every week, I was rocking a new hairstyle, trying to decide if I wanted to wear my hair up or down, curly or straight, tiara or no tiara. The MAC counter at Macy's also became a regular stop for me. Reggie, known as Regina and the most preferred MAC specialist behind the counter, hooked me up every time—experimenting with color. Although some days, his ass had me looking like a Rainbow Bright doll.

My choice of wedding colors changed daily and the only definite decision that I had made was to ask TaNaysha to be my maid of honor. I was also hopeful that my father would walk me down the aisle.

I ducked into my father's church and took a seat on the back pew. Bible study was almost over. He was in the pulpit with his head bowed and his eyes closed, praying over the few members who were in attendance. My mother and little sister were in place on the front pew. My mother had her arm endearingly wrapped around Shanelle's shoulders. The saying that *you don't know what you have until it's gone* rung true. I missed the comforts of childhood and being under the umbrella of my parent's love. But not more than I wanted to be with Slay.

After the last of the service lingerers had left, I faced my family. When Shanelle spotted me, her eyes brightened and her smile widened. She looked up at my father for permission to run and hug me, but he nodded his head no. She didn't budge. Nor did my mother. The three of them stood down in front of the pulpit, where at the end of each service, the deacons of the church sat out the chairs for the newly saved or for those who were just standing in need of prayer. "The doors of the church are now open," my father would say.

He had control over my mother but not over her emotions. She cried when I embraced her. Shanelle did the same and I joined in. Everyone was shedding tears except for my father. When I went to wrap my arms around him, he stepped back and looked at me with disdain. I felt like, if it was in him, he would have burned me at the stake like other cultures in third world countries did to their women who disobeyed or strayed from their families and their religion.

"Why are you here?" He asked.

"I miss you and Mom and Shanelle. I just wanted to see how you all were doin'."

"We're fine." He spoke to me with no emotion. We had become strangers.

"Mom...I'm gettin' married."

I flashed my left hand in front of them.

"Did your drug-dealing boyfriend buy that for you with his dirty money?" My father spat.

I ignored him. "Dad...I want you to walk me down the aisle. I want all of you to be there."

"Ummph," my father gasped. "You're living the life you want and as long as you're living that life with that man...we will have nothing to do with you. There're consequences to the life you're living...many consequences. Losing us is just one of them."

My father had closed the doors of the church and those to his heart behind me. I sat in my Benz crying with my head buried in the steering wheel. At that point, I didn't give a fuck if Slay and I got married at the courthouse.

"Hey...hey."

Even the frigid air of the approaching winter months couldn't keep crackheads in hibernation. They were always on the prowl, looking to score their next high.

"What the fuck!" I looked up to see a crackhead named Vera, knocking on my car window.

Every generation in the hood had a representative from their era who "should've" made it—if it wasn't for crack. Vera was her generation's. She was one of those too-far-gone crackheads— itching, scratching, hallucinating and shit. Before she got hooked,

Vera was beautiful. Her legs stretched for miles. They were runway-model long. She used to rock an Afro, big earrings and stayed fly. I knew because Ms. Trina had a shoebox full of pictures of everybody back in the day in the hood, including some jailhouse shots of herself.

I cracked the window. "What the fuck you want, Vera?"

Her hair was scattered all over her head. Her once flawless skin was filled with bumps, craters and open sores. Her legs looked like two long straws. She had on a sweater with some shorts, socks and flip-flops. *What the hell?*

"You Slay's other girl?"

"What the fuck you mean...other girl?"

"Nah...nah. I didn't mean nothin' by it. You seen him?"

"Seen who?"

"Slay...I need to get somethin' from him."

"Get the fuck outta here. Go get that shit from Cheez."

"Cheez shit ain't no good...not like Slay's. You see him...tell him I'm lookin' for him. That I'll suck his dick..."

I knocked Vera to the cold concrete ground with the driver-side door of the Benz. She tried to stammer to her feet, but I pushed her back down and lost count of how many times I stomped the heels of my boots into the crevices of her body. When she stopped moving, I stopped kicking.

* * *

"Fuck! Fuck! Fuck!" Never in my life had I been consumed with so much rage. I didn't know if Vera was dead or alive. I had just left her there, unconscious and bleeding in the middle of the street like road kill, in front of my father's church. The police, depending on if they were in the mood to answer a call in the hood, could have possibly been on the scene already. And if there was one thing that I learned from watching CSI and shit, it was to never go back to the crime scene. But sooner or later I knew that they'd come knocking. I paced from the kitchen to the living room back to the kitchen. Slay was gone out of town on business again, this time in Texas. I didn't know what the fuck to do.

My legs felt like Jell-O when I heard the loud banging on the front door. The police-when they did answer a call, rarely did it in the hood in less than forty minutes much less solved a crime that didn't take months to investigate. *Fuck!* There wasn't shit I could do. I answered the door.

Tyrell pushed his way inside the condo, shut and locked the front and back doors.

"Strip."

"What?"

"Take off all of your clothes and put everything in here. Your boots too."

Tyrell handed me a large garbage bag. He was decked out in all Black and wearing gloves. While I was shaking and shit, he remained cool, calm and collected—like he knew what the fuck he was doing and had done it before.

"What did you see?" I asked, shaking and shit.

"Everything."

"Is Vera…"

"Don't worry about Vera."

"I think I killed her. Oh my God! I killed her! She's dead…isn't she?" I was beginning to become hysterical.

"Just calm the fuck down. When you lose your cool…you lose control of the situation."

I took a few deep breaths and handed the garbage bag back to him. It was stuffed full with every article of clothing that I had on my back, including my bra, panties and socks.

"I need the keys to the Benz."

"What?"

Tyrell had his right hand out, palm up, staring directly into my eyes and not at my bare body.

"Slay will…"

"I'll have it back to you before he makes it back in town. And Shar," he said as he turned to leave. "Not a word…to anyone."

* * *

The buzz around the hood was that Vera had got into an altercation with another crackhead over a piece of chicken they had found in a discarded KFC box. It sounded like some shit LuLu had made up. The good news was that Vera was alive. She hadn't arrived at the hospital by ambulance but by car. Someone had dropped her off in front of the ER entrance and after being treated, she was released.

The Shell station's phone number flashed across the screen on my cell phone.

"Hey."

"Damn…you sound sad as hell. You alright?" TaNaysha asked.

"Yeah, I'm cool. Just a little under the weather. That's all."

"Bitch, I know. It's cold as hell out there. My own damn nose is runnin' and shit. Anyway, guess what?"

"What?"

"Bitch, somebody fucked Vera up. She walkin' around the hood with a limp and shit."

"Forreal?"

"Yep. The story in the hood is that her and another crackhead got in to it but that shit ain't true."

My heart raced. "How you know?"

"Vera told LuLu that shit wasn't the truth, but she's not tellin' who beat her ass up though. She just said that she felt sorry for the person who did it."

"Sorry...why?"

"Beats me. She just said that the person was full of sorrow. She saw it in their eyes."

"What?"

"Bitch, I know. I didn't know crackheads could be so deep. But, I'm still tryin' to figure out who the hell would beat up a two-pound crackhead? Shit, a cool breeze could knock Vera's skinny ass over. That shit was wrong. Anyway, I gotta go. I can't let Mohammed catch me on the store phone."

I hung up the phone, feeling lower than the scum of the earth.

Chapter 13

WHAT'S YOURS IS MINE

The police were never called the night I regretfully attacked Vera and the doctors and nurses at the hospital gave a fuck less about what had happened to her. To them, she was just a junkie who had already thrown away her future. They didn't even take x-rays of her injuries, just handed her a prescription for some painkillers. For a couple of days she was back on the streets and then, like smoke, she vanished into thin air. As it should have, guilt ran through my veins like crack ran through hers, as I imagined her passing away—alone and somewhere behind a dumpster from the internal injures that she possibly sustained from the tips and heels of my boots. And just like the police and the hospital staff, I too, could have cared less if the crack Slay polluted the streets with had killed her as opposed to her dying from my wrongdoing. Either way, some of her blood was on my hands.

Just as he had promised, Tyrell had the Benz in the driveway before Slay returned home from Texas. It was squeaky clean inside and out. Like looking into a mirror, I could see my reflection in the hood. Any and all of the evidence linking me to Vera had been destroyed. Tyrell tossed me the keys and hopped back into his black Tahoe. The windows on the SUV were tinted but besides that, there weren't any other additions that would call attention to the vehicle: no thousand-dollar rims, no thousand-dollar stereo system and no thousand-dollar paint job—all factory shit. The Tahoe, in its' simplicity, was indicative of Tyrell. He was a simple nigga who had a lot but didn't need much. And most noteworthy, he was a nigga who kept his promises. And those he couldn't keep, he didn't make. Unlike niggas like Slay, who were the type to promise a broad the moon and the stars without taking a leap into the sky to try and retrieve them. They promised unreachable and unattainable shit. Slay had promised to love, protect and provide for me. Of course, he said that he loved me— on numerous occasions. But, how the fuck does a nigga who had never been loved love anyone? And, he was more possessive than protective. However, Slay did financially provide for me. Anything with a price tag, no matter the cost, I could have had. Looking back, all I wanted was to be emotionally provided for—to be loved and respected. But, that's some shit you don't find out until you've been through some shit.

Slay came back from Texas sick as hell. He was coughing, vomiting, breaking out in cold sweats and had even dropped a few pounds. I saw it as my chance to be there for him—to take care of him and offer him the only thing I had to give, my love. Like a mother nursing her sick son back to good health, I tended to Slay's every need: mopping up vomit, wiping the sweat from his forehead with cold washrags and serving him spoonfuls of cough syrup every four to six hours. He adamantly refused to go to the doctor and shamefully stupid, I enjoyed him being sick. For one, he was home. And two, taking care of him gave me something to do since I didn't have a job or wasn't enrolled in school.

After a few days in bed, Slay was up and moving and in a hurry to get back to taking care of business—although Tyrell seemed to have everything under control. But, as Slay so bluntly reminded me, he was the "motherfuckin' president" and Tyrell was just the VP. "The president always needs to know what the fuck is goin' on...at all times," Slay said.

Kendra Dunn

He was in the shower when his phones started buzzing, one after the other. He had four of them total and someone, other than me, had all four numbers and was desperately trying to contact him. *Aleesha's ass.* I peeked at the name and number popping up on the cell phone screens. *Molly? Who the fuck is Molly? Fuck this!*

As time had passed, I had become much bolder. Shit, Slay had already struck me. The fear of him putting his hands on me was gone. At worst, I thought, he'd blacken my eye. After the pain, there was still going to be a woman inside of me that still loved him. I stormed into the bathroom and pushed the shower curtain back.

"Who the fuck is Molly?"

"Molly?"

"Sounds like some White bitch to me."

"Shar...yo' ass better be glad I don't have the strength to knock yo' ass out."

"Answer the question. Who the fuck is Molly? I put up with Aleesha's ass, but I won't put up with another bitch."

Slay grabbed a towel and stepped out of the shower, pushing me up against the sink. He pressed his naked body up against me and stared me down.

"You been answerin' my phones?"

"No...I just looked to see who was callin'."

He leaned further into me. His dick was hard and poking Ms. Kitty. He cupped my breasts and started biting my nipples through the fabric of my t-shirt.

"That...that shit is...not...gonna work," I said, arching my back and trying not to give in to Slay's advances. But, shit, we hadn't fuck since he'd been sick. He lifted me up on the bathroom counter, next to the sink, and spread my legs wide open. The back of my head was pressed against the bathroom mirror. He didn't remove my panties. He just slid them to the side. I watched him lick his fingers and then put one and then two and then three of them inside of me followed by his tongue and then his dick. He had both of his hands on my waist, stroking his dick in and out of me. Slow, at first, to tease me and then faster to please us both.

"Molly is Tyrell," he whispered in my ear after he caught is breath from coming so hard.

"Huh?" I wiped the sweat from my brow. He had given me a total-body workout.

"Tyrell is listed in my phone as Molly...just in case some shit went down and the police confiscated my shit. They wouldn't give a fuck about a bitch named Molly."

It made sense and I bought it.

"You happy?" He asked.

"Very." I hugged and kissed him.

* * *

Molly or not Molly, Tyrell *had* been trying to get a hold of Slay. One of the broads Slay had transporting weight got busted at Sky Harbor International Airport as soon as she landed, working the Kansas City-Phoenix route. Slay took a major loss and had to put another broad on the job ASAP. To make matters worse, the broad he and Tyrell had working as the receptionist, for the moving company, Keisha, had called in sick due to baby-daddy drama. She was legit and hadn't been plucked from Slay's other operations to work in the position. She was hood but soft enough around the edges to work in an office environment. I was her temporary replacement.

Slay had leased space in a small office complex to be the face of the day-to-day operations of the legal side of the company. The space, itself, was small. When you entered the office, there

Kendra Dunn

were three chairs against the wall on the right and a round table that seated four on the left. It was for client consultations; although, most of the company's business was conducted by phone and onsite at the clients' residences where an inventory of the amount of furniture, appliances and boxes to be moved could be taken. The receptionist area was a desk located in the middle of the office. It was equipped with a phone, computer, fax and printer. Towards the back of the space was a bathroom and an office the size of an apartment closet. Cheez couldn't have fit half of his big ass in it. That's how small it was.

Parked outside of the backdoor were the moving trucks. Initially, Slay had only purchased two of them. The left over square footage in the back of the truck not populated with the client's collateral was packed high and wide with Slay's products. Drops were made along the way. Some trips called for detours before the client's possessions were delivered to their intended destination. Pleasing the company's clients came second to making sure the niggas Slay associated with in the streets got their shit first. The money from the moving company was pocket change to Slay. But, to keep the "front" in place, he played the role and compensated clients angry about their shit being late with hefty discounts.

The truck drivers were longtime workers of Slay. They all were in the game. The actual movers were Mexicans who couldn't speak a lick of English and didn't have a clue that they were participants in a drug-trafficking ring. But, they knew how to count the cash that they were paid under the table. And they worked hard, carrying pianos and other elephant-sized objects down three flights of stairs from third floor apartments—doing shit niggas would quit a job over. And, they didn't ask any questions. Niggas asked questions and the more they knew, the greedier they got.

"Makin' Moves Truckin' Company. We deliver anything...anywhere. How may I help you?" I answered the phone, sticking to the company script.

"Keisha...where's my son? Don't fuckin' play wit' me. I wanna see my son."

"Nigga, this ain't Keisha."

"Oh...where she at?"

"Nigga, I don't know. She called in sick and don't be callin' here with that bullshit again. This is a place of business."

I hung up the phone; glad that Slay and I didn't have a seed to complicate things, although I thought it would be joy at first. Shit, the amount of time Slay spent away from home and in the streets would qualify me as a single mother. I wasn't aiming to raise a child by myself. *Condoms.* I made a mental note to pick some up. Slay and I had been lucky thus far but shit, luck always ran out.

I explored the desk drawers. There were the essential office supplies: stapler, staples, Post It Notes, pens, pads of paper, paper clips and other miscellaneous items. The lower drawer to my right was locked. I searched for the key and found it in an envelope indiscreetly marked "key to locked drawer." *Keisha's handwritin',* I guessed. The drawer must not contain anything too confidential. If so, Keisha wasn't the brightest bulb in the pack. I unlocked the drawer and began glancing through the paperwork in the files. My eyes widened when I spotted my name, social security number and birth date on a copy of the lease. *Oh, hell-to-the-nah.* I also found a copy of the company's business license; Makin' Moves Truckin' Company was licensed in my name. I was the owner and therefore responsible for all of the company's activities and actions of its' employees. The Mexican movers weren't the only ones in the dark. I was too.

Slay was gone, roaming around in the hood and making sure his corners were covered. Tyrell was in the back office with two Mexican niggas, paying them for a week's work. I waited outside the office door.

"Aqui´ esta´ tu salario mis amigos."

Tyrell, apparently, was fluent in Spanish. *Who is this nigga?* I asked myself, listening in but not understanding shit being said.

"Gracias." They thanked Tyrell. That word I knew. It was amazing how I had aced Spanish I, I and III in high school but couldn't decipher the conversation between Tyrell and the two men. I felt like an illiterate hoop star that had been accepted to college on a four-year athletic scholarship, barely knowing how to spell my name. Life had its' ways.

Smiling, with an envelope full of money—enough to survive in America and send some back home to Mexico—the two men exited out the backdoor and I entered the office, holding up the contract for the office lease.

"What is this?"

"What is what?" Tyrell never looked up at me but kept his eyes on the computer screen.

"This." I slammed the paperwork down on the desk. "Makin' Moves is in my name. Who authorized that move?" I asked, with my hands on my hip.

"That's between you and Slay. As you know, I'm the VP, not the President." As usual, Tyrell kept his answer short and didn't elaborate. I was tired of his act.

"What the fuck did I ever do to you?" I asked him. "I mean…at the park…the way you looked at me…at the bookstore that time you was talkin' my ear off and shit. Now, that you're workin' for Slay…you hardly say shit to me and treat me like you don't know me. I mean...you took care of that situation...you know...for me...but..."

"Are you done?"

"Fuck you."

I stormed off, back to the receptionist area, not trusting the nigga I loved and mad at the one who really loved me.

* * *

Slay stayed at the house with Aleesha that night. I stopped lying to myself, thinking that he was actually out all night—from dusk to dawn—handling business. He had to rest his head somewhere, at least for a few hours. When he came home, I was sitting on the couch with my legs crossed, nervously tapping my right foot on the floor and biting my bottom lip. My arms were crossed and copies of the lease and business license were sprawled out on the coffee table before me for Slay to see. He assumed that I was upset that he had stayed out all night.

"Babygirl." he came up behind the couch and kissed me on my neck with a pre-prepared excuse. "I gotta keep an eye on the niggas and bitches I got workin' the corners for me. They think I'm slippin' on my hustle because of the movin' company. I can't let them think that."

I pointed to the coffee table.

"What's that?" He asked.

"I don't know. Why don't you tell me?"

Slay walked around the couch and scooped up the papers in his hands. "Looks like paperwork for the movin' company."

"You used my information...without my permission...to start a company...that smuggles drugs across the fuckin' nation!" I screamed. "Looks like you're protectin' your own ass if the shit hits the fan...leavin' me out to dry. Is that what's goin' on? Huh, Slay?"

"Shut the fuck up, Shar, and listen to me before I…"

"Before you what? You already fucked my face up once."

Slay attacked me faster than a lion leaping to kill its' prey. He pinned my face down into the sofa cushion with the palm of his hand.

"Why do you constantly make me do shit like this to you?" He asked.

I know this motherfucker doesn't expect me to answer, I thought. Shit, I could hardly breathe.

"I put the business in your name so that if anything ever happened to me you could continue to run the legit side of it if you wanted to or sell it. Anything in my name, Aleesha would fight your ass for it."

He let me up. "Y'all not married so what the fuck would I have to worry about?"

"Aleesha's ass is crazy. You don't know her like I do. She would try anything to get some dough." Slay had calmed down. "Plus, Babygirl, we are about to be married. That's what married people do…they use each other's information for shit. What's mine is yours and what's yours is mine. Isn't that how it works?"

"Yeah, I guess so." To be so smart, I was acting real dumb.

Chapter 14

WOMAN TO WOMAN

Keisha began a pattern of calling in sick for non-health related shit, most of her excuses having to do with her baby daddy, Wayne. If he wasn't threatening to kidnap Lil' Wayne from daycare then he was threatening to whoop Keisha's ass for one thing or the other. I thought Slay and I were the new Ike and Tina but compared to Keisha and Wayne, we were the beloved Cliff and Claire Huxtable. Slay may have tried some WWE Smackdown shit with me and Aleesha but Wayne was using UFC street fighting techniques on Keisha's ass. If she wasn't limping because of a sprained ankle, she was slurring her words from taking one of Wayne's knees to her lips.

Now, no broad deserved to get the fuck beat out of them under any circumstances—I know that now. Actually, I knew it then but chopped it up as a small consequence of loving a nigga like Slay. But, I'd be damned if a short, ugly and unemployed, anorexic-looking nigga like Wayne would be beating my ass. He was all of four feet-fifty pounds. He wasn't in the game, in school or even looking for a job. The only thing that he was good at was making babies. He had another son, also named Lil' Wayne, from another broad in the hood and two other children. The little nigga's dick must have been good. Other than that, he didn't have shit going for himself.

Thanksgiving was just a few days away and Slay had grown unsympathetic to Keisha's baby daddy drama and all of her other problems. His plan was to hand her a turkey and fire her ass—he had purchased a bird for each of his workers from the ones on the corner and those serving his white collar clients to the truck drivers and broads making airdrops. He even gave the Mexicans that worked for Makin' Moves turkeys. Tyrell had him running his operation like he was head of a Fortune 500 company or some shit. He too wanted Keisha's ass gone.

But, I liked Keisha and begged Slay not to fire her. She was unreliable, lazy at times and constantly had drama but she was the only other broad besides TaNaysha, Khalilah and Big Steph that I trusted around Slay. She stayed the fuck up out of his face unlike some of the other hood rat-project chicks he had working for him. And, to be honest, I felt like I would be on the road to redeeming myself for what I did to Vera if I helped Keisha keep her job. It was the least I could do since Vera was her mother.

"Please, baby, don't fire her. The money she gets from workin' at the office...on the days she comes to work...is all she has. Wayne ain't helpin' her out with Lil' Wayne...with his sorry ass and Thanksgiving is on Thursday. It's not a good business practice to fire someone around the holidays," I pleaded on Keisha's behalf.

"That's why I'm givin' her ass a turkey to take with her."

"Slay, baby, you know I'm always at the office now anyway whether she's there or not. I can handle things."

"Shar, if her ass calls in sick with that bullshit one mo' time...I'mma have Tyrell fire her ass. She gots to go. I don't know why you takin' up for her ass anyway. Her life's too damn messy...don't let Wayne's little elf lookin' ass show up at the office startin' no shit either. I'mma kill her and him."

"Thanks, baby. I love you." I reached up, hugged and kissed Slay. He had just presented me with another I'm-sorry-I-put-my-hands-on-you-let's-kiss-and-make-up gift: three diamond encrusted white gold bangles. Guess he figured I had too many tennis bracelets.

"Love you too, Babygirl."

At that moment, I thought Slay and I were going to head up to the master bedroom and partake in some mind-blowing-make-up sex. But to my disappointment, he said that he had to go take care of some business and that he was stopping by Ernie Pain's for a minute.

"Call me if he has any cute purses in stock," I said.

"Babygirl, Ernie got that swap meet shit. You too good for that fake shit. One of your joints cost more than his whole collection of purses."

"Well, get us some DVD's. See if he has anything new."

"Will do."

"You…never mind. Be safe," I said under my breath.

There was no use in asking Slay if he was coming back home. I wasn't going anywhere if he did or if he didn't.

* * *

TaNaysha embarrassed the hell out of a young broad, about thirteen or so, trying to steal a pack of Bubblicious, grape bubblegum and some condoms from the Shell station—which reminded me that I still needed to get some myself.

"Ummm…excuse me little mama…can we have our condoms and gum back?" TaNaysha tried to be cordial.

"You can't have shit," the girl snapped back. Her hair, not even five inches long, was gelled up into a ponytail. Her eyelids were covered in glitter and she had on a pair of tarnished earrings, a black and gold Baby Phat coat, too-tight-for-her-age jeans and a pair of dingy tan knock off Timberlands.

"Fast-ass-little-girl…you don't know who the fuck you are talkin' to. Your ass is too young to be fuckin' anyway."

"Bitch, you don't know me and you ain't my mama."

"Bitch?" TaNaysha looked at me. *I know the fuck she didn't.* "Look here, hoe…little hoe…either pay up or get the fuck outta here before I knock that fake ass gold grill out of your mouth. Take your ass home and do some homework or somethin'…out here fuckin'…probably got the virus already any damn way."

"Oooooooohhh, she told you," the girls' friends instigated. They were all out of school for the Thanksgiving holiday and I know their parents were wishing they weren't.

"Fuck her." The girl threw the condoms and bubblegum on the gas station floor and fled.

"Bad ass little girl." TaNaysha shook her head. "Her mama needs to lock her ass up in a dungeon somewhere and throw away the key."

"We'll see her ass walkin' around pregnant this time next year. Bye, girl," I said. "I'll be back to scoop you up when you get off."

TaNaysha's lemon of a car that she had copped from a Buy Here, Pay Here place broke down on her. It just started smoking and shit and then died. I was back to my taxi duties, chauffeuring her ass around.

Before I left the Shell station, she handed me the grocery list I had asked her to make for me. Since I couldn't call my mother for guidance in the kitchen, I leaned on TaNaysha, once again. She had actually been thinking about quitting the community college and going to culinary school but hadn't decided yet. I simply told her to follow her heart, which depending on the outcome of a person's choice could be good or bad.

I had no idea how Thanksgiving day was going to go—which part of the day Slay was going to spend with me and which part he was going to spend with Aleesha. Whatever his plans, I planned on cooking or attempting to cook an entire Thanksgiving dinner without incident this time. *No takin' a shower while anything is in the oven,* I had to remind myself.

The grocery store was packed with people, mostly women, piling their carts full and preparing to cook Thanksgiving dinner for their families. I remembered all of the years I had lagged behind my mother in the same aisles during the holidays as she shopped, throwing items she didn't have on her grocery list in the cart. This Thanksgiving was going to be my first with Slay and without my family. It was bittersweet. The thought had me teary eyed and before long, I was sobbing in the middle of Kroger. I couldn't see shit through my blurry eyes as I pushed the cart along.

"Oh." I rammed my cart into another shopper. "I am so sorry."

Like death and paying taxes, some shit in life was inevitable—Aleesha was pushing the shopping cart that I had rammed into. We were standing face-to-face, eye-to-eye and woman-to-woman right in the middle of the cake aisle. We had managed to escape the moment for months up until then. There was no age limit on broads acting a damn fool over a nigga. I didn't expect anything different from Aleesha's now thirty-eight-year-old ass.

Bitch, hoe, slut, tramp—all of the names I was waiting to be called and had called Aleesha under my breath didn't slip from either of our tongues. We stared at each other in an awkward silence. She took in my long tresses that hung past my breasts. I took in her blonde-streaked quick-weave. It wasn't the worst weave job I'd ever seen. She took in the chocolate diamond, hoop earrings in my ear. I took in the diamond studs in hers. My Louis Vuitton was in the cart. She carried a Coach bag over her shoulder. My ring was bigger than hers—a small victory for me. I stared at the scar above her right eye, courtesy of Slay. *She needs to put some Mederma on that shit.* It was the only blemish on her damn-near flawless skin. I wondered if my face would one day be scarred for life due to Slay's doing. *So far...no scar.*

"You're the same age Slay was when I met him. He was eighteen and just out of juvee...motherless and fatherless. I took care of him when he didn't have shit. Whatever he needed me to be I became...his mother...his therapist...and his lover. So, you see...a nigga will switch therapists and take on many lovers but he'll never...ever...leave his mama," she said, pushing her cart past me.

I didn't have asthma but I was having a motherfucking asthma attack. That bitch had cut my air supply off with the shit she said. The lack of oxygen must have made me lose my damn mind. I grabbed the back of her motherfucking quick-weave, pulled her down to the ground and proceeded to fuck her ass up until the store manager pulled me up off of her. Like the little girl at the Shell station, I fled the scene, knowing Aleesha would never press charges—not if she knew better. I was betting on Slay whooping her ass again for even saying some shit to me in the first place and then on me being next in line for a beatdown for fighting her ass.

I tried to call TaNaysha to tell her about me mopping the grocery store floor with Aleesha's ass. Usually she answered her cell phone at work, not giving a fuck about Mohammed getting mad at her for taking personal calls. But, she wasn't answering. I tried the Shell station next. She nor Mohammed answered. I was on my way home but decided to stop by the gas station. I needed to vent, badly.

Three police cruisers, flashing their lights and sounding their sirens, pulled in behind me as I turned into the Shell station.

That bitch. My first instinct was to reach into my purse and grab my cell phone to call Slay. But then I thought about Amadou Diallo, Tyisha Miller and Sean Bell—all victims of trigger-happy police officers guilty of mistaking an innocent gesture for a nigga or a broad reaching for a gun. I respected Al Sharpton and Jesse Jackson, but I wasn't trying to become the cause of their next protest. I put my hands in the air.

The police officers rushed past me, sitting in my Benz and waiting to get arrested, into the gas station with their guns pointed. *What the fuck is goin' on?* I hopped out of my car and raced behind them, leaving my car door open and the keys in the ignition.

"Nooooooooooooooooooo," I screamed.

Chapter 15

ALL CRIED OUT

Mohammed was sitting on the floor of the gas station with his back against the cash register counter, holding TaNaysha in his arms. He had taken off his usually pristine white head wrap and pressed it into the hole in her chest. It was blood soaked. As one of the officers checked TaNaysha's wrist for a pulse, Mohammed cried out prayers in his native language. The officer looked back at his colleagues who were holding me back. He shook his head, grimly.

"Please...please...just let me go and hold her hand," I begged the officers. "Please."

"Mam, I'm sorry...we can't. She's gone and we need to secure the crime scene."

"Gone." For the second time in one day, I was left breathless.

The bad ass little girl that TaNaysha had argued with earlier had come back with her mother's boyfriend's small .22. She shot TaNaysha twice, point blank in the chest.

"Take this, bitch," she reportedly said before pulling the trigger.

Three hours later, her ass was arrested at the mall—not for killing TaNaysha but for stealing some four-for-twenty-dollar panties from Victoria Secret. Confiscated with the stolen merchandise was the .22 caliber handgun. It was stuffed inside the pocket of the same Baby Phat coat she had on earlier in the day.

Surprisingly, since most murders in the hood went unacknowledged by outsiders, TaNaysha's death had made the six o'clock news.

"Eighteen-year-old store clerk TaNaysha Raye Jenkins was shot and killed by thirteen-year-old Jazmin Hill. According to the storeowner of the Shell station where Jenkins worked, the two were involved in an argument earlier in the day when Jenkins tried to stop Hill from stealing a pack of bubblegum. Hill returned with a .22 caliber handgun and shot Jenkins twice in the chest," the anchor reported but failed to mention the condoms Jazmin had also tried to steal.

Mohammed—bloody and shaken—and Ms. Trina and I—too hysterical, all turned down the on-scene reporter's request for an interview. Of all of the other witnesses and onlookers, the reporter picked LuLu to interview.

She adjusted the bandana on her head. For a moment, my mind wandered from thinking about the death of my best friend to hoping that the camera man didn't point down to get a shot of LuLu's house shoes. They were the same ragged and dirt stained ones she always wore. *I'mma give her ass five dollars to go down to Family Dollar...*

"Okay, I'm ready," she told the reporter.

"Mam, what can you tell us about what happened here today?"

"All I know is that TaNaysha didn't deserve to die like this. I just can't believe she's gone. Lord...it's just tragic. That fast ass little girl needs her ass beat. I'm sorry...I didn't mean to cuss on camera. You can just edit that out can't you?"

"Yes, Mam, we can. Thank you for your time."

By the time the ten o'clock news aired, the story had developed into much more. They showed footage of Jazmin's mother's boyfriend being lead away in handcuffs. He was a Rick Ross-Biggie Smalls looking nigga.

"Get that shit out my face," he said to the camera man, putting the palm of his hand up against the lens.

"Was it your gun that Jazmin used to kill the store clerk?" The reporter asked, sticking the microphone in front of his face.

"You think I'm stupid enough to admit that shit on national T.V.? Stupid-ass White boy...fuck you."

They then aired an interview the reporter had conducted with Jazmin's trifling ass mother. The same black eyeliner she used to draw on her eyebrows, she used to line her lips. The liner showed through the red lipstick that she had applied and she was dressed like she was about to go to Club Pulse. Her short hair was curled to perfection like she had visited the salon just minutes before the interview. I thought back to how Jazmin's hair had been gelled up into a nappy-ass ponytail while her mother's shit was styled and permed.

"Don't that hoe know that it's cold outside," LuLu said as we all stared at her sagging breasts hanging out of the sleeveless, black, halter dress she had on.

Jazmin was one of her five kids, three of which were in foster care. They had been taken from her for neglect and abandonment. Jazmin and her older brother were suppose to be under the care of their grandmother but had recently moved back in with their mother and her boyfriend.

"My baby is innocent. She didn't do nuthin'."

"Bitch, if you weren't laid up with that Smokey-the-Bear-lookin' nigga and was payin' more attention to your damn kids this shit probably wouldn't have ever happened," I cursed the television.

Ms. Trina just shook her head and puffed on the Newport between her fingers. She was on her third pack for the day. Her eyes were swollen from crying and sadness rested between the wrinkles in her face.

"I 'otta go whoop her ass," LuLu said between the puffs she was taking.

My purse buzzed. I dug deep into it to find my phone. It was Slay. I hadn't spoke to him since earlier in the day, I had been over at Ms. Trina's house since the incident.

"Babygirl, you okay?"

"Yeah...I guess so."

"Let me know if Ms. Trina needs anything...tell'er I got'er."

"Okay, but Mohammed is pretty much takin' care of everything...the funeral costs and stuff."

"A'ight...I'll be home when you get here and Shar..."

Awwwh hell, I thought, thinking that he had spoken to Aleesha's old ass and was about to go all-the-way-the-fuck-off on me.

"I love you. You know that...don't you?"

"Of course...I love you too."

* * *

People were flocking to Ms. Trina's house in herds. Like a child's birthday party always ended up becoming a full-fledged adult house party, the gestures of niggas and broads paying their respects turned into a get-together. Ms. Trina's house was packed—mostly with Ms. Trina's old running crew. Cigarette and weed smoke filled the air along with the stint of Crown Royal, Hennessey and Coke. Both a domino and spades table had been set up and niggas were making toasts in TaNaysha's honor.

Kendra Dunn

Gladys Knight's voice soared from the old-ass-hell, cassette stereo that Ms. Trina had in the corner of her living room. TaNaysha had tried to hip her mother to CD's, but Ms. Trina refused to throw away her tapes. She had shoeboxes full of them. "As long as that shit plays when I hit PLAY...I'm gonna keep it," she argued. *I would rather live in his world than in mine without him...on that midnight train to Georgia.* Gladys was singing her ass off. A broad loving a nigga with everything in her wasn't no new shit.

I went back to TaNaysha's room and sat on the edge of her brass daybed, staring up at two faded posters of Ginuwine and Tupac. I remembered her taping them to her closet door when we were back in junior high. I looked down at her bookbag on the floor and lost it. She was the one trying to do something with her life, working and going to school. I wasn't doing shit but shopping and getting the fuck beat out of me every other week—as soon as one bruise healed I was receiving another.

A lot of shit went down in this room, I thought and smiled. It was where me, TaNaysha and Khalilah first explored the workings of a condom—tearing the package open with our teeth (a no-no) and rolling it over a banana. It was where we practiced giving head on cucumbers and took our first puff of a cigarette—one of Ms. Trina's Newports. Khalilah and I both choked. TaNaysha was use to the smoke. She inhaled and exhaled like a pro. It was where TaNaysha told us about her first time "doin' it."

"Depending on how big the nigga's dick is...it will hurt at first but then that shit gets to feelin' good. Your legs get to shakin' and shit...whewwww," she said, pretending to fan herself. We hung onto her every word. She was the leader of our pack.

I dried my eyes and started shifting through the clothes hanging in her closet. Ms. Trina had asked me if I could pick out something for TaNaysha to be buried in. *Bitch, don't have me lookin' a hot ass mess*, I imagined TaNaysha saying to me. I chose a long sleeved, black wrap dress. I didn't want to send her to the pearly gates scantily clad. It was matronly compared to the majority of her fuck-him dresses but it had a sexy neckline. I paired it with silver accessories.

At the time, I didn't know anything about how the dead were buried—that they were laid to rest barefooted. TaNaysha's shoes were lined up on the floor of her closet, some in boxes and others not. In the back left corner of the closet underneath a Nine West shoebox was a black case. I grabbed the case by its' handle, sat it on the daybed and opened it. It was the .40 that she had fired at the gun range. I don't know why, but I stuffed the gun into my purse. I put the case back in its' place and left the dress, accessories and shoes out on the daybed for Ms. Trina to gather and take to the funeral home.

The crowd of visitors hadn't thinned out one bit. Actually, more air and space had been taken up by Cheez's big ass. TaNaysha's grandmother's sister was Cheez's grandmother. He had stopped by to check on Ms. Trina, looking like he needed to be a contestant on the Biggest Loser and smelling like hamburger grease and ketchup.

"Whud up, Shar?" He asked. "Lookin' good."

Wish I could say the same, I thought. "Thanks."

"When you gonna drop that zero and get wit' a hero?"

I wanted to throw the fuck up, getting with Cheez would have been like feeding myself to a beach whale. "When you gonna hop on a treadmill, motherfucker? And wait until I tell Slay that shit."

"Ain't nobody scared of that flossin' ass nigga."

"Fuck you."

"Now, now…calm that shit down," Ms. Trina mediated.

"Cheez, my daughter needs a baby daddy for this new baby she 'bout to have," LuLu said, trying to hook Porsha up.

"Mama!" Porsha yelled from the spade's table. "My baby got a daddy."

"He ain't doin' shit," LuLu said.

"That's okay, LuLu. I'll pass," Cheez slyly grinned, like he had already been there and done that. Just envisioning his ass naked, alone, was some nasty ass shit.

"I'mma head out." I hugged Ms. Trina. "I'll meet you at the funeral home in the mornin'."

"Okay, baby," Ms. Trina said, all cried out.

* * *

Tyrell was leaned up against his Tahoe.

"Sorry about yo' girl. She was cool."

"Not cool enough for you to give her any play. She liked you…you know?"

"I'm not the type of nigga to lead a broad on…not my style. I wasn't feelin' her like that."

"Who you feelin' then…some chicken head, project chick, hood rat…gold digger?"

"Why do you care?"

"I don't."

I left Tyrell outside and went inside the condo. Slay had fallen asleep on top of the bed comforter. He hadn't even kicked his shoes off. I took the .40 out of my purse and hid it in my panty drawer, thinking that would be the last place Slay searched for anything. I grabbed a t-shirt from his side of the dresser and slipped it on. He stirred, tossed and turned but didn't wake up when I removed the brand new throwback Jordan's from his feet. He was sleeping so peacefully that I didn't even attempt to remove his jeans. I snuggled up under him and breathed him in. He reeked of the perfume I smelled on Aleesha when I was on top of her whooping her ass. He had been with her and hadn't even bothered to wash her off. As much as the thought upset my stomach, I would have preferred him smelling like fish oil, baby shit or even hamburger grease and ketchup...anything other than her. I turned the other way; he scooted up behind me and draped his arm around me. I wanted to cry but the tears wouldn't come.

Gladys Knight sung me to sleep. *I would rather live in his world than in mine without him...*

Chapter 16

TANAYSHA REINCARNATED

Ms. Trina didn't show up at the funeral home. I found her curled up in the fetal position on TaNaysha's bedroom floor in her nightgown. She was just lying there with her eyes wide open and her hair scattered all over her head. She had sunk into some kind of depression and wasn't functioning normally. She wasn't speaking, eating or sleeping. Nor was she smoking—that's how I knew the shit was serious and that somebody other than her had to take on the responsibility of planning TaNaysha's funeral. The task fell on my shoulders.

Willy & Sons wouldn't have been my choice of funeral home but it was the one Ms. Trina had instructed the coroner's office to release TaNaysha's body to on the day of the shooting. For over thirty years, the funeral home had been a staple in the hood—known for taking great care of the dead. But, when Willy Sr. passed away, the customer service died too. Willy Jr. and his brother Larry were running the business now and they were some shiesty ass niggas, using watered down embalming fluid and stealing jewelry and shit off of the bodies in their care. Numerous complaints had been filed with the Bureau of Better Business for the trifling shit they were doing, but they still received most of the hood's business.

Black on Black crime had contributed the most to Willy Jr. and Larry's bank accounts. Over the years, they had buried more of the young and vibrant than the old and ill. It seemed like a wake for somebody's son or daughter was being held at Willy & Sons almost every week. This week, it was TaNaysha.

The day of her visitation, I stopped by the funeral home to view her body before the official start of the wake. And, I'm glad I did.

"This is a Black funeral home. I shouldn't have to tell y'all asses that her make-up is too damn light...looks like y'all just brushed her face with some damn baby powder or some shit...got her lookin' like Casper The Friendly Fuckin' Ghost. I brought her make-up up here. That shit y'all used ain't MAC. Do I need to do it myself?"

"Ms. Reid...just calm down...we'll get it taken care of."

"Better...don't nobody have time for this shit. The wake starts at five. I'll be back at four. Larry, don't make me cuss your ass out again."

I wasn't sure about the effect embalming fluid was suppose to have on the deceased but except for TaNaysha's make-up, her body appeared normal. I just kept reminding myself that her body was just the shell that housed her spirit and that she was very much alive, hopefully in heaven. But to be honest, for a few days, I could have sworn she came back and took over my body. I was cussing out everybody and their mama.

Kinko's was my next stop, to pick up the programs. The photo that I had chose to be printed on the front of the program was of TaNaysha on graduation day in her cap and gown. I thought it was necessary to show that she had accomplished something and was full of hopes and dreams. She was smiling and blowing a kiss into the camera. Minutes before the picture was taken, she had refused to follow tradition and throw her cap in the air like the rest of us had done. I smiled and shook my head at the thought. She was in classic TaNaysha form that day. "Hell nah, I paid too much for this shit to risk throwin' it up in the air…losin' and gettin' it dirty and shit." I, too, was in classic TaNaysha form. "Bitch, what do you mean they're not ready?"

"Bitch, who you callin' a bitch?" The broad on the other line asked. I imagined her head bopping and neck rolling.

"Bitch, you."

"You do not know me," she said.

"I know you ain't T.I. and the programs I already paid for better be ready for pick up when I get there."

Her ass hung up the phone in my face. Apparently, she didn't know who I was—TaNaysha reincarnated.

I stormed into Kinko's like Sophia looking for Harpo in *The Color Purple*. I scanned all of the Kinko employees behind the counter. No one fit the description of the broad I had imagined on the other end of the line when I called earlier. No weaved up, ghetto fabulous broad picking her teeth with her back in the day, CoCo-from-SWV acrylic fingernails.

I calmed my ass down and took a deep breath. The last thing I needed was for someone to be picking up some programs for my funeral service.

"Excuse me…I'm here to pick up some funeral programs that I had printed. My name is Shar Reid."

"Yes, Mam," the tall, lanky Kinko's employee said. "They're ready…the young lady that you spoke to earlier had your order confused with another order. I do apologize."

"Not a problem."

I stopped by the condo for a quick shower and to change. I hadn't just been buying up casual clothes. I had copped a few pantsuits but never with the thought of wearing one of them to my best friend's funeral. I pulled the tags off of a black pantsuit and laid it on the bed. Slay wasn't home. It wasn't a surprise, but I wasn't worried about his whereabouts. Making sure that TaNaysha had a proper funeral and burial was my first priority. He was where he always was, in the streets. I was beginning to suspect that maybe I couldn't depend on him like he had me believing I could. But, if a broad couldn't depend on her own nigga who the fuck could she depend on? I called him.

"Babygirl, I gotta handle some business here at the office. I'll try to make it."

"Okay."

I didn't even bother to alert his ass that he was lying. I had stopped by the office on my way home. Keisha was the only person there. Lil' Wayne was with her. She said that Slay hadn't been in the office one time the entire day and I believed her. The first thing he would have done when he saw Lil' Wayne sitting in the lobby coloring was call me and complain about how he wasn't running a damn daycare.

Larry's ass must have called in the MAC cavalry. TaNaysha's make-up was applied flawlessly. As the old folks would say, she looked good. Ms. Trina, on the other hand, didn't. LuLu and Porsha had been taking care of her while I was busy making all of the funeral arrangements. They had bathed and dressed her in a black dress. Her hair was pulled back into a Black scrunchie. I was mad as hell at LuLu for not even attempting to do something with her hair.

"LuLu." I pulled her to the side. "I thought you were a hairdresser. What's up with Ms. Trina's hair? You could of at least tried to put some curls in it or somethin'."

I looked over at Porsha consoling Ms. Trina who was rocking back and forth in her seat, just a few feet away from TaNaysha's casket.

"Child, I tried. Every time I brought the curlers close to her head she tried to block the curlers with her arm. I almost burned her the first time she freaked out. She's gone." LuLu started crying. She was referring to Ms. Trina, not TaNaysha. She went to fill in for Porsha.

I stayed in the back, ushering folks in. I felt an arm slide around my waist. It was a familiar touch.

"Baby, you made it."

"Babygirl, you need me and I wanted to be here for you. Just like I know if I ever needed you…you'd be there for me."

"You know I would do anything for you." I hugged and kissed Slay. It was true. No matter how much I tried to deny it, I was becoming a down ass chick who would do anything for her nigga.

The visitation went as I had predicted, a whole lot of tears and niggas and broads not even close to TaNaysha falling over and into her casket. I think some of them had made their way over from the other two wakes going on in the funeral home. It was one big hood affair. I was glad that I had decided on a closed casket funeral for her. The casket would be open upon the family and attendees' arrival but after everyone was seated, it would be closed forever.

* * *

New Hope Baptist was the church Ms. Trina was raised in and where she had TaNaysha baptized as a baby. Technically, it was TaNaysha's church home and where I saw fit to have her funeral service. And like most of the niggas and broads in the hood, she had mad respect for Rev. Turner because—unlike my father—he tried to reach out to all of the people in the hood and not just the saved and sanctified. Some nights, he could be found on the corner talking to the dope boys while they chased cars. "God said trust in Him but don't be no fool," he joked about wearing a bulletproof vest under his suit while he was out on the block. He was a jolly man, short, stubby and balding with a welcoming smile that made drug dealers, prostitutes and crackheads comfortable crying in his arms.

Slay swore that when he use to work the corners, he witnessed Rev. Turner saving a nigga's life with the Word— literally.

"Rev. Turner...that nigga's a Bible-toting superhero...for real," he said.

According to him, Rev. Turner was praying for a nigga named Pooch. He had one hand on Pooch's forehead and a Bible pressed up against his chest with the other. Then, out of nowhere, an Aerostar van full of niggas rolled up on the corner and niggas started shooting. Slay described it as an all-out shootout. Everybody who was packing was shooting. No one was seriously injured that Slay knew of. But, if it weren't for the Bible that Rev. Turner had pressed up against Pooch's chest, he would have been killed instantly. The bullet entered the Bible between the space of Rev. Turner's index and middle fingers and stopped, mid air, a centimeter before tearing into the pages of the book of Revelations. Slay swore to it.

The shit that went on in the streets didn't faze Rev. Turner. He knew that the streets had the power to destroy lives, but he was all too familiar with a God that held all power in His hands.

Rev. Turner's daughter, Regina, was a recovering drug addict. She had completed one year of college before dropping out and drifting into the streets. She became addicted to heroin and contracted Hepatitis B. Rev. Turner would be out at all times of the night searching for her. He'd find her, bring her home, feed her, pray over her and sprinkle her with Holy oil. The next morning she would be back to her old habits, but Regina's recovery is a testament that there is power in prayer. Rev. Turner found her halfway dead in the abandoned house that now serves as Cheez's crack factory. Rev. Turner prayed her off of her deathbed and back into the church's choir where she sung as a child. She wasn't bigger than a fishing pole but her voice was thunderous. She could sing her ass off.

Regina had everybody in tears with her rendition of *Precious Lord*. It was the song that I recalled being sung at every funeral I ever attended, but I should have known better. The song ignited a shouting-and-crying spree that went on for almost an hour. Personally, I had no problem with it but TaNaysha used to joke about not wanting to have a long ass funeral that lasted from dawn to dusk and back around to dawn. *At least I got her make-up hooked up*, I thought, looking around at the theatrics. Things really got out of hand when Regina sung *I Won't Complain*.

> *I ask the question… "Lord…why so much pain?"*
> *But He knows what's best for me*
> *Although my weary eyes cannot see*
> *And I say, Thank You Lord…I won't complain…*

Ms. Trina had awoken out of her trance. She leaped up from her front pew seat and started running around the perimeter of the church, asking…why? Regina sung on.

"She's in a better place now," LuLu tried to console Ms. Trina.

> *God has been good to me*
> *He's been so good to me*
> *Better than you or this old world could ever be*
> *He's been so good, He's been so good to me…*

I sat, crying softly and taking inventory of everyone in attendance: me, Slay, Tyrell, Ms. Trina, LuLu, Porsha, Cheez and his crew, Ernie Pain, Big Steph and her girls, Keisha, Wayne, Khalilah and Carlo and a church full of others. I wondered what "this old world" had in store for us and if our good days would outweigh our bad ones.

Chapter 17

YOU TIRED?

Thanksgiving was two days after the funeral. I wasn't in a very thankful mood and stayed in bed the entire holiday; although, I should have been thankful for the fact that my ass was still above ground. Slay, of course, had slipped out that afternoon to go over to the house to see Aleesha. He didn't even try to deny his whereabouts and had the fucking nerve to come back home with a plate. *This motherfucker.* As much as I thought it was disrespectful of him to offer me some shit she had cooked, I had unwisely accepted the situation from the jump because I loved him that much. In turn, I had long disrespected myself.

I know his ass don't think I'm about to eat this shit...bitch ain't about to poison me. I was pissed and it was written all over my face. I pulled the comforter over my head. Slay snatched it off of me completely and tossed it on the bedroom floor.

"Shar...don't start no shit."

"You the one who came up in here with some shit your side piece cooked. Fuck you and her. I'm tired of this shit."

"You tired of this shit? Huh? You tired? Get the fuck up." Slay jerked me up by my arm.

"Stop! Let go of me!" I thought he was about to throw me down the stairs. Instead, he dragged me down them.

"You tired of livin' like a motherfuckin' princess...not havin' to work for shit? Huh? Is that what you're tired of? You tired of drivin' around in a Benz and not havin' to pay a fuckin' car payment? You tired of gettin' your fuckin' nails done and shit…shoppin' and shit…you tired of all of that? Get the fuck out."

Slay pushed me outside the condo door and locked it behind him. I was standing outside in nothing but my t-shirt and panties. No socks. No shoes. No jacket. Not shit. It was cold, my shirt was wet from my tears and my knees were tingling from the carpet burns I had just sustained. *God help me.* I tiptoed over to the Benz. The doors were unlocked. *Thank You Jesus.* I hopped in. The keys were inside the condo, but I had left my phone in the car. I had forgotten to take it off the car charger after returning home from TaNaysha's funeral. I was that distraught and never came back out for it. I stared at the phone. I had no one to call. My best friend was dead and I was dead to my family. *Khalilah.* I dialed her number. "Sorry, this Sprint PCS number is no longer in service." *What the fuck?* There was only one other person I could call, Tyrell. He had me meet him around the block from the condo. I stomped my ass down the street in a pair of three-inch stilettos that I had found in the backseat, my t-shirt and panties. *This is some bullshit.*

It took Tyrell a few minutes to show up, but he rolled around before I froze to death. I hopped into his Tahoe, shivering and with my teeth chattering. He took off his jacket and handed it to me.

"Thh…thh…anks."

Fifteen minutes later, we were pulling into a gated apartment community. We drove around to the buildings in the back of the complex. Tyrell parked, got out and came around to open the passenger side door for me. I took his hand to keep from falling out of the SUV but quickly unlocked my hand from his when I was on solid ground. I followed him up three flights of stairs. *Damn.* I was out of breath. Just because a broad was skinny didn't mean her ass was in shape. I, clearly, wasn't.

Tyrell was holding the door open when I finally made it to the third floor. His apartment was immaculate: Italian leather couch and matching sofa, dark cherry wood end tables and a ceiling-to-floor entertainment center that occupied his living room. Portraits of Malcolm, Martin and Marcus hung on the walls. There were no pictures of Tony Montana or any other mob gangsters in sight.

Meticulously placed within the cubbyholes of the entertainment center were several photos of the same two women. Both as dark skinned as Tyrell with perfect facial symmetry.

"Who are they?" I turned and asked.

Tyrell was standing behind me with his hands in his pockets. "My mother and little sister."

"They're both very pretty. Where do they live?"

"Is it important?"

"I just asked. Damn...you act like they in the witness protection program or some shit." I didn't ask Tyrell shit else about his family. His ass was as secretive about his life and family as the military was about a covert operation.

Without his permission, I roamed through the apartment's three bedrooms. One of which had been converted into a small gym and the other a library. All of the walls in the library showcased bookshelves populated with hundreds and hundreds of books: W. E. B. DuBois' *The Souls of Black Folks*, Booker T. Washington's *Up From Slavery*, The Autobiography of Malcolm X, *Selected Writings and Speeches of Marcus Garvey* and *The Measure of a Man* by Martin Luther King Jr.—just to name a few. In the middle of the room was a black swivel chair and matching ottoman.

"Is that where you read?" I pointed.

"Yeah…I could sit in here for hours." Tyrell lightened up.

It was the first time I had seen him smile since the last time at the bookstore, before he found out that I was the boss' girl.

"Why do you like readin' so much?"

"As they say…knowledge is power…you hungry?"

I couldn't deny it. My stomach was growling. He must have heard it. "Yeah…starvin'."

I followed Tyrell into the kitchen. He pulled a pan of turkey and dressing out of the oven. "You cooked?"

"Does that surprise you?"

I hunched my shoulders. "I figured you for a takeout-type-of-nigga."

"Guess you figured wrong. There's a bathroom down the hall to the right where you can wash your hands."

The hallway bathroom was decorated in red, black and white—Chinese themed. The shower curtain was designed in a step-and-repeat pattern of love, peace and faith printed in the language. *This nigga is too deep for me.* I washed my hands but before heading back to the kitchen and dining area, I peeked into Tyrell's bedroom. There were only two items in the room: a mattress in the middle of the floor and a painting on an easel. I looked closer. It was a painting of me in the red sundress I had worn to the park on the day that TaNaysha, Khalilah and I first met him. I didn't know what to think. On one hand, it was some sweet shit. On the other, it was some stalker-type shit.

"You done snoopin' around my apartment?" Tyrell came up behind me.

I bit my bottom lip in guilt. "I was…just lookin' around. That's all."

I took a seat at the dining room table, debating whether or not to question Tyrell about the painting. I left the issue alone for the time being. He fixed me a plate of turkey and dressing, cranberry sauce, mashed potatoes, green bean casserole, sweet potatoes and buttered rolls. My mouth was watering. *Who does he think he is...the hood's G. Garvin?*

"All I have to drink is water and cranberry juice."

"Water's fine."

Tyrell fixed himself a plate and sat across from me. He blessed his food, which reminded me to do the same. He ate one item on his plate at a time. I didn't understand it but hey, to each his own. Over dinner, I did most of the talking—mostly about my childhood, my family and TaNaysha. Neither of us mentioned the shit that went down with Vera or speculated what the fuck ever happened to her. We sat in silence for a while, listening to our forks scrap our plates. And then Tyrell asked me a question that Slay had never posed to me: What did I dream of being?

"I always wanted to be an anchorwoman...to study broadcast journalism and deliver the news in a fair and objective way. There's bias in the news. They always concentrate on the bad and forget about all of the good goin' on in the Black community. Granted, the good is sometimes hard to see. Plus, it was the only way I was goin' to be semi-famous since I can't dance, sing or act," I laughed.

"So, how does a girl with such big dreams get caught up with a nigga like Slay?"

"Trapped by love...I guess you can say."

"Love, huh? You think a nigga who puts his woman out on Thanksgiving Day...in the cold, naked and hungry...loves you?"

Instead of leaping across the table in attempt to stab Tyrell with the fork in my hands, I pretended not to hear his ass. *Don't nobody want to hear that shit right now.* If only I knew then that he was only telling me what I needed to hear.

"You know what? Fuck you." I couldn't let it go. "You walk around like you're a fuckin' saint or some shit...like the shit you move don't destroy people, families and communities. In my eyes, you're the worst kind of person...a hypocrite...reading W.E.B. DuBois and Booker T. Washington books...talkin' about knowledge is power and shit while you're pollutin' the streets with drugs. You're no better than any of the other niggas on the block."

"I don't know what the fuck you talkin' about. You done?"

Tyrell got up and took his plate and mine's, letting me know that he wasn't the type of nigga to incriminate himself in front of a friend or foe and that he did what the fuck he did for a reason other than street fame, money or material shit. There was a deeper reason, but he wasn't sharing.

After dinner, I volunteered to wash the dishes but Tyrell refused my help. He fetched me a pair of his boxers, sweatpants, an oversized black tee and bath towels.

"You got shampoo and soap?"

"Look under the bathroom cabinet."

Tyrell had cleaned up the kitchen and was sitting on the couch watching *New Jack City* when I stepped out of the shower. I plopped down on the opposite end and curled my feet into the soft leather. A few minutes later, Tyrell and I found ourselves engaged in a conversation about who we thought played the ultimate crackhead on screen: Chris Rock as Pookie in *New Jack City*, Halle Berry as Samuel L. Jackson's girlfriend Vivian in *Jungle Fever* or Angela Means as Felisha in *Friday*.

"Chris Rock." We both agreed and laughed.

Suddenly, there was a loud banging on the door. Tyrell pulled me close to him. His lips brushed up against my cheek. "Go into my room and lock the door. Don't come out for shit," he whispered in my ear as he pulled a .38 from underneath the couch. He peeked through the peephole with his finger on the gun's trigger and I raced down the hallway. Locked in his bedroom, I leaned my ear up against the door.

"Man, I fucked up!"

I recognized the voice. It was Slay, but I stayed in place.

"I don't know where the fuck Shar is. I put her out, but I promise I was just gonna leave her ass outside for a few minutes...teach her ass a lesson. When I went to let her back in the house...she was gone. I don't know if she's somewhere frozen to fuckin' death or if somebody kidnapped her or what. Man, what the fuck am I gonna do. I know I do some foul shit sometimes, but I love that girl." Slay was pacing the living room floor, I could feel the vibrations from his hard and deep footsteps.

"A'ight...just calm the fuck down. We'll find her." I heard Tyrell say, loud enough for me to hear, reminding me to stay put.

"What the fuck is that smell?" Slay asked. I imagined him sniffing the air.

"Nigga, what smell?"

"Smells like coconut or some shit up in here."

Fuck. It was the shampoo and conditioner that I had used to wash my hair. I prayed that Slay didn't follow the scent down the hall.

"Oh, shit! You got a bitch up in here. My bad, nigga. Sorry to disturb y'all. Shit, I'm glad. I was startin' to think yo' ass was gay."

"Never that, my nigga. I'm just selective about the broads I fuck," Tyrell replied.

"I hear you but pussy is pussy," Slay said.

Bastard. My hand was on the doorknob and if I didn't think Slay would have beat my ass into a coma simply for being in Tyrell's bedroom, I would have raced out and went haywire on his ass for the comment he had made.

"Until you run up in some infected pussy," said Tyrell. *Thank you.*

"You right, my nigga. Let me get the fuck up out of here and leave you and your girl alone. I gotta find Shar."

"A'ight. Let me get rid of this broad and I'll get at you, findin' Shar is most important." Tyrell played along.

"Thanks, my nigga."

Tyrell waited until the coast was clear to come back to the bedroom. He covered the painting of me sitting on the easel with a sheet and didn't say shit more about it.

"What you gonna do?" He asked, standing only inches away from me. I could smell his cologne easing out of his pores.

"I'm goin' home."

Tyrell snickered, disappointedly.

"Say what the fuck it is you need to say."

"I ain't got shit to say...you said it all," he said.

He made me shower, wash my hair again in unscented shampoo and conditioner and change back into the t-shirt and panties I had on before dropping me off exactly where he picked me up at. It wasn't the last time I would see him, but the last time was nearing.

Chapter 18

THE TAG ALONG

To redeem himself for putting me out—unclothed, barefoot and in the dead of winter—Slay surprised me with a weekend getaway to Miami. He knew that I had been longing to go on vacation since Carlo had whisked Khalilah to Hawaii. Miami wasn't Maui, but it did the trick. Once again, all was forgiven. But, I was soon discovering that—with Slay—nothing was as it seemed.

* * *

My suitcase was heavy as hell. *I know I didn't pack that much shit*, I thought as I grabbed the handle. Just as I was about to lift the suitcase out of the back of the Escalade, Slay came rushing towards me like he was coming to save me from a burning building. He grabbed the suitcase out of my hands and set it on the airport curb.

"Babygirl, let these motherfuckers work for their tip," he said, referring to the airport attendees. "You my lady and my lady don't carry her own luggage."

"It seems heavier than I remember," I said, trying to take a mental inventory of all of the shit I had apparently packed.

"'Cause your ass packed about twenty pair of shoes…that all look alike by the way."

"Because I got twenty different outfits and they don't all look alike," I said, playfully punching him in the arm.

"What the fuck y'all back there arguin' 'bout?"

"Why did you invite him?" I mouthed to Slay.

Gutt, short for Gutter, was a key player in Slay's operation. So was his brother Butter and a broad named Luxury. Slay had invited them all to accompany us to Miami. I was not pleased. But shit, I didn't have much of a say in the decision.

Gutt was a tall, lanky, brown skin nigga who usually piled on layers of baggy clothes to make his ass appear to be bulkier than he actually was. He was a nigga who didn't give a fuck about taking a bullet or taking a life—something him and Jazmin Hill had in common. Slay liked him because he would do anything to get the job done. If Slay asked him to make a drop on the moon, Gutt would find a way to make it happen. But, while Slay was worried about Cheez being the thorn in his side, let's just say I had a gut feeling that Gutt's ass was the one to watch. After Yo's death, Gutt had gotten a little ill when Tyrell joined the team and started heading up Slay's operation. He thought for sure that he was the next nigga in line to be Slay's right hand man. I could see the animosity building up inside of him. He was a loose cannon.

Butter, on the other hand, was a smooth operator—hence his street name. He and Gutter shared their mother's features but each had different fathers. Butter was shorter and lighter than Gutt. And unlike Gutt, Butter didn't necessarily need to hustle. He had big brown eyes and dimples that ran the broads in the hood wild. They were lining up to take care of his ass, taking food out of their children's mouths and using their government checks to keep him fitted in the latest gear and fresh kicks. He had them eating out of the palm of his hands and he could talk his way out of any situation. He could have a nigga believing the sky was purple and the earth was square. Slay kept him on the payroll simply because of his boyish and innocent looks and his million-dollar mouthpiece.

On a scale of one to ten, Luxury was an eight. If I weren't a ten, I would have really been fucked up about her tagging along. Slay had recruited her from Big Steph's assortment of girls to come and work for him. I'm sure he and Big Steph worked out a deal that benefitted them both. Luxury was one of Big Steph's top-money-making hoes. She got her name because in car-talk, Big Steph's other girls were Geo Metros and Fiestas while Luxury was the Bentley of the group.

Out of her clear, plastic, stripper shoes and "working girl" gear, Luxury looked like the all-American-girl-next-door. Days before we left for Miami, Slay paid for her to have an extreme makedown instead of makeover. Under the globs of make-up she wore, she had pretty golden skin. Her hair hung an inch or two below her shoulders and was dyed platinum blonde. It was now a soft brown color with highlights. He paid for her an entire new wardrobe, proper for a kindergarten teacher. Instead of standing out like a sore thumb, she now walked through the airport looking homely and unsuspecting of her old lifestyle of turning tricks or of her new one of moving weight.

"Babygirl, they've been workin' hard, puttin' money in the bank for me and therefore for you," Slay tried to convince me. "They deserve to go on vacation too. Gotta keep my top employees happy."

What about keepin' your "lady" happy? That's the question I wanted to ask his ass, but the bruises on my arms and wrists and the carpet burns on my legs had just healed from when he drug my ass down the condo stairs and out the door.

"I understand."

"I know you do, Babygirl."

Like he was the head of the FAA, Slay briefed us all—me, Gutt, Butter and Luxury—on the airport's travel policies.

"Nigga, we fly more than you. We know what the fuck to do and not to do," Gutt responded.

"Nigga, I'm just remindin' y'all's asses. Don't fuck up."

"We won't, baby?" Luxury spoke up.

Who the fuck is she callin' baby? Before I could utter a word, Slay stared me down with a don't-start-no-shit-right-now look.

Slay and I removed our shoes and placed them in the small gray bin in front of us. I grabbed another bin for my purse and jewelry and watched Slay walk through the metal detector. Usually he carried around a rubber-banded wad of hundreds but that day, he only had three twenties in a money clip on him and was dressed clean-cut without all of the bling he normally wore. We breezed through the security checkpoint without incident and waited on Gutt who was in the line to the left of us and Luxury and Butter who were in the line to the right of us to pass through.

"You look like you 'bout to bust?" The security officer smiled at Luxury. "This your first child?" He asked.

"Yes, Sir." Luxury patted her fake bulging belly like she was truly with child.

The day before we left for Miami, Luxury was a thick-size twelve with a tiny waist. The morning we picked her, Butter and Gutt up, her ass came walking out of her apartment looking nine-months pregnant. Slay had already warned me not to ask any questions that I really didn't want to know the answers to.

"Gonna have ourselves a little boy," Butter interjected. "You got children officer? Maybe you can give us some useful parentin' tips."

"Got five of'em."

"Five!" Luxury repeated.

"Yep...all by the same woman, my wife. Y'all two married?" The officer asked Butter and Luxury.

Both Butter and Luxury held up their ring fingers, displaying a matching his-and-hers wedding set. *What the fuck? Them niggas need to be nominated for an Oscar.* I looked up at Slay. Beads of sweat had popped up on his forehead like a bad case of the measles. I grabbed his hand. It was sweaty as hell too.

"Yes, sir. Goin' on two years now." Butter was lying through his teeth. He and Luxury couldn't stand one another and had argued the entire drive to the airport.

Another security officer whispered something into the ear of the officer who was conversing with Butter and Luxury. I could feel Slay's heart racing through the veins in his palm.

"Ya'll folks have a nice trip. Gotta keep this line movin'."

"Thank you, officer." Butter smiled, showing off his dimples.

Slay hadn't wiped his brow yet. Gutt was still in line and as soon as he walked through the metal detector, the shit went off—beeping loud as hell.

"Step back, please, Sir," the officer manning the area asked Gutt. He ran the handheld wand across Gutt's arms and torso, over his crotch and down his legs.

"It's over for his ass," I heard Slay say between breaths.

"Officer, come on man, it's my grill...see." Gutt smiled big and wide. "I can take'em out if you wanna see'em. You should try'em on...see how you look in'em."

The officer nodded his head as if to say *damn nigger.* "Move it along," he instructed Gutt.

* * *

As a child, I use to get excited about going on our annual family vacation. No matter what our destination was, we would always find a Holiday Inn to rest our heads. I thought the free pastries and orange juice that they offered in the morning after our night's stay was the best thing in the world. Those were simpler and happy times under my father's roof that I would always cherish. But, rolling with Slay came with an upgrade to The Ritz Carlton. The door to the suite opened up to a living area with floor-to-ceiling windows, displaying a wrap around terrace with a breathtaking view of the Atlantic Ocean. The suite itself was larger than the average size one bedroom apartment with its' own living room, bar, kitchen and dining area. The interior was ultra modern and sleek—dark cherry wood furniture and earth-toned décor. The hotel offered every amenity available: pool, spa, hair salon, fitness center, laundry valet, restaurants, private cabanas, a car and limo service and a safety deposit box—which Slay had open wide.

"Thanks, Baby." I threw my arms around his neck.

"For what, Babygirl?" He gripped my waist.

"For bringin' me here. It's beautiful."

"How many times do I have to tell you…anything for you, Babygirl."

"I'mma go look around."

"Okay, Babygirl. I'mma be up here handlin' some business."

"Slay, we're suppose to be on vacation."

"We are." he kissed me and proceeded to unpack.

I was planning to explore the hotel but not before I paid Luxury's ass a visit. I hadn't forgotten about that *"We won't, baby"* comment she had made at the airport. I was one hundred percent sure she was referring to Slay when she said that shit.

Slay had made it clear with his actions or non-actions that Aleesha was a permanent fixture in his life. He wasn't getting rid of her. I knew that in my heart, but I refused to put up with some new bullshit. From the abuse I suffered from his hands and me attacking Vera and Aleesha—I thought of myself as a seasoned fighter. Shit, I could take and give a blow. If necessary, I was ready to go head-to-toe with Luxury and any other broad who had their eyes on Slay.

Her hotel room door was cracked. I pushed it open and walked in. Gutt and Butter were sitting on the edge of Luxury's bed. She was bent down on her knees in front of them—stroking Butter's dick with one hand and using the other to grip Gutt's nut sack as she sucked his dick. *What the fuck!* I watched as she licked the length of Gutt's dick and juggled his balls between her cheeks before taking him whole again in her mouth. Luxury was gifted at sucking dick. I had forgotten that she was a hoe by trade.

Thrown in the middle of the bed was the fake belly Luxury had worn, several kilos of cocaine and bundles of cash. Luxury turned her head and smiled at me with her eyes. There was no shame in her game. Shit, she was getting paid.

Back in the suite, Slay had emptied all of my shit out of my suitcase and onto the bed. He had removed all of his belongings out of the two black duffle bags he had brought and was now stuffing them full of Saran-wrapped and taped blocks of cocaine.

"Call down to Luxury's room and tell her to bring my shit up here."

"She's busy suckin' Gutt's and Butter's dicks," I said. "Has she ever sucked your dick?"

"What?"

"You fuckin' heard me. Has...she...ever...sucked...your dick?"

"Shar, I don't have time for this shit right now. I got business to fuckin' take care of."

"Yes or fuckin' no. Answer the got damn question, Slay."

"Damn it, Shar." Slay rushed me and pinned me against the wall.

"No...but since you happen to fuckin' already believe she did why don't I go down there and let her suck the skin off my shit." He dropped me to the floor and headed for the door.

"No! Slay...I'm sorry. I'm sorry. Please don't go down there. Please."

Slay turned around and leaned up against the door. I dropped to my knees, unbuckling his belt and unzipping his jeans. His phone buzzed and he grabbed it out of his pocket before I slid his jeans to the floor. "Yeah, I got yo' shit...as long as you got my money motherfucker."

I took his dick in my mouth and imitated the shit I saw Luxury do. Slay clicked his cell phone shut.

"Damn, Babygirl. Ooooohhh, shit! You done learned some new tricks."

While I had been thinking that Gutt, Butter and Luxury were tagging along on vacation with Slay and I, the truth was that I was the tag along.

Chapter 19

WILL SLAY'S REAL MISTRESS PLEASE STAND UP?

Ms. Trina answered the door in a satin, mint green robe. Her hair was disheveled and she had a Newport hanging out of the corner of her mouth. She hadn't completely returned to being her old self but after losing her only child, I never believed she would.

She invited me in and the stench of burnt baking soda lingered up my nose. I figured it was the same odor TaNaysha had described smelling several times during her childhood. She was just five-years-old when she walked into her mother's bedroom and first remembered her nostrils being overcome with the drug-polluted air. She had also described becoming physically sick and suddenly, I found myself nauseated and rushed into the hall bathroom.

The stench in the bathroom was even stronger. Lined on the edge of the tub was a bent spoon, a lighter, a needle, an old worn-out leather belt and three small, clear, plastic bags. Two of which were empty and the last had a single, popcorn-kernel size rock enclosed in it. My breakfast came up and out of me. I cried but not because I was sick. Ms. Trina had been clean for eight years. With TaNaysha gone, she didn't have the will to say no to the old habit that had been waiting for an opportunity to re-enter her life. Jazmin Hill was now essentially responsible for taking two lives.

"Child, here." Ms. Trina took a face towel out of the bathroom cabinet, wet it and handed it to me. "And stop all that damn cryin'." She took a puff of the Newport.

"I'm okay," I said.

"How was Miami?" She tried to make small talk.

"Fun." I half smiled—not necessarily lying. After Slay had handled his business, we had a great time. He had rented a stretch Hummer limo for the weekend and we rode the streets like the King and Queen Pin of Miami: shopping, eating at fancy restaurants and hitting up different Miami nightclubs. Some of Slay's associates—some Panamanian and Columbian looking niggas—even joined us at several clubs. They were dressed in suits, smoking cigars and receiving lap dances from a variety of Miami broads. Gutt and Butter seemed to be thoroughly enjoying the entertainment. Luxury, on the other hand, seemed pissed. However, I wasn't sure if she was angry with Gutt and Butter for paying her ass no attention or at me for sitting where she wanted to be—up under Slay's arm.

"I'm glad you had a good time," Ms. Trina said, standing in the bathroom doorway. "When I'm high...the pain goes away," she said.

"You don't owe me an explanation," I said.

"I know, but I want you to hear me out."

I nodded my head to let her know that I was listening. She instructed me not to worry about her and to stop checking in on her, which I had been doing every week since the funeral. She said that I had been making it harder for her to move on, seeing me without my partner in crime in tow.

"Every time you come through the door, I hold it open, hoping TaNaysha is somewhere behind you," she said. I hadn't thought about my presence being a burden in her life. I was doing what I thought TaNaysha would do for me—being there for her mother during such a difficult time.

"I believe in God and I know He heals in time, but the shit got to be too painful...thinkin' about TaNaysha every second of every day. I just couldn't deal with it anymore. It's just the way I'm copin' with the situation right now. I cope with my problems with drugs...you cope with Slay beatin' your ass and fuckin' around with them other bitches with material shit...the jewelry, clothes, cars and money all replace the pain with moments of pleasure. But, you know as well as I know...the pain always comes back."

* * *

Makin' Moves Truckin' Company wasn't making too many moves during the winter season; business on the legit end of the company was slow. So slow that Slay began instructing Keisha and I to work up paperwork for non-existing clients. He purchased cheap furniture and stored it in the back of the trucks, continuing to use the interstates to move major weight. Tyrell was against the plan completely. He wanted to keep the trucks off the highway during the winter season as much as possible stating that people didn't relocate as much in the winter as they did in the spring, summer and fall. But, Slay wasn't hearing him and wanted to keep his product moving by any means necessary—on the corner, in the air and on the interstate. He had cash coming from all directions.

The day the office was scheduled to close for the Christmas and New Year's holidays, Keisha came to work with her arm in a sling. Wayne had beaten her ass once again. Watching her try to fill out paperwork with her left hand was amusing. Her left-handed writing skills weren't even compatible with that of Lil' Wayne's.

"Why the fuck you let Wayne's broke ass beat you like that?"

"The same reason you let Slay's rich ass beat you up." Keisha had made her point, she and Ms. Trina both. From then on, I tried to stay the fuck out of her and Wayne's business.

Slay stopped by the office every couple of hours or so but for the most part, he was out keeping surveillance over his corner operation. Tyrell was in the back office on the phone, but he wasn't discussing business. He shut the office door, but the office walls were thin.

"I'll be there, I promise."

Must be talkin' to a broad. I shook my head. *How the fuck he gonna have a paintin' of me in his room and shit and be makin' promises to another broad?* The next question I asked myself was: *Why do I care?* I stared down at my engagement ring. Slay was my nigga and soon-to-be husband. Slay, not Tyrell, had my heart and I'd given up too much for him just to up and throw what we had away.

Twenty minutes after the office had closed, Keisha was still outside waiting on Wayne's ass to pick her up. She was crying, going on and on about how he probably was out riding another broad around in her car. Which, was more than likely true than not. She needed a ride to pick Lil' Wayne up from daycare and to the grocery store. I offered since I didn't have shit else to do but go home to an empty condo.

Lil' Wayne didn't exactly attend a licensed daycare in a building with a playground, actual teachers or a set curriculum. After a half-a-day at preschool, he was dropped off over at a broad named Niecy's apartment. She charged a monthly fee of $250 per child—a steal for childcare that could cost as much as $400 a week and she offered a discount to those families with more than one child. She took infants and kids up to age eight, ten at a time. When their bad asses started talking back and disrespecting her, she instructed their parents to find childcare elsewhere and then took the next child on her six-month waiting list. She was running her shit like it was officially registered to do business in the state—another hood entrepreneur.

There was no yelling, screaming or any sounds of kids running and playing coming from Niecy's apartment. *Damn, she must have spiked their bottles with Benadryl or some shit,* I thought. It was quiet enough to hear a pin drop. When Keisha and I walked in, five of the older children—including Lil' Wayne—were sitting on Niecy's plush, forest green sofa engrossed in an episode of General Hospital and eating Cheetos. Lil' Wayne didn't budge at the sight of his mother—not until Niecy nodded her head and gave him permission to greet Keisha. She had signs taped around her apartment: *No Runnin', No Jumpin'* and *No Fuckin' Cussin'* along with posters of the Alphabet and the United States of America. But at two o'clock, the time slot for General Hospital, all learning for the day ceased.

Keisha helped Lil' Wayne put on his coat. After which, she dug into her purse and pulled out two hundred dollar bills, handing the money to Niecy.

"Where's my other fifty?" Niecy still had her hand out. "Keisha, you know I don't play about my money. Plus, I gots to finish my Christmas shoppin'."

"I'm sorry, Niecy. Wayne was suppose to give me the other fifty when he picked me up after work but as you can see his ass didn't show up. That's all I got."

"Wayne ain't shit and ain't gonna ever be shit," Niecy said, as if Keisha wasn't aware of what Wayne was.

"Here." I handed Niecy $300—the fifty Keisha owed and $250 for the next month. She took the money and stuffed it inside her bra.

"Thanks, Shar," Keisha said.

"It's the least I can do," I said, with Vera in mind.

* * *

Keisha ran into the Save-a-Lot while Lil' Wayne and I stayed in the car. He didn't scream after her but remained entranced with the action figure in his hands. He was a cute little boy with thick, long eyelashes. The only real resemblance to his father was his nose and the braids he wore, which was a blessing. I wondered what he'd grow up to be. If he would follow in his father's footsteps down a path of irresponsibility or would he overcome his circumstances and grow up to be a productive member of society: a doctor, a lawyer, an engineer, a teacher, a basketball coach, an architect, a firefighter, a business owner, an actor, a barber, an astronaut, a painter, an actor or even the president. He could be anything that he wanted to be. I hoped that he knew it.

I reached into the backseat to hand him a Kleenex. His nose was running. Out of the back windshield and across the street, I saw Gutt and some of Slay's corner workers coming out of a warehouse that I had always assumed was abandoned and property of the city because of the barbwire fence and *No Trespassing* signs. I squinted my eyes and looked harder, seeing the back of what I believed to be Tyrell's Tahoe, Slay's Escalade and the two Makin' Moves trucks. I suspected that it was ground zero for Slay's operation, where he manufactured his products. All of the windows of the warehouse had been covered by sheet metal and the front entrance of the warehouse had been bricked over. Traffic flowed in and out of the building from the back. There was one way in and one way out and cameras were strategically mounted on the roof to capture every angle of the property. The uninvited were not welcome.

My cell phone vibrated. It was Slay. One of the cameras on top of the warehouse roof was aimed directly at the Save-a-Lot parking lot.

"Where the fuck you at?"

I knew damn well that my Benz was in Slay's view. "Wayne didn't show up to pick up Keisha and she needed a ride to pick up Lil' Wayne from daycare and to the grocery store."

"You don't shop at Save-a-Lot."

"I don't, but Keisha's does."

"Hurry up and get the fuck home. I'll be there soon."

"How soon?" I asked, knowing that soon to Slay didn't exactly mean he would be home within the hour. Then again, some days it did and some days it didn't.

"Soon enough."

I didn't see Slay until the next morning. We were engaged but he was already married—to the game. I was his mistress.

Chapter 20

REVELATIONS

Months into our relationship I had a revelation—I had fallen in love with Slay-the-street-star-with-major-swag before I had gotten to know Slay-the-man. All that I knew of him personally was what he had chosen to share with me. His mother was a prostitute who, in the end, he couldn't protect from the hands of one of her Johns who strangled her to death. He never knew his father and to his knowledge, he didn't have any siblings. He shared these things, emotionless and I believed that with each dollar that went into his pocket, he was trying to fill the void of "not having" shit as a child. He didn't have a mother. He didn't have a father. He didn't have a home—the streets were his refuge. He didn't have clothes to put on his back or shoes for his feet if he didn't steal them. He didn't eat if he didn't deal. But, he wasn't empty inside. He was full of rage. I knew that for sure. And, he was increasingly becoming the type of nigga he despised—a selfish one that made mistakes and let greed guide him.

Nevertheless, I loved him and I believed that he loved me.

* * *

For more than a few days, the same unknown number kept popping up on my cell phone. I didn't have any debts. So, I knew it wasn't a bill collector. Still, I wasn't answering. I tossed my phone aside and returned my attention back to decorating the Christmas tree I had bought. I had the condo looking like an overly decorated department store during the holiday season. I had two stockings dangling from the fireplace mantle with Slay and my name embroidered on them. I even had a Christmas CD playing in the background and was attempting to do some White people shit—string popcorn.

Christmas had always been my mother's favorite holiday. She loved to decorate the house, outside and in. I suppose I was trying to recreate the feeling of family in the condo even though it was just Slay and I. He was all the family I had since my own had disowned me or as they saw it, I had walked away from them for a no-good nigga. Hindsight was always 20/20.

I imagined my mother hanging cherished ornaments that my sister and I had crafted as gifts to her in the past on the same White Christmas tree that my parents had purchased back when I was in elementary school and before my little sister was even born. It had faded to a dull white over the years, but my mother refused to throw it out. "There are memories attached to this tree," she always said to my father when he tried to talk her into donating it to the Goodwill and buying a new one. I pictured him trying to untangle the lights he always strung up along the front door and windows and then I pictured my little sister inspecting the gifts under the tree, shaking each box for telltale signs of what was inside. I wondered if, without me there, they were still enjoying themselves.

I stared under the Christmas tree at the presents I had bought for them. A pair of Stacy Adams for my father—he was old school—a couple of Kenneth Cole items to update his attire and a Rolex watch. My mother was still carrying the first Dooney & Burke purse she had ever purchased; I copped her a new one along with some perfume, a gift card to Macy's and a pair of diamond earrings. Most of the gifts under the tree were for my little sister: Dora-the-Explorer everything, all of the Bratz Dolls, roller skates, an Ipod and a MP3 Player along with a spring and fall wardrobe of True Religion clothing.

I loaded the gifts into the Benz, slightly hesitant about personally delivering them but it didn't seem logical to mail them since my parents' house was a quick drive away. And even so, I hadn't communicated with them since the last time I tried to share what I thought was good news with them—my engagement to Slay.

I parked in front of the house where most of my childhood memories were made. My mother had opened the curtains to showcase the infamous white Christmas tree to those passing by. I could see her and my father dancing in the middle of the living room. He had his hands around her waist and she had her arms around his neck. They were moving slowly in a circular motion, laughing and smiling at each other. I suspected that they weren't listening to Christmas music, maybe some Marvin Gaye or Teddy Pendergrass. My father acted holier-than-thou but every now and then he took a moment to enjoy life without the fear of persecution. My parents looked happy—even without me in the picture. I was fooling myself, thinking that my absence from Christmas dinner was going to spoil their holiday fun.

Fuck it! I put the Benz in drive and drove my ass away. They hadn't once tried to reach out to me since I had been gone—to see how I was doing or even to see if my ass was alive. They could have at least tried to conduct an intervention or some shit—anything to show that they cared. In fact, the parents on A & E's show *Intervention* cared more about their drug-addicted-prostituted-and-pimped-out-mouthwash-drinking kids than my parents did for me. On the show, parents of junkies loved their children enough to risk their own lives, driving around in the hood looking for their strung out sons and daughters—asking questions like they were the police. *That's some shit!* I guess my parents had resolved to leave the situation in God's hands. *Fuck them! They ain't no more saved than Slay.*

I wasn't trying to go through the hassle of returning the thousands of dollars worth of shit I had bought. On my way back to the condo, I took a detour into the hood and handed out the presents that I had bought for my mother, father and little sister to anyone I saw walking the streets: kids, adults and crackheads. I knew most of the shit would end up in Ernie Pain's hands—most of the hood's crackheads sold the new shit they came across to him—or in the pawnshop.

"Bless you child," Bop said when I handed him the Rolex and the pair of Stacy Adams. Bop was in his fifties and a certified crackhead. He didn't give a fuck about sucking a nigga's dick for drugs or money to buy drugs. He'd bop and slob on a dog's dick for one hit of the pipe. He was that gone. He slipped the watch on his wrist and traded the jailhouse slippers he was wearing for the Stacy Adams.

"Oooohhh, I look sharp. Don't I?" He smiled, showing nothing but his gums. All of his teeth had rotted out from years of drug abuse and lack of proper oral hygiene.

"Yeah, Bop, you look sharp," I said, staring at the dirt-stained jean jacket and green jogging pants he had on. "Here." I handed him the last of my father's gifts that I hadn't yet given away. It contained a gray Kenneth Cole sweater and black slacks. He tore the wrapping paper off the box like an anxious little boy.

"Oooohhh, that's nice. I might just go to church." Bop held up the sweater. "I'mma go change right now."

"Okay, Bop. Take care and Merry Christmas."

"Merry Christmas to you too. God gonna bless you…watch and see."

I watched Bop walk towards Ernie Pain's.

* * *

Slay was laughing so hard that he couldn't breathe. He was barely audible on the other end of the phone. "Oh my God...my side hurts," he said. "This shit is so funny."

"What's so funny? And where are you?"

"Babygirl, Bop is in the middle of the street in front of Erine Pain's house tap dancing. Somebody done gave that crackhead-nigga a pair of Stacy Adams and now he thinks he's Sammy Davis Jr."

"Nigga, them ain't tap-dancing shoes," Slay yelled out. "That nigga crazy and he wearin' them Stacy Adams with some green sweats. I'mma give that nigga a discount on his order today just for makin' me laugh."

A discount on his order. Slay always talked in code over the phone and out in public. He never stated that he sold drugs. Mainly not to incriminate himself, but I also believed it was partly because he didn't want to own up to the responsibility of ruining people's lives—those addicted to drugs and the family members who loved them.

"A'ight, well, I'mma stop by the grocery store and then I'll be home." I didn't mention to Slay that I had played Santa earlier in the day and had supplied Bop with the shoes.

"Okay, Babygirl, I'm right behind you."

I pulled out the very same list that TaNaysha had helped me make for the Thanksgiving dinner that I had planned on cooking but didn't. In honor of her, Slay, and my first Christmas together, I decided to prepare a grand feast. I snuck into the grocery store, hoping the store manager who broke up the fight between Aleesha and I wasn't working. I was sure he'd recognize me and either call the cops or throw me out of the store. I peered down every aisle and around every corner as I shopped, trying to avoid a run-in with him. And then there were the memories of the last time I was in the store. Of course, of me whooping Aleesha's ass but sadly of the day I lost my best friend.

Bags of groceries had replaced the load of gifts that were in the trunk of the Benz earlier. By myself, it would have taken me three trips out to my car to carry them all in. I was glad Slay had made it home before me. *Good, he can help me with these groceries.* I parked next to the Escalade.

"Honey, I'm…what the fuck happened?"

The Christmas tree had been knocked over and the silver and blue ornaments that had adorned its' limbs had been smashed all over the living room floor along with the lights and plastic star that I had graced the top of the tree with. I felt like I was walking on eggshells, literally. The Christmas stockings that I had hung up had been ripped from the fireplace mantle and the garland and red bows that I had decorated the staircase with had been removed and tossed on the floor. But what had disturbed me the most was seeing the baby-Jesus-in-the-manger figurine that I had set in the middle of the coffee table broken into pieces. *Lord, I didn't do it.*

The gifts that were under the tree hadn't been stolen. They were in middle of the mess on the floor, which ruled out a break-in. I raced up the stairs. Slay was laying in the bedroom floor with his head buried in the carpet. I could see the rise and fall of his back. He was alive and hadn't physically been harmed from my view. I rushed to his side.

"Slay, what happened?"

He looked up at me with tears in his eyes.

"Baby, what's wrong? What's the matter?"

I sat on the floor with my back against the dresser drawer with Slay in my arms. He was crying like a newborn baby.

"I'm sorry, Babygirl...for destroyin' your decorations and the tree and shit. I lost it when I came in and saw the tree...lights stockings and shit." He sniffled and gained his composure. "It's just that...I grew up hatin' Christmas. It was just another day for me. Most Christmas mornin's, I was mad that God had woke me up. Shit, there was nothin' for me to wake up to. No tree...no presents...no mother and no father. I would've been thankful for a ninety-nine-cent Hot Wheel or some shit. The closest thing I got to receivin' a gift was some rotten apples and oranges from the landlady."

"Baby, I'm so sorry for everything that you went through and everything that happened to you." I stroked my hand back-and-forth over the waves in Slay's hair. "But, I believe that what doesn't kill us only makes us stronger."

"True, Babygirl. That's why I had to do what the fuck I had to do to make it. Now, everyday is Christmas. I don't make it rain...I make it snow."

Chapter 21

Part Three

MAN TO MAN

The line to get into The Tap Room was wrapped around the building. Broads were in line, shivering in outfits that exposed almost every inch of their bodies. Frontin' ass niggas were flossin' on their cell phones like they were making a call to someone inside the club who could actually get them in. *Stunters.* I pulled into valet parking driving my Christmas gift from Slay—a White Range Rover with wood grain and butterscotch colored interior. I tossed the keys to the attendant and swayed my ass right up to Big Tiny, the bouncer on duty. At birth, he was given the name "Tiny" because he was born premature. In high school, he started lifting weights and drinking protein shakes and shit. Soon, he was walking around the hood looking like the Michelin Man. That's when niggas prefixed the Tiny with Big.

"I ain't tryin' to get clowned," Keisha said. "Maybe we should just get in line."

"Me neither," said Niecy.

"Just bring y'all's asses on," I said.

I should've come by my damn self. Inviting Keisha and Niecy to roll with me had proven to be a mistake. My plan was to arrive at the club by ten but we didn't arrive until close to eleven. First, I had to wait on Keisha because she was waiting on her little cousin Ciara to come over and watch Lil' Wayne. When we went to scoop up Niecy, she was undecided on what to wear. She tried on three different outfits before deciding on a yellow halter dress. She looked like a giant-sized banana. It was hideous, but if she thought she looked good who was I to rain on her parade.

"Hey, lil'mama," Big Tiny said as he unhooked the velvet rope to let me, Keisha and Niecy in. He, too, was on Slay's payroll.

The club was packed to capacity. Like roaches in a colony, niggas were damn near on top of each other. The smell of funk, cheap ass cologne and perfume along with dial soap and burnt-curling-ironed hair floated in the air. And it was hot as hell. Broads had sweated their edges out and make-up off and niggas had stripped down to their white tees.

Keisha and Niecy made a run for the bar. Looking for Slay, I sashshayed my ass through the crowd in an extra small silver and black dress, black liquid tights and a pair of black strappy stilettos with a silver heel that complimented my dress. I had straightened out my hair and wore it parted in the middle. For a more dramatic look, I applied black eye shadow and fire-engine red lipstick. I can't lie; I was feeling myself.

"Damnhummm, Shawty. You fine ass hell." A nigga in the crowd grabbed my hand. I wanted to say *I know* but didn't want to come off brash.

"Thanks," I said and kept it moving.

The deejay was spinning Webbie's *Independent*. "Ladies, if you own your own crib…wave your hands in the air," he screamed over the microphone. Broads who I knew for sure lived in government housing, received a check on the 1st and an EBT card were waving their hands in the air and singing, "I-N-D-E-P-E-N-D-E-N-T…she got her own house…drive her own whip." I sung along too, knowing damn well that I didn't have shit that wasn't given to me by Slay. If anything, I was D-E-P-E-N-D-E-N-T on a nigga for my every need. Slay was my lifeline and without him I didn't have shit—no money, nowhere to lay my head at night, no transportation and no family. It was no longer about me *wanting* to be with Slay. I had put myself in a position in which I *needed* him or else I was going to be shit out of luck.

Tyrell was in his usual spot, leaned up against the wall with the brim of his New York Yankees cap bent down over his face with a drink in one hand and his other hand stuffed deep into his jean pocket. He was nodding his head to the music and ignoring all of the broads trying to throw free pussy his way. They were the same broads who always approached him, persistent and hopeful that he'd one day give them a chance to unravel the mystery of him.

Lately, he and Slay had become distant. I didn't know what the fuck was going on between them, just that the duo had unglued themselves from each other's hips.

The countdown to the New Year had officially began. "Fifty-nine…fifty-eight…" *Damn it!* I was frantically searching the club for Slay. He had some business to take care of before coming to the club but promised to meet me there before the clock struck midnight. I didn't want to start out the New Year without him by my side—the start of the New Year was indicative of how it would end.

"Ten…nine…eight…"

Fuck! I was pissed but my thoughts were quickly consumed with thoughts of being kidnapped, beaten, raped and possibly killed as I struggled to kick and scream myself free. Some nigga had attacked me from behind, muzzling my mouth with his hand and pulling me into a storage room that was off to the side of the bar area of the club. Everyone was so occupied with counting down to the New Year that no one saw what had happened.

The storage room was no larger than a jail cell and it was the only place in the club not being filmed by the plethora of cameras Frankie and Carlo had in the corners of the club. I turned around to face my attacker.

"What the fuck are you doin'?"

"Happy New Year's!" I heard the crowd cheer as they clinked their champagne-filled glasses together. Sharing the moment with Tyrell would have been nice if he was my nigga, but he wasn't.

"I can't believe this shit."

"Slay's not even here."

"What?" I asked with major attitude.

"He was here, but he left...told me to keep an eye on you."

"What the fuck you mean he left?"

Tyrell was coming closer and closer to me. With my back against the wall, I had nowhere to go. "Leave with me," he whispered in my ear.

"You talkin' crazy."

"Leave with me," he repeated.

"And go where?"

"We can go anywhere....Trinidad....Jamaica..."

"The only place I wanna be is with Slay."

"You love him?"

"Yes, I love him."

"More than your own life...your own freedom?"

"Yes." I didn't hesitate in answering.

Tyrell backed away from me. "Seriously, Shar, you think that nigga really loves you? He be fuckin' all of Big Steph's girls and you think that nigga loves you." He laughed, wickedly.

"Why the fuck you hatin'?"

"Hatin', huh? I'm just tellin' you what you already know or what you don't want to see. There's more goin' on at Ernie Pain's house than niggas playin' fuckin' dominos. What the fuck you think be goin' on in those other rooms?"

"Fuck you! Let me the fuck out of here." I tried to side step Tyrell, but he blocked my efforts to free myself.

"You know why I do what the fuck it is I do?"

I didn't answer.

"My little sister...I started hustlin' to make her dream of attending college come true. I hustle to make sure my moms don't gotta worry about shit. I don't hustle for street credit, cars, rims, and shit...I don't hustle for selfish reasons."

"What the fuck you tryin' to say?"

"I'm sayin' that a smart man gets out of the game faster than he got in and I'm tellin' you to get out while you still can."

I had been warned.

* * *

Tyrell disappeared into the crowd, leaving me to digest the shit he had said. In my head I knew that it was probably true. When Slay wasn't physically in the streets, at the warehouse or the office, he could be found at Ernie Pain's. It wasn't hard to believe that Big Steph and Ernie Pain could possibly have an arrangement that allowed her to run her business out of the backrooms of his house in exchange for money and free pussy. But as much as the shit made sense, my heart wouldn't let me believe that Slay was fucking around on me with any broad other than Aleesha—especially not with one of Big Steph's girls. Confronting him about it would only give him an excuse to open up a can of whoop ass on me and once he learned that Tyrell was the nigga pouring salt in his game and breathing down my neck and shit, all hell was guaranteed to break loose. *Maybe his ass would act right knowin' that another nigga was on my jock.* I hightailed it out of the storage room, on the prowl for Slay again.

Niecy was hugged up at a table with a nigga old enough to recall the Last Supper. Everything about him screamed, "I'm old ass hell!"—from the brown polyester suit that he had on to the tassels on his dusty ass church shoes to the fresh Jheri Curl on top of his head. I could smell the chemicals seeping from his scalp. I knew Niecy smelt that shit too but apparently it didn't bother her. She was on him like white on rice, rubbing his leg and nibbling on his wrinkled ass ear. The shit was disgusting.

"You gonna start runnin' a nursin' home along with the daycare?" I asked, laughing my ass off.

"Whatever pays the bills...a bitch gotta handle her business."

The nigga just nodded his head and kept on smiling. When he turned to face Niecy, I saw the hearing aid in his ear. It must have been turned down on low.

"Wow!" That was all I could say. "You seen Slay or Keisha?"

"Nah, I ain't seen Slay and the last time I saw Keisha...Wayne was snatchin' her ass up off the dance floor."

"Wayne up in here?"

"Yep."

I left Niecy alone with her sugar daddy to go find Keisha, hoping that Wayne didn't have her hemmed up in a deadly headlock or some shit. Just when I spotted them in a corner of the club arguing, I bumped into Khalilah. Needless to say, it was an awkward moment. She had been acting brand new ever since hooking up with Carlo. Her and TaNaysha weren't on speaking terms before the accident and the last time I had spoken to her myself was at TaNaysha's funeral. It was a brief exchange.

Because of Carlo and Slay, we had both changed and were headed in different directions.

"I've been tryin' to call you," she said.

"Really? Well, I tried callin' you once just to find out that your phone number was no longer in service."

"Yeah, Carlo got me a new phone on his family plan. I had to switch carriers." She hunched her shoulders like she didn't have a choice in the matter. "How are you?"

"I'm cool."

"How's Ms. Trina?"

"I guess you wouldn't know since you haven't stopped by or called to check on her," I said, staring her dead in the face.

"Shar, TaNaysha's death has been hard on me too."

I just rolled my eyes and shook my head.

"Look...there's somethin' that I think you should see. Carlo and Frankie have a videotape showin'..."

There was commotion coming from the direction where Keisha and Wayne were, I pushed past Khalilah and through the crowd. Wayne had his hands around Keisha's neck. She was gasping for air. The sorry ass niggas who were looking on didn't do shit to stop his ass. I stomped Wayne in the middle of his back with the heel of my stiletto. Blood gushed everywhere and Wayne started screaming like a little ass girl. I grabbed Keisha up from off the floor and headed for the exit. Niecy was right behind us.

"What the hell happened?"

"Just get my ride and pick us up around the corner."

Keisha was coughing and gagging, trying to catch her breath. Tears were streaming down her face. She looked up at me and I could see fear in her eyes. She had come close to dying at the hands of a sorry-ass nigga. Wayne had clearly shown that he had no regards for her life—the mother of his first son. I wondered if I would ever find myself in the same situation at the hands of Slay—me fighting for my life. There was no way to predict when the next physical altercation between us would end tragically; when the next head butt would cause me to have a major head injury; when the next jab would break my jaw; when the next kick to my side would rupture my spleen; when his hands would strangle the life out of me. It was a wake-up call for both Keisha and I but only she would take heed and finally break away from Wayne. I had made my mind up to be with Slay for better or for worse.

Niecy came screeching around the corner in the Range Rover like the police were behind her, but I didn't hear any sirens. The coast was clear. I helped Keisha into the backseat and hopped in beside her. Niecy peeled rubber down the street, thinking her ass was Dale Earnhart Jr.

At Keisha's apartment, Niecy and I helped her stuff two suitcases full of her and Lil' Wayne's belongings. We dropped Ciara off at home and then dropped Keisha and Lil' Wayne off at her Uncle Jimmy's house. He was a stubborn man and told Keisha she could stay for a few days but then she had to get the fuck up out of his house, which was known as Fort Knox. He had been in the military and was an expert in explosives. Niggas didn't step foot in his yard without permission, afraid they'd misstep on a Jimmy-made landmine or some shit. Wayne was crazy but not that crazy. Nobody fucked with Jimmy.

What a fuckin' night? Happy Fuckin' New Year! I said to myself, looking down at Wayne's blood that had dried on the silver heel of my shoe. Tyrell was nowhere around to help me get rid of the evidence this time and I suspected that he was done coming to my rescue.

After I dropped Niecy off at her apartment, I rode by Ernie Pain's. Slay hadn't shown up at the club and I doubted that he was home. I eyed the vehicles parked in Ernie's yard, praying that Slay was anywhere but in one of the backrooms in Ernie's house fucking one of Big Step's girls. I exhaled, breathing a sigh of relief. He wasn't there and there was no reason for him to be at the office in the wee hours of the morning. But, there was always a chance of catching him at the warehouse. It was my next stop.

Bingo. Slay's Escalade was parked in the back next to Tyrell's Tahoe. The fence door had been left unlocked. Quietly, I snuck in—knowing that if anyone was paying attention to the camera monitors, they were fully aware of my presence. But, I had a feeling that Slay and Tyrell were the only ones there and from the sounds of it, they were in a deep conversation.

"I'm here, man to man, to let you know that I'm out," Tyrell said.

"What? You out. Niggas don't leave the game that easy. It don't work like that partna," Slay said. I saw him stand up and put his hand on the .45 tucked in his boxers.

He and Tyrell were standing face-to-face, only a couple of inches from each other. Slay was slightly shorter than Tyrell but he wasn't a nigga to back down. His model was, "The bigger they are…the harder they fall."

"What…you gonna shoot me? Here the fuck I am. Shoot me." Tyrell spread his arms wide open, giving Slay a clean shot at this chest.

"Nah, nigga, I ain't gonna shoot you. Leave if you wanna leave. You'll be back when your stash dries up. That's guaranteed."

Tyrell walked out of the warehouse—a very smart man.

Chapter 22

ONE SHOT, ONE KILL

Large concrete columns were scattered throughout the warehouse. I guessed they were in place for structural reasons beyond my construction knowledge. A set of stairs led to an upper level that I assume was constructed for those in management positions to peer down at the workers on the production floor back when the warehouse was an up and running distribution center for refrigerator parts. It was still a distribution center but for another kind of commodity.

I imagined Slay staring out of one of the glass offices on the upper level down at his own employees—making sure that every particle of the substances they produced was packaged and not snorted up their noses, smoked or shot up in their veins.

The lower level of the warehouse was divided into several different stations—the lab where glass flasks, prongs, pots, and hotplates rested on the tables; the cutting area where razor blades and small scales were stored; the packing area where boxes of Saran Wrap and plastic bags of all sizes were stacked; the shipping and receiving area where a scale large enough to weigh five niggas the size of Cheez was located—that was equivalent to five beach whales; and a 600 square foot glass greenhouse in the back corner of the warehouse home to a marijuana garden.

Slay was by no means stupid, but I didn't wholeheartedly believe that he was the mastermind behind the running of such an efficient operation—not by his damn self. With Tyrell out of the game, I wasn't sure if his operation would continue to operate on the level it had evolved into and I knew that the Makin' Moves office would soon close shop; although, Slay continued to use the trucks to move weight up and down the interstates.

Along the back wall of the warehouse, white lab coats were strung on a line of hooks. *They actin' like they are real scientists up in here.* There were also pallets stacked high with boxes full of Arm & Hammer baking soda and a month's worth of other inventory. As I looked around more, I noticed that some of his workers—the longtimers—had decorated their work areas like they were fucking cubicles in a legit work environment. They had pictures of their families, posters, calendars, inspirational quotes and scriptures taped to the walls and tables. *They are doin' way too much.*

And where niggas worked hard, they played hard. The breakroom was more like a lavish lounge with black leather sofas, a 52" LCD TV mounted to the wall, a PlayStation, X-Box and a bin full of DVD's and games. But, it was the motherfucking stripper pole in the middle of the lounge that fucked with my psyche.

"What the fuck is that?"

"What?"

"Nigga, that." I pointed to the pole.

"I don't see shit," Slay joked.

"Bitches be in here strippin'? Huh, Slay?"

"Calm the fuck down. Why would I give you a tour of the warehouse and show you this shit if I was guilty of bein' apart of such degradin' activity?" He smiled.

"You fuckin' lyin'."

"I'm done defendin' myself...believe what you want to believe."

Slay slumped down in the middle of the sofa facing the pole. He spread his arms across the back of the couch and sat with his legs wide open. I stood there with my lips poked out, arms crossed and right foot tapping. He stared at me with a sly ass grin on his face. I huffed, puffed and rolled my eyes—knowing exactly what he was thinking. He wanted me to strip for him and give the pole a twirl.

What you don't do for your nigga...another bitch will. TaNaysha had spoken those words to Khalilah and I years earlier when she shared with us the very first time she had sucked a nigga's dick. "You can play goodie-two-shoes if you want to," she said. "A nigga wants a freak in the bedroom."

Seductively, I danced out of my dress and tights—standing in front of Slay in a black lace bra and panty set and my bloody stilettos. He unzipped his jeans and exposed his dick through the opening of his boxers. His shit looked like a brown pickle on steroids: big, fat, long and juicy. He gripped it.

"Damn, Babygirl, just watchin' you gets my shit hard."

My hair touched my ass as I threw my head back. I wrapped my right leg around the pole and swung around it. Then I unhooked my bra, slung it in Slay's direction and hopped on the pole like a motherfucking pro. Shit, I surprised my damn self. I crisscrossed my legs around the pole and flipped myself up side down, spreading my legs wide open in the air. Slay walked over, his dick concrete hard. He positioned himself in my mouth and then proceeded to spread my legs wider and fed on Ms. Kitty. He had a way of taking my mind off of all the dirt he did.

"Slaaaaa...Slaaaaa...oh my...oh my...oh myyyyyyy gaaaawwwwd," I cried as Slay pleasured me. His dick slipped out of my mouth—my concentration was on coming.

Usually I liked to refer to us having sex as making love but that night, he fucked me hard and good. When it was all said and done, we were both drenched in sweat and panting feverously. I was too tired to grill his ass on where he was and what or who he was doing when the New Year rung in. Besides, questioning him about his whereabouts would only result in me wasting my breath. Slay and I were sprawled out on the couch, butt ass naked. Our bodies were still intertwined, yearning for another round. My head rested on Slay's chest and my bare breasts were pressed against his stomach. As he played with my hair, I felt my nipples hardening again. I began to rotate my pelvis in a circular motion. Slow and easy, I eased on top of him, squeezing my vagina walls tight around his dick. His hands reached for my breasts as I moved Ms. Kitty up and down this groin.

"I can't...I can't...take this shit...awwwwwwhhhhhhh shhhiiii..."

"Do I got that platinum pussy or what?" I asked Slay, while riding his dick. "Do I?" I sped that shit up.

"Got damn...yes! Yes!"

"Say it. Say I got that plantimum pussy."

My plan was to remind Slay of the good pussy he had at home. Although, I knew that a nigga was always going to be a nigga and make ignorant-ass-nigga decisions when pussy of any kind—good or bad—was involved.

"Baby...Babygirl...you...you...got...that...plat...platinuu uummm...I'mmmm commmmmin'."

Slay exploded inside of me. "I love you," he said.

In the sack, a nigga always thought he loved a broad more than he actually did—if at all, but those three little words were still music to my ears.

"I love you too," I said, forgetting about all of his indiscretions.

We fucked each other into a deep sleep. Slob drained from my mouth onto his chest. We were knocked out like someone had slipped us both the date-rape drug and we would have stayed that way if I weren't stirred out of my sleep by the strong sense of another presence among us. When I looked up, I saw Gutt towering over us with an AK47 in his hands, aimed and ready to fire. Slay was still sleep, snoring louder than a motherfucker and oblivious to what the fuck was going on.

"Slay!" I pounded on his chest with my fists. "Slay! Wake the fuck up."

"Huh!" Slay jumped up. "What the...nigga, put that shit down. You done lost your motherfuckin' mind...forreal."

"Nigga, I was just playin'," Gutt laughed.

"Motherfucker, it ain't a laughin' matter." I picked my clothes up off of the breakroom floor. "One slip of your finger and we would've been dead. Slay, you need to check that nigga," I said, fastening my bra.

"Shar, don't tell me what the fuck I need to do. I got this. Just go home. I'll be there later."

I gathered the rest of my shit and left but not before witnessing Slay shatter Gutt's jaw with his piece.

* * *

Niecy had left two voice messages on the pink Razor. The first was of her giving me an update on Wayne's status. The injury he suffered from me stabbing him with my stiletto wasn't life threatening. He was taken to the hospital, stitched up and released. When the cops showed up to question him, he gave them a false story about slipping and falling on an ice sickle. If he had told the truth then he would've had to recap almost strangling Keisha to damn death. Nor did he want to admit that a broad had stomped a hole in his motherfucking back and since the police weren't able to round up a single eyewitness—not that they tried too hard to do so—I had gotten away scotfree. It was the second time in months; first with Vera and then with Wayne. The only difference was that Wayne deserved what he got, Vera didn't.

The second message was also about Wayne. He was dead. He hadn't even made it out of the hospital parking lot alive. Keisha had calmly walked up to him, shot him pointblank in the head and then turned herself into the police where she handed over the murder weapon and confessed to killing him. She had snapped. I suppose it was inevitable from suffering through years of physical and mental abuse and the longer I stayed with Slay, the stronger my chances were of ending up just like Keisha—fed up and deranged.

No one could have convinced me that Keisha was in her right mind when she killed Wayne. She loved and lived for Lil' Wayne. Now, he was a motherless and fatherless child, like Slay had been. Keisha's Uncle Jimmy handed him over to the social worker—not giving a fuck what happened to him and he was taken into state custody, which was a tragedy all in its' own. My heart broke as I imagined him being moved from one foster home to the other—feeling unwanted and unloved. Or worse, being abused by pedophile foster parents, beaten and left to starve to death in a cage or something—all shit that had been reported in the news at one time or another. I was aware that not all foster parents were evil and just out for a check. Nor did all children fall through the cracks of the foster care system in America but according to the statistics, most did.

What the fuck now? My cell phone buzzed again. I wasn't interested in hearing anymore bad news. I just wanted to go home, get under the covers and fall the fuck asleep. Being surrounded by so much death, violence and crime was exhausting. If I had chosen to go away to college I would have been exhausted for reasons that benefited my future—up all night studying for finals or pledging a sorority.

I had long regretted my decision to allow my self to fall in love with Slay, realizing that he didn't have as much to offer me as getting an education would have. He offered me more pain than pleasure, more fear than security and more nightmares than dreams. I was learning that love may have been the foundation of a relationship, but it wasn't the glue that held it together. The glue was comprised of a lot of shit—shit that Slay and I didn't necessarily have. Starting with a monogamous fucking relationship. Of course, my ass could have vamped. Slay and I didn't have any kids keeping us together. Nor, was I scared of what he would do to me if I did leave. I stayed because I had nowhere to go, no one to run to and because I loved him. Maybe those were the same reasons why Keisha continued to fuck with Wayne. It sure as hell wasn't because his pockets were deep in dough.

My cell phone buzzed again. *Damn.* It was the same mysterious number that I had been ignoring for days. I answered, remembering that Khalilah had mentioned she had a new number.

"Hello," I said, sounding irritated and annoyed.

"Shar, it's me." It *was* Khalilah.

"Oh, hey. What's up?"

"I was tryin' to tell you at the club that there's somethin' I think you need to see…before all that shit went down with Keisha and Wayne."

"Yeah…I remember you were about to say somethin'."

"It'll be better if you saw it with your own eyes than me tryin' to tell you over the phone."

"Khalilah…Lilah…what-ever-the-fuck   you're   callin' yourself these days, stop bullshitin' me and just tell me," I said, getting frustrated with the whole conversation. From the sound of her voice I knew it wasn't good news—like Slay had decided to get out of the game, turn his life around, get a regular nine-to-five gig, marry me forreal, move to the suburbs, have 2.5 five kids and live happily ever after. Or, that Aleesha had moved to Africa or some shit. It wasn't good news. "Spit the shit out."

"Just stop by club…come back to the security room. That's where I'll be."

"I'm on my way."

Fuck! If it wasn't one thing it was a motherfucking another. There were only two things that Frankie and Carlo could have caught on tape that involved me. One was of me stabbing Wayne with my shoe, but Khalilah and I had crossed paths before any of that shit had went down. What she had to show me was caught on tape before the incident with Keisha and Wayne. The other I guess was of Tyrell and me in the storage room closet. *Shit!* They had footage of Tyrell breathing all down my neck and shit and the simple fact that I didn't push him away was enough to convince Slay that I was thoroughly enjoying myself.

On the ride over to The Tap Room, all kinds of scenarios were swirling around in my head. One minute I thought that Frankie and Carlo would use the tape to try and bribe me, thinking I had access to Slay's money. In the same minute, I thought that maybe Khalilah would threaten to show Slay the tape—angry that I had grown closer to TaNaysha and further from her when she started dating Carlo. There was the possibility that Slay, Frankie and Carlo were somehow business partners in a venture that I was unaware of. Shit, there was a lot I didn't know about Slay or who he conducted business with. The truth was, I was more afraid of

Slay than I let on. Not of him beating me to damn death but of *him* leaving *me* with nothing—no money, no friends and no family. The one thing that frightened me could have been my biggest blessing—us breaking up.

Chapter 23

THE COLOR YELLOW

By the time, I pulled in front of The Tap Room, my heart was racing and my palms were sweating. It was the feeling I used to get as a child right before I got a whooping. The feeling of guilt mixed with the anticipation of pain.

I freely walked through the front door. It was unmanned and the club showed no signs of the previous night's New Year's celebration. The tables were wiped clean and I could see my reflection in the floor. It had been swept, mopped and waxed. *Hope I don't slip and fuckin' fall.* One of Frankie and Carlo's bodyguards was behind the bar fixing himself a drink. He must have been informed of my arrival through the wire in his ear because he wasn't startled when I walked through the door. He simply gestured his head towards the back of the club, letting me know it was okay that I joined Khalilah in the security room.

"What up, Shar?" A nigga sitting at the bar spoke to me.

I recognized him from the night at Frankie and Carlo's house, but I couldn't recall his name. I just remembered that he was on their security team. He had remembered my name and apparently what I looked like. I suppose that was his job, to observe and pay close attention to the company around Frankie and Carlo. He was dressed in camouflage pants, black boots and a simple black t-shirt that was tucked into his pants. He looked like he was about to go off to war or some shit, but he seemed cool so I spoke.

"I'm cool," I said, lying and drying my palms on my tights. I was still wearing the same outfit I had originally stepped into the club in. I hoped nobody noticed and I hoped what Khalilah had on tape wasn't as damaging as I imagined it to be.

"Hey, Shar?"

I looked back at the nigga before entering the security room. "Yeah?"

"Good lookin' out for your girl last night. You got to that nigga Wayne before I could reach him and don't worry...that part of the tape goes black."

"Thanks."

"My name is Jake by the way. Just in case you forgot."

A nigga named Jake? "Got it," I said, opening the door to the security room.

Khalilah was sitting behind a large mahogany desk like she was running shit up in The Tap Room. In fact, she looked the part of a businesswoman—unlike last night when she could have substituted for a call girl. She was covered from head to toe in a black pants suit and white shirt. None of the flesh that was exposed by the off-the-shoulder short dress she had had on just hours before could be seen. Pea-sized pearls had replaced the long, dangling, chandelier-like earrings that she had rocked with the dress and her hair was pulled back into a bun. To top the look off, she had on some Black-rimmed glasses. *Frontin' ass. She know she ain't never needed glasses.* I kept my remarks to myself.

"Where're Frankie and Carlo?" I plopped down in one of the chairs facing the wall of computer screens.

"Back in the office on a conference call with one of our vendors," she said, like she had a monetary stake in the club.

"Who does business on New Year's Day?"

"People interested in makin' money," Khalilah said, rather snidely. *Bitch,* I thought and not in the homegirl-sister-friend type of way in which we once referred to each other. I meant that shit in the most derogatory sense of the word.

"What is it that you have to show me?" I said, in a hurry to get the fuck up out of there before I said or did anything that would destroy any chances of us ever rebuilding our friendship. But, Khalilah decided to get some shit off of her chest before showing me the videotape.

"I know you don't like Carlo, but..."

I stopped Khalilah's ass right there. "It's the new you that I don't like. Carlo got your ass thinkin' that you're somebody that you're not."

"Oh...because I dress differently, wear my hair differently...talk proper English...you assume that Carlo's tryin' to whitewash me?"

"If that's what you want to call it." I rolled my eyes and smacked my lips.

"Shar," Khalilah paused. "When I met Carlo, I was a teenage girl."

Hoe...you still a teenage girl. I thought but quickly realized that Khalilah was referring to her mental growth.

"He has helped me evolve into the woman I always wanted to be...a more mature and confident one. That's what a man does. He lifts his woman up. He doesn't tear her down or bring her down with him. Carlo encourages me to dream...to make somethin' out of myself. Yeah, he got money...plenty of it, but at the end of the day...it's his money and not mine. Just like Slay's money isn't yours."

"That's were you're wrong," I boasted. "What's Slay's is mine."

Khalilah smirked. "And I thought I was the naive one of the group," she said under her breath but loud enough for me to hear. She had become much bolder too.

"Look, I didn't come down here for this shit. You gonna show me what you got or not?"

With the click of a mouse, videotape of The Tap Room appeared on the computer screens. The footage was of broads and niggas dancing up on each other, drinking and having a good time. *What the fuck is she showin' this shit to me for?* Just as I had that thought, I saw what it was that she wanted me to see. It wasn't of Tyrell and myself trapped in the storage closest. The footage cut from the inside of the club to the alley outside of the back entrance. From the desktop computer in front of her, Khalilah enlarged the shadowy figure standing up against the brick building adjacent to The Tap Room. Clear as day, it was Slay—getting his dick sucked.

My stomach turned, I raced out of the security room into the restroom and dry heaved over the toilet. I hadn't eaten since the previous afternoon. Nothing but clear phlegm was coming up. I heard the restroom door open and footsteps coming towards me.

"Shar, you okay?" Khalilah knelt down beside me.

"I'm cool," I said, wiping my mouth with my arm. "I gotta get out of here."

"Shar, I'm here for you if you need me. Regardless of how you see me, I'll always consider you to be one of my best friends. Really, if you need anything…"

"Khalilah, just shut the fuck up. That's what I really need you to do right now…please."

She left me in the restroom to myself. I replayed the videotape in my head, over and over again. *It's not real,* I told myself. *Motherfuckers tamper with videos all day long…puttin' other people's heads on other people's bodies. That kind of shit happens all the time. Niggas still debating if R. Kelley was the nigga in that tape that surfaced on the web...what if this shit gets...*

I ran back into the security room. Khalilah read my thoughts. "Don't worry...Carlo and Frankie haven't even seen it. I've been reviewin' the tapes lately." She handed me the tape. "It's the only copy."

"Thanks." I stuffed the tape into my clutch.

"And Shar..." Khalilah stopped me on my way out. "I meant what I said...anything you need."

I acknowledged her offer and sulked away—still in shock that Slay would let another nigga suck his dick.

* * *

Although the odds of Slay actually being at the condo before the sun went down were slim, there was still a chance and I wasn't for sure I could face him after watching the videotape—not so soon afterwards at least. Fabricated or not, the vision was stained into my conscious. My fear was that when I looked at him, I would see him differently. However, I knew that I wouldn't love him any less. Nor, would I hate him enough to leave him.

I drove around for hours before ending up over at Niecy's apartment. Slay had called me a couple of times. If I hadn't answered, he would have continued to call until I did. I kept our conversations short and for the first time ever, I lied to him— saying that I had spotted a mouse in the condo and the exterminator couldn't make it out until the next day. I told him that I was staying the night over at Niecy's, which wasn't a lie.

From her living room couch, I watched Niecy stir the cabbage and then the black-eyed peas with the same spoon. She then turned the eyes down on the two pots and checked on the cornbread in the oven before frying the fish she had seasoned and battered. Unlike Niecy, I wasn't raised to believe in superstitious traditions like eating cabbage and black-eyed peas on New Year's Day—for prosperity and luck in the New Year. My father wasn't a man who believed in luck. He believed only in God's grace and mercy and that people were blessed according to their obedience to God. But, something like luck had to exist to explain why all of the disobedient and immoral motherfuckers in the world were escaping death and living lavish while the righteous and poor were dying and struggling. But, the thing about luck is that in time, it runs out.

"Damn-it-to-hell," Niecy cussed, getting attacked by hot grease as she lowered pieces of fish into the deep fryer she had set up on the kitchen counter. The outside of the deep fryer was stained with years of fish and chicken grease.

"You alright over there?" She yelled.

"Yeah, I'm cool," I said.

"Well, you ain't gotta tell me shit. You can stay here as long as you want, but after a month yo' ass gotta start payin' half the rent," Niecy laughed, but I knew her ass was serious.

Niecy fixed herself a plate and a glass of red Kool-Aid—strawberry.

"Help yourself," she said.

I sauntered into the kitchen. The floor was linoleum not real tile like at the condo. The countertops were laminate not granite like at the condo. All of the appliances were prehistoric compared to the stainless steel appliances installed in the kitchen at the condo. My eyes traveled over every inch of Niecy's apartment, comparing its' contents to those of the condo from the furniture to the paint on the walls. I was grateful for her hospitality and she kept a clean and fairly nice apartment. However, I had grown accustom to living lavish. It was as if, all of a sudden, nothing but the best was good enough for me. The thought scared me. I wasn't for sure if I was trying to give myself a reason to go back home—

to the condo and to Slay—or if I was slowly evolving into a gold digger who would do anything and everything from scheming to fucking in order to maintain a certain lifestyle; or, in my case, forgiving Slay for yet another fuck-up so that I could go back to living carefree and not having to worry about paying half the rent at Niecy's or anywhere else.

I raised my lips to the glass of Kool-Aid that I had poured myself. It tasted like straight sugar water. *Glad I'm not a diabetic.* I fixed myself a plate and sat down across from Niecy at her black and gold lacquer dinette set. As I was about to stuff a fork full of cabbage into my mouth, a loud beeping sound startled me.

"What the fuck was that?"

"Girl, nothin'…just my police scanner. I always got to know what the fuck is goin' on."

Niecy went to turn down the scanner and returned with a confession. "I always hated you," she said, squirting hot sauce and mustard on her fish.

Here this bitch go with that nonsense. Niecy hated me for the same reasons other broads did, with the exception of TaNaysha and Khalilah. They were the same reasons I didn't fuck with too many broads because jealously could be a bitch, but what these broads didn't understand was that in the long run, brains always outweighed beauty.

"I would always see you at the park on Sundays…swingin' your hair like you were filmin' a shampoo commercial or some shit. You and yo' girls walked around that motherfucker like yall was runnin' shit…gigglin' up in all the niggas faces…"

"You mean all the niggas were gigglin' up in our faces…correct that shit," I interrupted her.

"Yeah, you right," Niecy laughed. "Anyways, I always thought you were stuck up and shit, but you're cool as hell."

"That goes to show you that you can't judge a book by its' cover."

"Guess not."

From the jump, I had tried to keep my eye on Niecy while she moved around the kitchen simply because I didn't eat everybody's cooking and I was glad I did. Still, after her little confession, I was hesitant to eat my damn food. Although I believed she no longer had it out for me, I said a prayer before and after each bite—as a precautionary measure.

Over dinner, Niecy went from thinking of me as an enemy to thinking of me as one of her bestfriends. She told me all of her business; dating back to the first time her mother's boyfriend ever molested her.

"He was an ugly ass motherfucker," Niecy had said. "He had to pay for pussy and took it whenever he got the chance...nasty ass nigga."

Niecy had started to tear up when reliving the memory but quickly wiped her eyes. "That nigga can't steal no more of my joy. I won't let him."

The sad part about the shit was that Niecy's own mother didn't even believe her when she ratted that sick ass nigga out. At fifteen, she ran away from home and never returned. She ended up dropping out of high school but eventually she got her GED and took a few business courses at the local community college. After one or two office gigs, she realized that the only person she could ever work for was herself. Hearing the complaints of her friends and neighbors who made just enough money to be denied childcare assistance but were still broke ass hell after payday, she saw the need for reasonable childcare services in the hood. She set up shop in her apartment and Niecy's Daycare was born and even though she could take care of herself with the proceeds from her daycare, she still had niggas paying her utility bills and for her to get her hair and nails done—after years of being abused, she decided to never let another motherfucker fuck her for free. Niecy refused to fuck a broke nigga.

"Where're the dish towels?" I had volunteered to clean up the kitchen since she had cooked.

"In the far left drawer to the right of the sink," Niecy yelled from her bedroom where she was getting ready for a not-so-hot date. She was going out with that old ass nigga she was hugged up with at the club. Now I knew the reason why—she was trying to cop his social security check or at least some of it.

Niecy came out of her bedroom looking like a bumblebee. *Damn...yellow must be her favorite color.* I pursed my lips to keep from bursting into laughter. Her style was definitely all her own. She didn't give a fuck about coordinating the colors of her wardrobe with the different seasons. She had on a yellow dress with a black belt, stockings and boots along with a yellow purse.

"You love yourself some yellow," I said, laughing.

"It's my favorite color. It reminds me of the sun shining bright...when I was growing up I use to love the daytime when the sun shined. My mother's boyfriend never molested me during the day. He always waited until the sun went down."

My laughter subsided.

Chapter 24

DIRTY MOTHERFUCKER

"Shush." I heard Niecy whisper when she came through the door. *I know she is not about to fuck his old ass.* I was wide awake, lying on my back and staring blankly up at the ceiling. The television was on mute. There was enough noise in my head—me going back and forth with myself about whether or not I was going to confront Slay about the bullshit I saw on the videotape or not. Questioning him about it would undoubtedly send him into a violent rage. The real question was whether or not I was ready to die. The shit on that tape could be detrimental to his reputation. Slay would kill a nigga to keep that shit a secret, even me. And the fact that I believed that Slay would kill me—the woman he supposedly loved—should have been enough for me to pack my shit and leave his ass; along with the situation with Aleesha, all of the lonely nights, the physical abuse and the incidents with Vera and Wayne. But, I was getting good at coming up with excuses not to leave Slay and would rather him kill me than hate me. If I left him, he would have as much disdain for me as he had for his mother for abandoning him for a life of drugs and prostitution.

I closed my eyes as Niecy and her old ass date walked past me on the couch. Seconds later, I heard Niecy's bedroom door shut and then her bed squeaking. Her and that nigga were moaning and groaning like two elephants in heat. I tossed and turned, burying my head into the arm of the couch and covering it with the pillow I had taken from the linen closet.

Somehow, between the thoughts in my head and the activity in Niecy's bedroom, I was able to get a few hours of sleep. I woke up early, hoping to sneak out before Niecy and her company woke up. *Shit!* I heard the bedroom door crack open.

"Shar?"

"Yeah," I said, pulling the sweatshirt over my head. It was the top to the sweat suit Niecy had given to me to wear. When I knocked on her door New Year's Day, I was still rocking the same outfit that I had on New Year's night and smelling like cigarette smoke, alcohol and sex.

"You, gone?" She asked, coming into the living room and rubbing sleep out of the corners of her eyes.

"Yeah."

"Sorry about last night but that nigga stays in assisted living. He can't have company after nine."

Niecy nor I could hold in our laughter.

"His dick wasn't that bad for an old ass nigga. Plus, he's paying for these yellow Christian Louboutin boots I saw on the Internet."

Broads in the hood knew about Christian Louboutin before the celebrities jumped on the designer's jock. I had several pair myself. They weren't cheap. "Shit, you might as well have him pay your rent and car note."

"Nah, I got that. I just can't see payin' for those boots myself."

"I heard you."

"I bet you don't pay for shit," she said. "Your bank account must be fat. All the dough Slay probably breakin' you off with."

I just smiled. The truth was, I didn't have a bank account and therefore didn't have any dough saved up. The way Niecy thought reminded me of TaNaysha's mindset and now Khalilah's.

"I don't know what popped off with you and Slay last night that had you not wantin' to go home and I'm not tryin' to be all up in your business but one word of advice…don't fuck yo' money up. Get what you can when you can get it. He may be fuckin' other broads but you the one he's takin' care of. Well, you and Aleesha."

"Thanks, Niecy, for everything."

Mentally, I was in the back of the pack—the last one holding the baton. TaNaysha, Khalilah, Niecy and even Ms. Trina all understood the workings of the game—use it…don't let it use you.

* * *

Khlailah was right, I had been the naïve one—believing in love the way I did. The love Slay had for me wasn't keeping him from laying his hands on me, fucking other broads or getting his dick sucked by crackheads. Drugs, money, sex and power—I had forgotten that those were the things Slay lived for. Love wasn't listed; I wasn't listed. To him, I was mere arm candy until the next young broad came along. Ms. Trina had told me that a long time ago.

My mindset had changed. Loving Slay was no longer my priority. It was time that I worked the game but after getting my ass beat, the lies, and the cheating—I refused to leave with nothing.

It was too early in the morning for Slay to be home if he hadn't sleep there the night before. For the first time, I had prayed that he hadn't. He had been driving the Escalade during the winter months and had put the other vehicles in storage until the season ended. It wasn't in the driveway.

I put the Range Rover in park and hurried into the condo upstairs to our bedroom. I picked out the most valuable pieces of jewelry that he had purchased for me along with the ones that I had copped for myself. I stuffed the jewelry inside of an empty Crown Royal bag that he had lying around and left just enough in place for him not to be suspicious if he just so happened to look through my jewelry box, which looked more like a small treasure chest.

In the closet, I looked at the thousands of dollars of shit that I had purchased over the last few months. It totaled well over enough to pay for the college education I had forgone. I closed the door, deciding against the ideal to sell some of it on eBay. I didn't have time for that shit.

I looked around the condo. Nothing else was mine to sell. Plus, Slay really would have put me six feet under for selling any of his shit, especially his Play Station and X-Box. I hopped back into the Range Rover and drove over to Ms. Trina's house.

"It's Shar, Ms. Trina. Open up." I banged on her screen door.

"I'm comin'. Damn it. Hold on."

Ms. Trina came to the door looking like death itself. She seen the expression on my face and patted her hair down. It was matted and scattered all over her head. *Damn...even Vera didn't look that bad,* I thought to myself. Ms. Trina's situation saddened me but there was no time for tears. I had cried my last cry yesterday.

"I know I look bad," she said.

"I don't think you do," I said, not trying to sound harsh.

"Well, fuck you too," she said, stepping aside to let me in.

Ms. Trina's house was as much of a mess as she was. Dirty dishes and shit were scattered everywhere except for in the kitchen sink where they belonged. Drug paraphernalia and empty liquor bottles were out in the open. Filthy ass panties and boxers were lying around. I even spotted a used condom stuck in the carpet.

Even smoked out, Ms. Trina had more sense than me. The shit was still nasty. My stomach churned. It was doing a lot of that lately.

"How yo' Mama'em doin?" Ms. Trina asked, lighting up a Newport.

"I don't know. I haven't talked to them."

"That's fucked up how they're doin' you. I know I wasn't the best mother to TaNaysha but when I got my shit together, I was there for her. I would've never turned my back on her no matter how many fucked up decisions she made."

"You were a good mother," I said.

"Thanks."

"I need a favor."

"Name it," she said, without hesitating.

An hour later, after Ms. Trina had showered and looked decent enough to present herself in public, we pulled into the back of Lonnie's Pawn Shop. I handed her the Crown Royal bag full of jewelry. I wasn't worried about her making a run for it or gypping me out of any cash because one; I had promised to break her off a couple of hundred dollars and two; I had called the pawn shop earlier and verified that a check was cut for all items worth more than $500. I was sure all of the jewelry I had scooped up was more than a few thousands dollars. The rings, earrings and bangles that I had bought for myself totaled well over $10,000 by themselves. And strung out or not, Ms. Trina didn't take no shit. I knew she would bargain with Lonnie's ass until she was satisfied with the offer he made.

Thirty minutes later, Ms. Trina came back with a check in her hands. She handed it and the Crown Royal bag to me. It wasn't empty.

"Lonnie say that shit in the bag is costume jewelry."

"What!"

"Lonnie said…"

"I heard you the first time. Stay here. I'm goin' in."

I stormed into the pawnshop like a nigga about to go postal on some motherfuckers. I figured Lonnie was the potbelly White nigga walking towards me. The buttons on his shirt looked like they were in pain and about to pop. His hair was white and he walked with the assistance of a cane. He met me at the counter, smelling like onion rings.

"How may I help you…young'un?"

I dumped the contents of the Crown Royal bag on the glass counter. None of the shit I had copped for myself came tumbling out—just the diamond tennis bracelets, rings, earrings and necklaces that Slay had showered me with after each ass whooping I took from him. The tennis bracelet he gave me on my birthday was the only piece of jewelry that he had given me out of the goodness of his heart.

"My aunt just came in here tryin' to pawn this jewelry…she said you said it was costume jewelry."

"Yep, that's what I told her," he said, adjusting his glasses.

"What you mean it's costume jewelry?"

"It's fake."

"All of it?"

"Yep. I gave her a check for the pieces that were real."

Don't cry, I told myself, trying to fight back the tears welling up in my eyes. I took off my engagement ring and handed it to Lonnie, telling him the specs of the ring.

"Can you check this out for me? Tell me if it's at least real."

Lonnie took the ring out of my hands and examined it by eye first. He then turned around and inspected it under an instrument similar to a miniature microscope.

"Well…it's white gold not platinum as you thought and the three carats in the middle are cubic zirconia along with the diamonds set in the band."

"It's fake too?"

"Yep…the diamonds are faker than Pamela Anderson's boobs. I can offer you six-fifty for it."

"Is that all?"

"Retail…it probably sold for about eight hundred. I'm cutting you a pretty good deal."

"I'll take it."

"What're you gonna tell your fiancé?" he asked.

"Fuck him."

My next stop was the bank where Ms. Trina and I opened up a joint savings account. Neither of us could withdraw any of the money without the other being present or able to provide a death certificate for one another in the case that one of us had unfortunately passed away. We deposited both checks into the account and I had her withdraw the $200 that I promised her. After which, I had an even $11,000 in the bank. Even though the stipulation on the account prevented Ms. Trina from making any withdrawls on her own, the simple fact remained that she was a crackhead. She promised on TaNaysha's grave not to touch my dough. It was a promise I knew she would keep, in honor of her slain daughter.

* * *

While at the bank, I also rented out a safety deposit box where I stored the videotape of Bop sucking Slay's dick. I had a feeling that there would be a time and place in the future when having the videotape in my possession would benefit me more than I could ever imagine. Maybe even make me a millionaire if I played my cards right.

Slay was home when I arrived back at the condo from dropping Ms. Trina off. I came through the door wearing a fake ass smile—as fake as the costume jewelry he had fooled me with. I was surprised my fingers, ears, wrist and neck hadn't turned green from wearing that fake ass shit. Lonnie had said that it was the best looking costume jewelry that had every come across his counter. He added that if not worn everyday and taken care of, it could last for years. Not having a job gave me a lot of time to do miscellaneous shit, like cleaning all of my jewelry every other day. *That nigga had me cleaning fake as jewelry like it was worth millions. Dirty motherfucker.* The love I had for Slay was slowly evolving into hate.

"Hey, Babygirl," Slay spoke. "Where you been?"

"I went to see Ms. Trina."

"How she doin'?"

"Better but her car's been actin' up and she needed to run some errands. So, I gave her a ride," I said, knowing all too well that Slay had eyes on the streets. He probably knew that we went to the pawnshop and the bank.

"Did the exterminator come this mornin'?" He asked.

"No. The guy that they were sendin' out got into a wreck." I lied to Slay as easily as he had been lying to me about everything. I didn't know what about him was the truth or what was a lie. "They were suppose to be callin' me back to reschedule. Anyways, I didn't want to go back over to Niecy's again tonight. She brought some old ass nigga home with her last night. I had to listen to them fuck. It was horrible. Anyway, I just wanted to come home...rat or no rat."

"It's probably just a little mouse anyway."

"Probably."

"You okay, Babygirl." Slay came up behind me in the bathroom and wrapped his arms around me.

"'Remember the last time we fucked in here," he said, nibbling on my ear. I smiled through the flashbacks I was having of the videotape—envisioning Slay's hand on top of Bop's head, pushing it up and down as Bop sucked his dick in the alley behind The Tap Room.

"Ummmm," I moaned. "I do...but I'm not feelin' too good. I think it was somethin' I ate earlier. Ms. Trina and I stopped at a Chinese Buffet."

"Oh, shit...ain't no tellin' what you done ate, Babygirl."

"I know, right."

"Some dog or cat or somethin'."

"Stop...you're makin' me sicker sayin' that shit."

"Babygirl, I love you."

Lyin' bastard. I couldn't say it back. I dived towards the toilet like I was about to vomit. Slay jumped out of the way.

"Babygirl, that Chinese food really fucked you up. Do you need me to take you to the emergency room?"

I nodded my head no.

"Okay, what you want me to do?"

"I'll...I'll be okay. Just give me a few minutes."

"Okay, I'mma be downstairs. Just holla if you need me."

When Slay was out of sight, I got up. I turned the facet on to make him think that I was rinsing my mouth out. Like lying, acting seemed to come natural to me. *For the best vomit scene, the MTV Award goes to Shar Reid.*

"You good, now?" Slay asked, as I snuggled up next to him on the couch.

"I'm okay but you know what would make me feel even better?"

"What?"

"I saw this Gucci purse that I wanted and these amazing thigh-high boots. You would love them."

"I would love them or you love them?"

"I would feel much better if I had them in my possession. I could model them for you when I get them."

Slay stuck his hand down in his jean pocket and pulled out a rubber-banded wad of money. He handed my $2,500. I was hoping for more. At this rate, stacking my savings account was going to take longer than I had anticipated.

Chapter 25

GETTING IN THE GAME

Sex, lies and videotapes. The media had worn out that slogan in its' advertisement of everything from books to television shows to the sale of porn-filled DVD's, but it perfectly described the essence of what Slay and my relationship had dwindled down to. *So much for love, honesty and commitment.* I was becoming one of Slay's biggest enemies, right up under his nose.

Over the course of six weeks, I had hit him up for over $15,000. Every time he turned around, I had an excuse for needing more money: repairs for the Range Rover, repairs for the condo and more shopping sprees. I also asked for money to help Ms. Trina get her car fixed. I told Slay that she needed a new transmission when she really only needed a new alternator. He gave me two grand to get it fixed. But, sooner or later, I knew he would become suspicious of my requests. I calmed that shit down, realizing that I needed a new plan. I needed to get in the game.

Like I had predicted when Tyrell bounced, Makin' Moves went out of business. The office closed down, but Slay continued to use the trucks as a front to continue moving weight across states. His profits from the block had decreased because of the commitment of the new Chief of Police—a Billy Blanks looking nigga—to wipe the streets clean of drug dealers and the drugs they sold. The City Council approved the installation of cameras on each corner in the hood and the hiring of more police officers to patrol the streets. The niggas and broads on the corners were chasing less cars and screening buyers. New crackheads had to answer twenty questions before getting the drugs they had stole, fucked and sucked for. Shit on the corners was slow and after a major police sweep, most of the niggas and broads who worked the block were arrested for selling to undercover police officers— including some of Slay and Cheez's workers.

To supplement for the loss of profits that the nickel and dime game on the corners had brought in, Slay beefed up his drug trafficking operation—moving more weight than ever before. He was selling truckloads of marijuana and cocaine all over the United States. Even to niggas in Oregon, Wisconsin, Iowa, Idoha and Montana—states that I didn't even know Black people lived.

He paced the warehouse floor, in a state of panic. Losing money wasn't his only worry. Now that most of his workers in the hood had been arrested, he was worried about motherfuckers snitching. On top of that shit, Luxury was pregnant—forreal this time—and too sick with morning sickness to travel and make the drop she was scheduled to make in Atlanta. And, one of the moving trucks broke down on its' way to make a drop in Nebraska. Slay's thick ass, throwback Julius Erving jersey he had on was drenched with his perspiration. All I could think about was how he was nothing like Tyrell, who had the quiet calm of a Buddhist Monk. I had never seen Tyrell sweat. *Just calm the fuck down. When you lose your cool...you lose control of the situation.* Those were Tyrell's exact words to me on the night I lost it and attacked Vera. He didn't know it, but he had taught me more than Slay had ever offered to teach me about the game. But, I was still learning.

"Calm the fuck down," I told Slay.

"Who the fuck you talkin' to?" He ran up on me.

"Damn...I'm just sayin' calm down...take a breath and think the situation through." He backed up off me. "Who was the driver makin' the Nebraska drop?"

"Gutt."

Awwwwhhh hell. Slay's first mistake was not firing Gutt's ass when we returned from Miami. His second mistake was not firing Gutt's ass when he shattered that nigga's jaw. On the other hand, Gutt hadn't handed in his resignation letter to Slay. I had an inclination that he had revenge on his mind.

"Him and Butter were on this one," Slay added. "Babygirl, what the fuck am I gonna do?"

Slay continued to pace the warehouse floor. He wiped the sweat from his brow. Something was different about him. He wasn't just panicking. He was acting like he couldn't make a damn decision. He might not have had Tyrell's corporate business sense or cool demeanor, but he was a nigga who got rich slanging on the corner before venturing into distributing cocaine. He was street educated.

Slay pulled a vile of cocaine out of his jean pocket and emptied it onto the steel table in front of him. He broke the White powder up into three individual lines with a razor, rolled up a hundred dollar bill and sniffed that shit up his nose. *No wonder his ass has been actin' weird...sweatin' and lettin' niggas suck his dick and shit.*

"I just need somethin' to help me get my head right."
Even I—once a naïve preacher's daughter—knew the golden rule in the street game: never smoke what you were selling. Marijuana didn't count. Most niggas, in the game or not, smoked grass but all other substances were off limits.

"How long you been smokin'?"

"I'm not a fuckin' dopefiend. I just have a line or two every now and then. I got this shit under control so don't be questionin' me like I'm some kind of got damn crackhead." He wiped his nose.

"How much you pay Luxury to make a drop?"

"Why the fuck you askin' me that?"

I had $26,000 in the bank. Fifty grand was my goal. It would be enough for me to hop on a plane and start a new life wherever the fuck I wanted without having to worry about being strapped for cash. It was also the price I had valued all the bullshit at—the mental distress and physical abuse—that I had suffered at Slay's hand. He owed me at least that much.

"Can you please just answer the question?"

"Five hundred."

"Five hundred." I turned up my nose. "That's it?"

"I ain't tryin' to fund nobody's retirement account and that's more than she use to make in a week workin' for Big Steph."

"Double it and I'll do it."

"Double what and you'll do what?"

"Agree to pay me $1,000 and I'll make the drop for you."

"Don't I already take care of yo' ass? Why you tryin' to hustle me?" Slay glared at me.

"Ain't nobody tryin' to hustle you out of shit. Carlo's been teaching Khalilah all about the nightclub business. She's helping him and Frankie manage the club. I want you to teach me about your operations. I want to be a part of it all. Shit, if you can't trust me…your girl…then who the fuck can you trust. It sure as hell ain't Gutt's ass."

Slay took a few minutes to think before he responded to my proposal. "If you my girl and you love me, why I gotta pay you? As much money as I dish out to your ass…you should make the drop for free."

"Slay, that's just it. You give me handouts. I want to feel like I've worked for somethin'…to feel like I'm makin' my own money. Who better to work for than the man I love?" *Use to love.*

"We'll be like Bonnie and Clyde. We'll be the hood's Beyonce and Jay Z."

"Shar, this drug game is forreal. It ain't no play shit. It can get dangerous. Niggas can lose their lives…get locked up and shit. You hear me talkin'?"

"If I get locked up…you'll get me out, won't you?"

"Of, course, Babygirl. You know I got you."

"You'll hire the best lawyers."

"The best money can buy."

Slay's word wasn't worth much, but I refused to believe that he would let me sit and rot in jail without making an effort to get me out if the drop went wrong. It was a risk I was willing to take.

Sewn into the lining of my suitcases were blocks of cocaine wrapped in scented pampers. *If Huggies only knew.* There were a total of fifteen bricks between the suitcases-seven in one, and eight in the other. Each weighed a little over a pound and had a street value of approximately $22,000. I was moving over a quarter of a million dollars in weight.

Lip biting, foot tapping and stuttering were all signs of nervousness that Slay said airport police looked for when trying to sniff out drug traffickers. Luckily, I didn't have any nervous habits. The only tell-tale sign that I was up to no good was the racing of my heart. After a few deep breaths, I was good to go.

Slay reminded me of my instructions for the umpteenth time. "I got it," I said.

"Babygirl, be careful and I love you."

"I will," I said, wishing he would stop saying that shit— that he loved me when he really didn't mean it. He hugged me like we would never see each other again. I broke away and disappeared into the airport crowd.

Initially, I was scheduled to fly out during the middle of the week. I convinced Slay to switch my flight to Friday evening—the time when the airports were the most congested with weekend travelers and more likely to be dealing with complaints of lost luggage and irate passengers than closely inspecting the contents of people's luggage. To be honest, because of my physical characteristics, I was more worried about being suspected of being a terrorist than of getting caught smuggling drugs.

I eased through the security checkpoint, making small talk with the nigga running my belongings through the x-ray machine. He mistook my friendliness for flirting and was too busy smiling in my face than examining the monitor that displayed the contents of my purse. He was a nigga who was easy to distract. I figured his contact with beautiful women was probably limited to the confinements of the airport and that the right amount of cleavage would have him drooling all over my chest rather than doing his job. For future reference, I made a mental note to remember his name, *Kelvin*.

Seated on the plane, I relaxed a little and went over the instructions for the drop in my head. Once at Hartsfield Jackson Airport in Atlanta, arrangements had been made for me to pick up a rental car at the Enterprise counter. After which, I was instructed to go directly to my room at the Westin and empty my personal belongings out of the suitcases. Then I was given directions to meet a nigga named Q in the parking garage of the hotel and hand the coke-lined suitcases over to him. *Seems easy enough.*

I looked out of the window at the other planes on the runway. We hadn't yet taken off. I didn't wear watches. I took a sneak peek at the one on the man's arm in the middle seat next to me. It was 7:03 pm. The flight departure had been scheduled for 6:50 pm. We weren't moving. *Just be calm,* I told myself and leaned back against the headrest and closed my eyes. When I opened them, two air marshals were coming down the aisle of the airplane. *Oh, shit!* There was nowhere for me to run and nowhere for me to hide. *When you lose your cool...you lose control of the situation.* I grabbed one of the magazines stuffed inside the pocket on the back of the seat in front of me. I pretended to glance through it, trying not to make eye contact with the armed Federal Marshals. Both officers had a piece of paper in their hands. They glanced at it periodically. I guessed that it was a photo or sketch of the passenger they were searching for—me.

Just when the Air Marshals approached the row I was sitting in, a deranged looking White man seated in the back of the plane jumped up and started screaming at the top of his lungs. He was cradling a little girl in his hands.

"She's mine!" He yelled. "I won't let you have her!"

This is some wild ass shit.

"Sir," one of the air marshals said. "Just calm down. No one's trying to take your daughter away from you. We just need you to come with us. Your wife is looking for you both."

"She said that she was going to leave me," the man broke down and started crying.

One of the Air Marshals lifted the little girl out of the man's hands. The other guided him off the plane. I was just glad that it wasn't me they were leading away in handcuffs.

* * *

The elevator opened. A black BMW with pitch black tinted windows was parked directly in my view. I pushed the cart that I had borrowed from out of the hotel lobby to lug the suitcases on, towards the back of the car. A caramel colored nigga stepped out of the driver side door. He had a doo rag on but slid if off and threw it in the passenger side seat of the car. He was only about five foot ten but his swagger was tall. He rocked a gray and black hoodie with gray and black low top Nike's to match. He had on jeans that appeared to be washed out and rugged, but they were new. I noticed the chain that was linked from his front to his back jean pocket. It was some skateboarder-White-boy shit. I was expecting him to be a grimy ass nigga, but he was surprisingly the opposite.

"I'm Quincy," he extended his hand. "But you can call me Q."

"Shar."

"Welcome to Atlanta."

"Thanks."

"How was your flight?"

"Memorable," I said and went on to tell him what transpired on the plane.

"That's some crazy ass shit," he said, loading the suitcases into the trunk of the car. "How long you here for?"

"'Til Sunday."

Slay wanted me to turn right around and fly back home until I explained to him how suspicious that shit looked. I also wanted to see what all Atlanta had to offer since I was on the lookout for a new place to call home.

"You wanna hook up later on...not hook up...but hang out? I can show you around the city."

"That's cool."

"A'ight...I'll be back in about an hour to scoop you up. If that's cool."

"I'll be ready."

True to his word, Q came back for me. He was parked in the same spot, waiting for me. I stepped off the elevator looking like a motherfuckin' model. I was feeling myself until I almost tripped over my own foot trying to switch my ass to Q's BMW. *Embarrassed.* Q hopped out of the car and opened up the passenger side door for me. He was on the phone but stopped talking to the person on the other end of the line to acknowledge me.

"Damn, Shawty, you pulled a Clark Kent on a nigga."

"A what?"

"A Clark Kent...you went into the telephone booth and turned into Superwoman."

"Oh, thanks, I think."

"You look nice. That's all a nigga's tryin' to say. 'Dem boots are hot."

I was rocking a short black dress with the back cut out and those thigh-high boots I had hit Slay's pockets up for. My hair was slicked back into an elegant ponytail and I accessorized with gold jewelry—some real shit I had copped for myself.

"I'mma hit you back." Q clicked his phone shut.

We rode down Peachtree Street and then circled through Atlantic Station, making small talk.

"Slay didn't tell me he had a bad bitch like you workin' for him," Q said. "And before you go off on a nigga...that was meant to be a compliment."

"Guess he wanted to keep me a secret."

"Or, all to himself." Q looked my way and licked his lips. He was sexy as hell, but I wasn't shopping for another nigga like Slay.

Chapter 26

GONE BABY GONE

Everywhere we went Q was greeted like a celebrity. It didn't take long for me to realize that he was a major player in the streets of Atlanta. He had fans on deck, hoes and niggas. Each club that we hit up, we were escorted through the back and straight to the VIP area where celebrities that I had only seen on television were snorting lines on the abs of groupies. I couldn't believe some of the shit I was seeing. *Ain't that...* At one popular nightspot in the ATL, I recognized a well-known rapper hugged up with a broad that appeared to be another nigga in drag. That shit reminded me of the videotape clearly showing Bop giving Slay some head. I needed to get out of VIP and catch my breath.

Q continued to circulate VIP while I made my way around the dance floor. *So much for catchin' my breath.* It was musty as hell on the lower level of the club. *They need to spray some Glade...burn some candles or some shit down here.* I pinched my nose as I roamed around. Atlanta was the south's Hollywood— everybody in the club, VIP worthy or not, thought of themselves as a superstar and walked around like they had a "S" on their chest. *They partyin' like rockstars up in here.* I wasn't hating. In fact, Atlanta seemed to be the place to be.

I scoured the dance floor with my eyes. Niggas and broads were grinding on each other close and hard enough to start a wildfire. Niggas were spilling drinks on their kicks while they danced and broads were trying discreetly to pull their panties out of the crack of their asses. At least, those who were wearing some did. I spotted a nigga on the opposite side of the club, leaning up against the wall. There was something familiar about his stance, the way he moved his head to the music and held his drink in his hand. He was rocking a New York Yankees fitted hat. It was Tyrell.

I pushed my way through the traffic on the dance floor. "Excuse me. Oh, I'm sorry. My bad." I was bumping into niggas and throwing elbows, trying to make my way over to him. I wanted to tell him that he was right about Slay and that I was wrong.

"Shawty, let me holla at you." I jerked my wrist back from a nigga trying to get my attention. "Damn, I'm just tryin'to introduce myself," he said, wearing a three-piece, grapefruit colored suit. "You act like you in a hurry or somethin'.

"I am," I said, turning my nose up at him.

"Well, fuck you then."

"Fuck you too...lookin'like you about to say an Easter speech in that loud ass suit."

He walked away and when I turned my attention back in Tyrell's direction, he had disappeared. *Fuck! Fuck! Fuck!* I did a 360° turn in the middle of the dance floor. He was headed towards the back door. The same entrance that Q and I had entered through. I tried to zigzag my way through the crowd but couldn't catch up with him. I watched as he gave dap to some niggas on the way out and then he was gone. He didn't leave alone. A long-legged model type was clinging to his arm. My heart dropped into the pit of my stomach.

Pissed and ready to go, I headed back to VIP to find Q. He was chatting it up with a Latina-looking broad but quickly dismissed her when he saw me.

"Shar, I was startin' to worry that you had bounced on a nigga."

"Nah, but I am ready to go."

"Not a problem, but there's somebody I want you to meet first."

Q grabbed my hand and escorted me over to one of the tables in VIP where a group of broads—each representing a country in the United Nations—surrounded three horny ass looking niggas.

"Shar, this is Lavar Jackson."

The tallest and best dressed of the three niggas stood up, took my hand and kissed it.

"Lavar, this is the chick I was tellin' you about," Q said with a big ass smile on his face.

"Yeah...yeah." He ran his eyes over me like I was a USDA prime grade steak. "She's cute."

Am I invisible or some shit? He spoke about me like I wasn't there. *And kids are cute...I'm a bombshell, motherfucker...with them shades on in the club. Who does that?*

"Can you sing...rap?"

Q saw the confused look on my face. "Lavar owns Ball Hard Entertainment. He's lookin for new talent."

"Besides being beautiful, I have no talent."

Q and Lavar laughed.

"Beauty always comes before talent," Q said. "Why do you think we have synthesizers? Half the bitches out now with albums can't sing. I want to get you in the studio...see what you're workin' with. You already got the look."

"No thanks, I'm not lookin' for a record deal."

Lavar reached into the inside pocket of his pinstripe suit and handed me his card. "Hit me up if you change your mind."

"Will do."

Q and Lavar exchanged a few words and then we jetted.

"You should seriously think about what Lavar said. He can make you a star."

"It may be hard to believe, but everybody doesn't want to be famous."

"But, they do want to be rich."

Khalilah was right. Slay's money wasn't mines. Lavar was offering me an opportunity of a lifetime to be rich and famous and the ATL had something else that I wanted, Tyrell. My mind was made up, I was going back home for two reasons: to get my money out of the bank and to pack my shit. I was leaving Slay, sooner than I had planned. Twenty-six thousand dollars was enough to get settled in the ATL. My decision was final. All I had to do was plan my escape.

* * *

The airplane ride back home was uneventful, unlike my flight to Atlanta. There were no delays or deranged men trying to kidnap their daughters.

I picked up the new luggage that I had to cop from baggage claim and went to wait on Slay. I had tried to call him before boarding my plane but wasn't able to reach him. I had left him three messages already, informing him that my flight had landed. After an hour, I was thoroughly pissed and called a cab.

The Escalade wasn't anywhere in sight. Nor was the Range Rover. I suspected that Slay had taken it to the dealership to be inspected after all of the lies I had told him about it needing so many repairs.

Seconds after walking into the condo, my phone buzzed. It wasn't Slay. It was Niecy.

"Hello."

"Where are you?"

"Just gettin' home."

"You at the condo?"

"Yeah."

"You gotta get the fuck outta there. I'm listenin' to the scanner and the po-po's are on their way over there right now."

"What?"

"Shar, they been bustin' niggas left and right. They callin' it Operation-Get-These-Niggas."

"Fuck! Do you know if they got Slay?"

"I…"

My phone went dead. *Shit!* I couldn't lug around the suitcases I had so I grabbed a duffle bag and stuffed as much shit into it as I could. I opened up my underwear drawer and emptied it out. At the bottom of it was the gun I had taken from TaNaysha's closet. I stuffed it into the bag too, I found my charger and grabbed my purse. *My keys. My keys. Shit!* I didn't have any transportation.

The cabbie. He was still outside waiting on me to come out and pay him. I had given my last few dollars to the airport attendee in Atlanta who had helped me with my luggage. I kept a stash of cash in the condo. Not that much, just a couple of hundred, I told the cabbie that I would be back out with the cab fare I owed him. He was still there.

"Go!" I yelled at the cabbie.

"Where's my…"

"Just go. Now!"

The cabbie pulled off, making a loud screeching sound. He hauled ass down the street, barely stopping at the stop sign. As he turned the corner, a parade of police cruisers and unmarked cars sped past us. Out of the cab's back window, I watched as DEA agents swarmed the condo. I instructed the cabbie to roll past the warehouse. *What the fuck?* The street was blocked off. While half of the police department was busting into the condo, the entire fire department was fighting a massive fire at the warehouse. I could see the flames from the cab. They stretched into the sky amongst black smoke. My bet was that Slay had started the fire himself or paid someone to do it. I wondered where Aleesha's ass was and if the house had been raided. I pulled my phone out to call Slay again but stopped before pressing the call button. If he was locked up, his phone would be in police custody as well. I would have to wait for him to contact me.

"Here." I handed the cabbie a hundred dollar bill. He let me out about a block from Niecy's apartment. I walked the rest of the way, constantly looking over my shoulder for the patty wagon to come and sweep my ass up.

"Who is it?"

"Me," I whispered.

Niecy let me in with a hell-nah-you-can't-stay-here look on her face.

"Don't worry, I just need to stay the night…until the bank opens in the mornin'. Then, I'm out."

"Cool. 'Cause you know I can't have the po-po's bustin' up in here over some shit that ain't got nothin' to do wit' me."

Didn't I tell this bitch I was out in the mornin'?

"Anyway," Niecy continued. "The new police chief ain't fuckin' around. He havin' motherfuckers arrested West to East and North to South." She turned the television on to the ten o'clock news.

"New Chief of Police Roswell Jones is sticking to his promise to eliminate crime, violence and drugs in our neighborhoods. The local Narcotics Division along with the DEA rounded up over thirty suspected drug dealers over the weekend," the news anchor reported.

The screen spilt to footage of officers leading niggas away in handcuffs and stuffing them into the back of police cruisers. I recognized most of them as Slay's workers.

"Ain't that that nigga Gutt?"

The news coverage showed Gutt, Butter and Luxury being whisked away from a mansion in a White neighborhood called Heaven Hills. The house stretched over two acres of land and was bigger than Frankie and Carlo's crib. Any outsiders looking in would suspect that the residents of the house would need a team of hired help to maintain the premises—inside and out. In the circular driveway was a slew of luxury vehicles including Slay's Escalade and my Range Rover.

"Damn. Who the fuck lives there?"

"Aleesha," I said, without any doubt.

"That's fucked up. Slay got you all cramped up in that condo and Aleesha's livin' in a mansion in Heaven Hills."

I mean mugged Niecy. If looks could kill, she would have been dead.

"Anyway, girl, Curtis is comin' over. I thought I'd go ahead and tell you."

"Who the fuck is Curtis?"

"You know Curtis...the old nigga I'm fuckin'."

"Oh."

I gathered that Niecy wanted to talk about her and Curtis' apparent relationship, but I didn't want to hear that shit. I needed to find out where Slay was. It was funny how easy it was for a nigga to walk away from a broad and how damn hard it was for a broad to walk away from a nigga. Even though I was falling out of love with Slay, I still had love for him. He was the first man that I had ever loved and before I left for Atlanta, I needed to know that he was still breathing.

Throughout the night, I kept staring at my phone, hoping that it would ring and "My Boo" would pop across the screen. I tossed and turned on Niecy's couch, trying to tune out the noises coming from her bedroom. *Fuck this!* I got up. I was going to look for Slay.

* * *

It was unusually quiet around Ernie Pain's. Besides his junk cars and the Chrysler that he drove, his yard was empty. Those niggas who weren't arrested in the weekend raids were hiding out. There were only a few stragglers on the corner.

I knocked on Ernie's door, to see if he knew where Slay was. He came to the door with a gun in his hands. It was late; I didn't blame him. He pulled me inside his house and looked out the door, making sure no one was following me. He locked all three locks on the door. *Awwwhhhh-hell-to-the-nah.*

"Have you seen Slay? I can't find him."

I saw an almost empty bottle of Jack Daniels and a plate of chicken bones resting on the coffee table in front of the couch. Old episodes of Sanford & Son were showing on the television.

"Whooooo 'dat you talkinnnn' 'bout?" Ernie was slurring his words. He was drunk as hell.

"Ernie, have…you…seen…Slay…Sean…Sean Rodgers?" I asked.

"Oh, Slaaaayyy. Yeah, I…I…thinnnnkkk they got him."

"Who is they?"

"Five-O…the po-po's."

"You…you neeeeddd a new purse?" Ernie showed me some fake-ass-imitation Louis Vuitton, Gucci, Michael Kors, Coach, and Chanel purses. "I got sommmme DVD's."

"Nah, Ernie. I'm cool." I reached to unlock the door. Ernie walked up on me, with his dick hard.

"Get the fuck up off me," I said, kicking and screaming as he grabbed me and threw me on the couch. He pulled his pants and drawers down to his ankles. *Got damn!* The rumor about his dick being the size of a boa constrictor was damn near true. His shit hung down to the middle of his thigh and was thick as a soda can. *Fuck that!* I kicked him in his nut sack and busted the bottle of Jack Daniels over his head. He stumbled to the floor and passed out. I stood over him, watching his chest rise and fall. He was still alive. I stepped over his body and grabbed the keys to his Chrysler. I planned on returning it before he regained consciousness.

I turned into Heaven Hills. It was a gated community with a twenty-four hour security guard monitoring who came and went. The iron gate looked heavy and able to withstand a car crash. I decided against trying to ram the Chrysler through it. I would have to lie my way into the subdivision.

"Evening, Mam. Are you a resident or a visitor?"

"Actually, I'm a realtor in town and I left my office keys in one of the houses I showed earlier. I don't recall seein' you earlier," I lied.

"No, Mam. I work the third shift. I'm not here durin' the day." He pushed a button and the gate opened. "Hope you find your keys."

"Thanks."

I drove around the subdivision until I pulled into the circular driveway of the mansion that the news showed Gutt, Butter, and Luxury being escorted out of to police custody. All of the cars that were lined up in front of the house earlier were gone—confiscated in the raid. The front door of the mansion was left unlocked. The police had gone on a rampage, searching for dirty money, drugs and drug paraphernalia. All of the furniture had been tossed and turned. The sofa cushions had been slashed, along with every mattress in every bedroom of the house. Sledgehammers had been taken to the drywall in certain spots of the mansion, revealing the installation. And thrown about the destruction were broken pictures frames with photos of Aleesha and Slay, smiling and looking like they were a couple in love—a happily married couple at that.

Chapter 27

A MAN'S JOB

I sat in the dark, on the stairwell that led to the second floor of the mansion, thinking back to my very first encounter with Slay. He had captured me with his street swagger and I admit that I was blinded by the bling and the glamorous life that it represented. But, I was also just twelve-years-old. He was an adult and in essence had raped me of my future. He had already made up in his mind that one day I was going to be his. In my heart, I believed that Slay wanted to love me but could never figure out how. In turn, I became just another one of his possessions—a thing and not a person in his life that he owned and could discard at his convenience. However, with the exception of not being able to love me, as I deserved to be loved, Slay had held me down—giving me everything and anything that I asked for; money and material shit for the most part. That's why I wasn't fucked up over seeing how high and mighty Aleesha had been living, tucked away in Heaven Hills. And despite all of the other reasons I had to hate Slay, I didn't. The hate and resentment that I would eventually feel towards him didn't come until later.

There was more to lose than to gain being a hustler's girl. Beyond the glitz and the glamour was a life filled with broken promises, lies and abuse. Slay and I hadn't even been together for a whole year, but I felt like I had been through a lifetime of bullshit. Not to mention that I had let my goals and dreams fall to the wayside while caught up, loving him and living hood fabulous.

I was ready for a fresh start and hoped to hop on the first morning flight to Georgia. There was so much that I wanted to do, starting with going to college. Being a news anchor, reporting all the bad shit that happened in the world, wasn't appealing to me anymore. Once in Atlanta, I planned on enrolling in The Art Institute of Atlanta and majoring in fashion design or something. And maybe, one day, open up a small clothing boutique. *Yeah, that's what I'm gonna do.* I didn't plan on hooking up with Q or his boy. Something told me that Lavar Jackson's business stretched far and wide beyond the music business. I was trying to get out of the game, not dive deeper into it.

But, first, I needed to find Slay. I had never planned on saying goodbye—just getting my shit and vamping. But, as fucked up as it sounds, I felt like he needed me. I was officially a DAC and refused to abandon Slay while he was down and out. Aleesha had been there for him when he was a no-name nigga on the block and I wanted to show him that, paid or not, I would be there for him just the same. I was done trying to convince myself that I didn't love Slay anymore. Deep down, I did and always would.

A car pulled into the circular driveway, dimming its' lights as it stopped in front of the double-glass doors of the mansion. *Shit!* I raced up the stairwell and peeked down into the foyer, hoping to get a good look at the intruder as he walked through the door. *Thank God.* It was Slay. He looked like he had been through hell and high water, literally. The white tee he had on was ripped, exposing his chest. His jeans were torn and his once-all-white kicks were muddy.

"That nigga is a dead man walkin'. Believe that shit," Slay said, speaking into his cell phone like it was a walkie-talkie. He cut his conversation short and slid the phone into his back pocket, picked up a lamp from off the floor and threw it at the wall. "Fuck! Fuck!" He held his face in his hands and fell to his knees. His entire operation had been burnt to the ground; his hustle had been stifled.

"Slay!" I ran down the stairwell.

"Babygirl." He hugged me tight.

"What happened?"

A mixture of blood and mud were dried up on Slay's face and arms. He was scratched up terribly, like he had been in a catfight.

"That nigga Gutt set me up."

It wasn't the time for any I-told-you-so's, but I had warned Slay about Gutt's shady-acting ass. Tyrell had warned him too.

"I drove the other truck to go and pick him and Butter up from off of the side of the road. We moved the weight from one truck into the other. Minutes after we took off, a state trooper pulled in behind us. Butter and I hopped out the truck and took off runnin' into the woods and shit. Gutt didn't move from the driver's seat. He was laughin' and shit...like some psycho ass nigga."

"Where's Butter?"

"I don't know. We separated. I've been hidin' in the woods for two motherfuckin' days, underneath a pile of fuckin' leaves, tree limbs and shit...gettin' bit by fuckin' squirrels and shit. After the police search was called off, I went back to the highway and caught a ride back into town." Slay buried his head in my stomach. "Babygirl, I ain't got shit. I tried to get here before the feds did but they beat me. They got everything. My money...my vehicles...this house…the condo. Everything's been seized." All Slay had left of his empire was the two-grand he had in his pocket.

"You got me," I said, resting my chin on the top of Slay's head. "I got some money saved up. We can take it and get the fuck up outta here."

I wasn't at all worried about the feds seizing anything of mine because I didn't have shit—only the money in the savings account that I shared with Ms. Trina. She had received a life insurance check from TaNaysha's passing; although, she had already cashed and smoked the money up. The feds couldn't prove that the money deposited into the account was mine and not hers.

"Babygirl, what the fuck else am I gonna do to make dough? I ain't got no college degree…no trade…no real work experience…nothin'. All I know how to do is hustle. Plus, money comes to slow workin' a nine-to-five."

"Just think about it…for me. Please, Slay…if you love me…you'll at least try." I had hoped that the fall of Slay's empire would be enough to convince him that it was time to get out of the game—to start living legit.

"Do you love me?" He asked.

"I wouldn't fuckin' be here if I didn't."

"I need a favor, Babygirl."

"What?" I asked, suspiciously.

"I need you to take out that fat motherfucker Cheez."

"What the fuck Cheez got to do with anything?"

"He's the only motherfucker on the block who didn't get busted and I found out that Gutt had been workin' with that nigga all along. He had infiltrated my operation, collecting information on how I ran my business for that nigga Cheez. I know you know how to shoot a gun. TaNaysha took your ass to the range. I knew about that shit but never said anything."

"You want me to kill for you?"

"Babygirl, I would do it for you. I promise…you do this…we can jet up outta here tomorrow. Go wherever you want…get married. I'll get out of the fuckin' game."

"You promise."

"To God," Slay said.

"What about Aleesha?"

"Fuck that bitch." It was the first time I had ever heard Slay call Aleesha out of her name.

"I'll do it." Slay had sucked me back into his world.

The plan was for me to get Cheez alone and then go in for the kill. "Aim for his head," Slay had said. After the deed was done, Slay and I had planned to meet up at Ms. Trina's house. And after hitting up the bank, we were heading straight to the airport— leaving the game behind.

* * *

I eased onto the premises of the abandoned house that Cheez operated out of. The grass stood as high as corn stalks and was littered with cans, bottles and McDonald's cheeseburger wrappers. The windows were boarded up and spray painted with gang signs and graffiti. The white paint was chipped and weeds sprouted up from the cracks in the cement. Camouflaged in the dark were two big ass pit bulls that barked and salivated at the sight of me. They charged towards me but were yanked back by the chains around their necks. *Whew!* I thought for sure that I was dog food.

The outside motion lights flickered on and a braided-up nigga, almost bigger than Cheez, came around from the back of the house—breathing all hard and shit.

"What the fuck you want?" He huffed and puffed.

"I need to speak to Cheez."

"What the fuck you want wit' Cheez?"

"Nigga, didn't I just tell you that I needed to speak with him."

"'Bout what?"

"'Bout none of your damn business. Just tell him that Shar Reid is here to see him."

"Wait here."

"Hurry the fuck up. It's cold out here."

His ass took his time walking back around the house and made me wait ten minutes before coming back out and signaling for me to follow him.

"How the fuck am I suppose to follow you with these damn dogs tryin' to eat me alive?"

"Lady and Man-Man…get back!" At the sound of his Barry White voice, the pit bulls backed up and let me walk freely around to the back of the house.

Another nigga patted me down and glanced inside my purse. The .40 caliber pistol was wrapped in a pair of my panties and hidden at the bottom of my purse, below the globs of other shit I had stuffed inside of it.

"Damn…you got cho' whole house up in there," the nigga checking my purse said, letting me through.

Cheez's operation was still up and running but like Slay, he had lost some workers in the raid as well. He was down to a handful of niggas and broads working for him and would soon be on a recruiting spree, trying to round up another crew. Two panty-and-bra clad broads sat at one of the tables scattered throughout the space, cutting marble-sized crackrocks into crumbs and weighing and packaging them. It was a much smaller scale operation than Slay's set up at the warehouse but the game was the same.

The inside of the house was much larger than it had appeared to be on the outside. All of the walls on the first floor had been gutted, creating one wide-open space. Even the bathroom walls had been torn down, leaving niggas without any privacy to shit if they needed to. *That's some foul shit.*

Cheez was in an upstairs bedroom. I don't know how his big ass made it up the stairs without the assistance of a crane but apparently he had managed to do so. The old wooden stairs squeaked as I climbed up them and I could only imagine what they sounded like under the pressure of his weight.

"The door on the right…go on in. He's waitin' for you," the braided-up nigga told me.

As soon as I opened the door, a mixed odor of sex, greasy-ass cheeseburgers and weed attacked my nostrils. The floor was barely viewable beneath the heaps of balled-up McDonald's sacks and cheeseburger wrappings, dirty clothes and beer bottles. *Filthy ass nigga.* Cheez was laid up in a twin-size bed. *Now he know he needs a king...two kings.* Flaps of his skin folded over the sides of the small mattress. He had a dingy white sheet covering his midsection and a money-counting machine hiked up on his mountainous stomach. He was inserting handfuls of dollar bills into the machine and didn't once look up at me. I should have shot his ass right then and there, but I didn't. Cheez was a slimy nigga but even a slimy nigga had a family that loved him. For a broad with a conscience, killing a nigga was easily said than done.

"You finally ready to get with a hero?"

I could have hurled all over his boat-size-bear-clawed feet.

"Slay's locked up," I lied. "I don't know what to do. I'm so use to a nigga takin' care of me. I thought...that maybe I...I could help you expand your operation. Be your right hand bitch."

Cheez laughed a hearty laugh. "Really, what the fuck you want?"

"I told you...I don't have no fuckin' where to go. You the only nigga still up and runnin' around this bitch. I need work. Shit, I'll chase cars if that's what the fuck you want me to do."

"What you gonna do for me?"

"Like I said, I can help you expand your operation...move major weight."

"No," he said forcefully. "What the fuck you gonna do for me?" He removed the sheet that covered his midsection. His dick was buried beneath his stomach but a .57 was resting on his leg. He reached for it.

"Do what the fuck I tell you to do. Put your purse down and take off all of your clothes."

I didn't sign up for this got damn shit, I thought to myself. The only thing I ever wanted to do was be with Slay, but I had discovered that loving a nigga in the game came at a price. A broad had to pay with her dignity, peace of mind and self respect. And sometimes with her freedom or even worse, her life.

"I didn't come here for this shit. Fuck you." I turned to leave but stopped at the sound of him cocking the gun.

"Take another step and I will bust a cap in your ass. You'll be walkin' around this bitch wit' one ass cheek."

I dropped the handle I had on my purse and let it fall to my side.

"Now, get naked."

If I run for it, I'm dead. If I stay and he rapes me, a part of me dies, I thought. Either way, I was shit out of luck. I removed my coat and then my shirt.

"Do it more sex-a-ly," Cheez instructed, waving the gun in my direction.

Nigga, sex-a-ly ain't even a word...dumb ass nigga. I rolled my eyes at him, while kicking off my boots and pulling down my pants.

"Now, what?" I asked, standing in my bra and panties.

"Now, take the rest of that shit off. I said get naked not half-naked."

Cheez grabbed his dick. It was so tiny that it disappeared inside the palm of his hand. He stroked it hard as I unfastened my bra.

"Take this shit over for me."

I needed to think fast and move quickly. I reasoned that giving Cheez a handjob would be less traumatic than giving him some head, which I believed was the next of his demands. Kneeling down next to the twin-size bed, I took the job over, squirming as my hand made contact with his dick. I felt like I was squeezing the life out of a glowworm. Cheez closed his eyes and leaned his head back against the wall, moaning and shit. I used my foot to kick my purse closer to me.

"Does that feel good to you, daddy?" I asked, trying to keep Cheez focused on the nut he anticipated was coming.

I eased the .40 out of my purse. As Cheez climaxed, I pulled the trigger.

Chapter 28

BETRAYED

Cheez's eyes rolled into the back of his head. His arms dangled at his side and his body jerked. I had aimed at his head but missed. The bullet landed in his chest. I scrambled to pick up all of my shit and hightailed it to the bedroom door where I met the two niggas I had encountered before. They were coming in as I was going out.

"The shot came from outside!" I screamed, acting all hysterical and shit for added drama.

"Cheez!" They ran to check his pulse.

I raced down the stairs and out of the house, zooming past the pit bulls but not before one nipped the back of my ankle. *Shit!*

I stopped in the alley leading to Ms. Trina's house to put on my clothes, ducking behind a dumpster when I heard the sirens pass by. The new Chief of Police wasn't only cracking down on the distribution of drugs in the hood but he had also dedicated himself to running a more efficient police department, ensuring faster response times to 9-1-1 calls that originated in the hood. The police were responding to hood incidents in record-setting time— some Usain Bolt-type speed. I pounded on Ms. Trina's door.

"It's too early in the got damn mornin' for this shit," she said, coming to the door. "Who the fuck is it?"

The sun was setting. Dawn was on the horizon. It had to be around six in the morning.

"Shar!" I yelled. She opened the door. "Slay here?"

"Hell, nah. Why the fuck would his ass be at my house?"

"He's suppose to meet me over here."

I pushed past Ms. Trina and went directly to the bathroom. Her house was still a hot-dirty mess. Just like the room Cheez was cramped into. I looked at myself in the bathroom mirror. The broad staring back at me was unrecognizable. I took a life that God had given. Possibly two if Vera was dead. Her whereabouts were still a mystery. I wondered where all of my morals and values that my parents had instilled in me since birth had gone. I had thrown them away like I had thrown away my future when I made the decision to choose Slay over a life of integrity. I was making one bad decision after another. The last—going after Cheez—being the worst. And it was all in the name of love—for a nigga not man enough to kill for himself.

The bite on my ankle wasn't as bad as I thought, but it hurt like hell and was bleeding profusely. I rolled up my pants leg and stuck my foot under the bathtub facet, running warm water over the wound. After which, I flushed the bite with alcohol and peroxide and bandaged it up.

"You got some Tylenol or somethin'?" I yelled to Ms. Trina.

"Got a big bottle of aspirin that I got from the Dollar Store. Look in the cabinet...behind the box of douche."

I heard someone banging on the front door. *Slay.* I hobbled back into the living room but not before hiding the .40 inside the vent in Ms. Trina's bathroom. The screws had been missing for years. TaNaysha had unscrewed the vent back when we where in middle school to hide the big bag of condoms and birth control pills that she had copped from the health department unbeknownst to Ms. Trina who would have killed her eleven-year-old ass for even thinking about fucking at that age.

Slay came storming through the door in a ski mask. "That nigga ain't dead. I thought I told you to aim for his head."

"You know what...fuck you. I'm the one who risked my fuckin' life and shit...almost got raped and shit to kill another motherfucker for your coward ass."

Before I fucking knew it, the back of Slay's hand made contact with my jaw. Ms. Trina grabbed a nearby beer bottle. "Nigga, I know you didn't." She swung at Slay. He ducked and then tackled her to the floor.

"Try that shit again and your crackhead ass will be layin' next to your daughter."

"Fuck you...sendin' a bitch to do a man's job. You ain't a real man...fightin' bitches and shit."

"Shut the fuck up!" Slay barked at her.

"I'm sorry, Babygirl. You know how I get sometimes. I can't control that shit. Let's just get to the bank and get the fuck up outta this bitch," he said.

Ms. Trina shot me a *bitch-I-know-you-ain't* look. Yes, I was about to hand over my savings to Slay. She put up a good fight against Slay, refusing to go with us to the bank. He had to drag her to the car, kicking and screaming. Looking back, it was obvious that she was just trying to look out for me as she would her own daughter.

At eight o'clock on the dot, we entered the bank. Ms. Trina had on the peach, satin nightgown that she had woke up in and a matching pair of house shoes. My cheek was freshly bruised and I was still limping from the dog bite. The teller looked at us suspiciously and even more so after she learned that we wanted to close the savings account, withdrawing every cent of the $26,000 that had been deposited into the account.

"Is there a reason why you're choosing to close your account with us?" She asked.

Bitch, because it's my money. My patience was wearing thin. "We're movin'."

"Okay, well because it's such a large sum of money, we'll have to issue you a cashier's check," she said.

"That's fine." The two-grand that Slay had in his pocket was enough for two plane tickets. We could cash the check whenever and wherever we landed.

"One moment." The teller excused herself and came back with the bank manager.

"Ms. Reid...Ms. Jenkins." He extended his hand to the both of us. "I just wanted to make sure that you were correct in stating that you wanted to close your account with us. We value our relationship with you all and would like to continue to be the bank that provides all of your banking needs."

"We're movin' and I believe that I have already informed Mrs. Baker here of our move."

"Ms. Jenkins, do you concur?"

"Con-what?" Ms. Trina scratched her head in confusion.

"Concur? Do you wish to close the account also?"

"Yes, she concurs. Now, give us our fuckin' money or there will be hell to pay."

The teller verified the spelling of my name and made the cashier's check out to me only upon receiving Ms. Trina's permission to do so.

"Where we goin'?"

"To take Ms. Trina back home."

"I thought she was droppin' us off at the airport and takin' Ernie back his car."

"I need to stop by Ernie's to pick up somethin'. He can give us a ride to the airport."

Ms. Trina hugged me before exiting the car. "Goodbye, Arabian Bombshell."

* * *

Ernie had regained conscienceness and was walking around his house, nursing the bump on his forehead with a pack of frozen peas. He didn't say shit to me when I walked into his house behind Slay. He kept his head down, avoiding any eye contact with me—the actions of a guilty ass nigga.

"Babygirl, go wait in the car. We'll be out in a second."

I hopped back into the Chrysler. This time in the backseat, leaving the front passenger seat free for Slay since he needed the legroom the front seat provided. Unconsciously and consciously, I always put his needs first—always before my own.

The screen door to Ernie Pain's house opened. Ernie came out, but Slay wasn't behind him. And then, out of nowhere, Slay pulled out from behind Ernie's house in his Escalade. It had been parked in the garage-sized shed in the backyard. Slay didn't stop for me. I jumped out of the Chrysler and chased behind the Escalade, waving my hands in the air.

"Please, please don't do this to me!"

Slay drove away, with my heart, my money and my sanity. The next thing I remembered was waking up with Bop standing over me. My jeans were unzipped, barely hugging my hips, and my vagina was throbbing. It felt like someone had lit a blowtorch inside of me and it was still burning. The pain was almost unbearable. The back of my head also ached and I was drifting in and out of consciousness.

"I didn't do it. It wasn't me." Bop put his hands up like the police had demanded him to do so. "I promise. Look."

He pulled up his jacket sleeve and showed me a bruise on his forearm and then turned around and showed me the one on the back of his calf.

"It was Ernie. He did bad things to you. I saw him with my own two eyes…drug you around to the back of his house…pulled your jeans down and put his thing inside you…right there in the backyard. I tried to help, but he hit me with a baseball bat. He hit you too…knocked your ass out cold."

"Where…where am I?"

"When Ernie went inside the house…me and my friend Otis picked you up. You at my house."

I was laying on a broken down, cardboard box in what appeared to be a tent city for the homeless. Bop and his tent-city friends circled in around me.

"You sure she ain't dead?" One of them asked. "She look dead."

"She ain't dead, fool," said Bop. "Didn't you just see her move her head?"

"What's her name?"

"I don't know, but she's a nice lady. She gave me this watch." Bop still had the Rolex that I had given him. "And these shoes." And the Stacy Adams.

"Ms. Nice Lady." He leaned over me. "You need a doctor." I heard Bop say before I drifted into a coma.

* * *

Locks of my hair landed on my bare feet. I ran my hand over my head. It was all gone, chopped off to no longer than an inch.

"There. Now, we're twins."

I looked up at Maureen, whom I shared a room with. Her hair was buzzed off military style. Our room door swung open and she jumped back.

"Hand them over," the orderly demanded.

"Hand what over?" Maureen asked.

"You know what."

Maureen handed him the pair of scissors that she had stolen from the nurse's station. "She said that she wanted it all gone…all cut off like mine's. She said that she didn't want to be pretty anymore…that being pretty got her into trouble."

"She's tellin' the truth," I said. "I told her to do it." I had convinced myself that if I were unattractive, Slay would have never been interested in me and my life would have taken a different course.

"Y'all both crazy as hell," he said.

Seconds later, the orderly was back with a broom, sweeping up my hair off the floor. He left and came back again, handing both Maureen and I a Dixie cup filled with water to wash down the two white pills he had placed in the palms of our hands. Figuring that I was already in a drug-induced state, I swallowed the medicine without putting up much of a fight. I knew where I was. I had been there for a while—on the sixth floor of the hospital, the mental ward.

The orderly led Maureen and I to the dining area. Two of the patients were engaged in an argument that had escalated into a food fight, each of them firing green Jell-O cubes at each other.

"He kicked my dog," one of the patients said.

"I did not," the other defended himself.

"You did to."

"Jim, your dog is okay." The orderly pretended to pet Jim's invisible dog. "Don't you hear him barkin'?"

Hell-to-the-nah. Most of the patients in the ward suffered from severe mental illnesses. Maureen was a manic-depressive—once married to a successful lawyer who cheated on her with his paralegal. She caught the two of them in the act, went home, laid down in the bed and never got out. She stayed in bed for three whole months before her husband finally committed her. It was some crazy shit.

I, on the other hand, was told that I had suffered a nervous breakdown due to traumatic stress, screaming and crying and shit after I had regained consciousness. The doctors and nurses had to drug me in order to calm me down. The next day, I was transported to the mental ward for a psychiatric evaluation.

I had met with a psychiatrist three times and each time I had put up a silent protest. It wasn't because I was mentally disturbed. It was because I didn't feel like fucking talking. Other than my refusal to communicate with the doctor, I didn't display any behavior that suggested that I was mentally ill. I wasn't having any hallucinations—thinking that bugs were under my skin or any shit like that. Nor, did I have any invisible pets. I wasn't crazy. I was a woman scorned.

Maureen and I sat at a table in the dining room and ate our food in silence. Some days we talked. Some days we didn't. It all depended on the mood Maureen was in.

"Reid, you ready for your visit with Dr. Harris?"

I sat in the doctor's office, staring up at all of his degrees, framed and hung on the wall behind his desk. He was old, bald and White. He wore a bow tie, brown tweed jacket and khakis underneath his white cloak, which reminded me of the jackets the ushers wore at my father's church. He didn't bust out any inkblot cards or pictures with black glob painted on them asking me what I saw or any shit like that. He just asked me a few questions, the same ones that I had refused to answer the three previous times we had met.

"Do you know your name?"

Not talking was the thing that was driving me insane. I decided that it was time to break my silence. "Yes." He looked at me and smiled. "Shar Reid."

"Do you know where you are?"

"Yes. On the nut floor of the hospital."

He cracked a smile. "Do you know why you are here?"

"Because I apparently had a nervous breakdown."

"Do you know what happened to you?"

"Yes."

"Do you know that you were brutally raped?"

"Yes."

"Do you know that the doctors had to remove your entire reproductive system...that you had to have a hysterectomy?"

"Yes. They told me when I woke up."

"Who's Slay? When you were emerging from the coma you where in, the nurses said that you called out for a person named Slay."

I locked my jaws and clenched my teeth.

"We can stop for today if you would like."

"He's the man I've been in love with every since I was twelve-years-old...the only man that I've ever been with. He's the man that I trusted with my well bein'...with my life. He's the man who betrayed me...the reason why I no longer have a relationship with my family. He's the man who beat me and left me in the hands of a rapist. He's the man I killed for. He's the man I now hate."

"He's the man that you thought would love, provide and always protect you," the doctor said.

I nodded, yes.

"Do you think that you're crazy, Ms. Reid?"

"Do you think that I'm crazy?"

"No, I think you're just heartbroken and deeply saddened by this man's betrayal, which is why I'm going to recommend that you be released and suggest that you seek counseling."

I was released but not on my own recognizance. Two DEA agents were waiting for me when I returned to my room.

Chapter 29

CHARGED

In an attempt to kill Cheez, I ended up saving his life. The bullet missed his heart by inches; however, during the surgery to remove it the doctors discovered that Cheez was days away from having a heart attack from the build up of cholesterol in his arteries—too many damn cheeseburgers. Word was that he was going to try and sue McDonalds. *Niggas always runnin' a scam or some shit.* When the police questioned him about the shooting, he refused to name the perpetrator who attempted to murder him. That nigga owed me, which is why he wasn't talking and neither was I.

The detective slammed his hand on the table and pointed his finger in my face. "I'm done bein' nice here," he said, his breath smelling like coffee and cigarette smoke. "You either tell us what you know now...and I mean right now or you're goin' away...to prison. Is that what you want?" He asked.

It was two o'clock in the morning. The detective and his partner had been taking turns interrogating me for twelve straight hours. They were tired and so was I. I hadn't had a sip of water since earlier on in the interrogation. My mouth was dry and my stomach was growling. Still, I kept my trap shut.

"You fuckin' Black broads kill me...would rather do time than give up your drug dealin' boyfriends. I feel sorry for you."

I didn't owe Slay shit and had every reason to rat his punk ass out. But, sending him to prison wasn't the revenge I was after. I had much worse in mind—for him and Ernie Pain.

The detective left me in the room, alone, to contemplate my fate. They wanted me to snitch on Slay, to provide them with information that would collaborate with Gutt's story. He had made a plea deal with the District Attorney's office and had laid out the dealings of Slay's operation, detail by detail. He was going to be in the witness protection program for the rest of his life. *Snitchin' ass nigga.*

The detective came back into the small, gray and cold interrogation room with a manila folder filled with photos of me: going in and out of the condo, driving the Range Rover and some of Slay and I together—none that proved I was ever involved in any illegal activity. But, I would soon find out that simply knowing of any criminal activity taking place and not reporting it was a crime all in its' self and that's exactly what I was charged with.

"You get one phone call."

"Don't need it," I said. There was no one for me to call.

The detective led me down to the booking area to be fingerprinted and photographed. The area was filled with broads who had been arrested during the wee hours of the morning, most for prostitution and solicitation. There was an old-head hooker in the group. She looked like she was currently pregnant with twins and her breast sagged in the lime green halter dress she was wearing. She had kicked her plastic-heeled, stripper shoes off and was rubbing her feet. She was in need of a pedicure, badly. The red polish on her toenails was chipping away.

"Oooohhh, shit." She massaged the balls of her feet. "Been on my feet all night."

"You mean your back," another broad in the cell said.

"Fuck you, Darlene...with your funky ass pussy."

"My pussy don't stank."

"That ain't what I heard."

The two worked the same block and were well acquainted with each other. They went back and forth before Henrietta, the prostitute in the lime green dress, shut the conversation down when she said that Darlene's pussy smelled like a dead gold fish. Darlene didn't have shit else to say after that. She even laughed herself. Physically, Darlene was the total opposite of Henrietta: light skin, skinny and more visible wrinkles on her face that showed that she had lived a hard-knock life.

"I can't stand your old ass," Darlene said.

"Shit, you older than me."

Henrietta and Darlene had been in the game their entire lives, a combination of a hundred and four years. They were born into a life of prostitution. Their mothers worked the streets together, performed tricks together, robbed and stole together and did drugs together. And the two of them ended up trapped in the same cycle. Henrietta had two children and Darlene had one. And both had no idea where their sons were.

"My son tells everybody that I'm dead," Darlene said.

"He's a selfish motherfucker...blames me for his fucked up childhood. He got money...lots of money but won't give me shit. Told me to continue trickin' since that's what I was good at."

"Mine's the same way," Henrietta said. "Act like I'm dead when I see they asses. I try to tell'em to leave 'dem streets alone...look at me...I say...look at what the streets did to me. They don't listen...just keep on sellin' 'dem drugs and won't give me a dime."

All women who gave birth weren't meant to be mothers. Henrietta and Darlene were two prime examples, consumed with living the street life and hanging out; instead of taking care of their children. And, like a stray bullet, the game didn't have a name on it. It would swallow, chew, and spit out any one involved. I was a prime example of that.

Darlene leaned her head back on the concrete wall. A scar circled the entire diameter of her neck, like someone had tried his or her best to strangle her, but she had survived.

"Henrietta Price," the jailer called out. "Time for your glamour shot," he joked.

Henrietta put her shoes back on and followed the jailer.

"I can make you feel good, Big Daddy." I heard her say, walking away.

"No thanks," he said. "I'd rather do a dog."

"Fuck you. Where's the Chief of Police? Get him out here right now. Tell'em Henrietta Price wants to talk to him. This motherfucker just disrespected me," she yelled.

"Lady, calm down and step behind the camera."

Henrietta smiled hard, showing her two front gold teeth. Darlene looked at me. We were both waiting our turn to have our mug shot taken and to be fingerprinted.

"Whoever cut your hair fucked it up," she said to me, reminding me that I had Maureen whack off my crown and glory. "You look like a little boy. I ain't sayin' you ugly though...a cute little boy. My son was cute when he was little. He ain't all Black...mixed with somethin', but I was workin' the streets when I got pregnant with him...don't know exactly who his daddy is."

"Darlene Rodgers," the jailer called, confirming what I had suspected. Darlene was Slay's mother, alive and still working the streets.

* * *

The courtroom was packed with niggas and broads waiting to be arraigned for the charges brought up against them and with their families present for support and praying for a miracle. The family of the nigga in front of the judge when my lawyer and I walked into the courtroom had their Bibles opened on their laps like God was going to rise up from the pages and save their son from a life in prison.

"How does the defendant wish to plead?" The judge asked.

"Not guilty, Yo' Honor," he said. "I didn't do shit. Y'all got the wrong nigga." The nigga was dressed in a blue suit and white shirt, probably at the suggestion of his lawyer. He looked uncomfortable.

"He didn't do it. My son didn't do it," his mother stood up and yelled.

"Quiet down! Quiet down!" The judge ordered.

"We ask that the defendant be released on bail, Your Honor," his lawyer said.

"Your Honor, the defendant is a flight risk," the state prosecutor said. "We ask that he remain in the state's custody until his trial date."

"The court agrees."

"Fuck you! The nigga spit in the judge's direction." The jailers hauled his ass back into custody.

My lawyer was an overworked and underpaid public defender who didn't give a fuck about whether I went to prison or not. He just wanted me up and off of his caseload. If I plead guilty, I was looking at five years in prison. If my case went to trial, maybe even more. It was my turn in front of the judge.

"How does the defendant wish to plead?"

"Guilty," I said.

"Do you understand the constraints of your plea?"

"Yes, Your Honor."

"The defendant will be remanded to the Topeka Correctional Facility for Women for sixty-two months."

* * *

The bus stopped in front of a one-level brick facility. On the outside, excluding the barbwire fence that surrounded the building, the premises of the facility looked more like a college campus than a prison. In my mind, I pretended that it was. Even shackled and chained, the thought of spending the next five years of my life behind bars hadn't yet soaked in.

Me and the other new arrivals were led off the bus and into the facility, passing by some inmates who were out in the yard.

"This don't look too bad," Janae said.

My story—the story of a young woman with a bright future being led astray by a nigga in the game—wasn't at all original. Janae's boyfriend was a nigga named Theo, a smalltime drug dealer who hadn't yet made a name for himself. Though he was on the rise, he wasn't a nigga that posed a threat to Slay. "The crackheads say that nigga sellin' candy...that mild shit." I remembered Slay saying about the quality of Theo's product. "He needs to go back into the lab with that shit."

One night, the police stopped him and Janae and searched the car they were in—called out the drug dog and everything. The dog sniffed out an Advil bottle of rocks that Theo had dropped inside Janae's purse. She took the wrap and was serving ten years for his ass. *Over some candy.*

"Fresh meat," some of the inmates yelled and whistled at us.

"Guess I spoke too soon," she said.

We were strip searched, given our prison attire—a week's worth of light blue shirts and dark blue pants—along with a bar of soap, two towels, a toothbrush, some toothpaste, a flimsy ass comb and brush and some thick ass maxi pads. Even though I didn't need the pads, I took them anyway.

We were then led to our cells. The fourteen-by-nine foot cell was smaller than my walk-in closet at the condo. Shit, the inside of the Range Rover was roomier than the cell. My cellmate was in the yard, I guessed. Her side of the cell was neat. *Good...can't stand no nasty ass broad,* I thought to myself as if I had a choice in the matter. She didn't have any personal items on display like photos of herself or her family or any posters, cards or letters taped up on the wall. Nothing in the cell indicated her racial identity, not that it mattered. As long as she wasn't some Nazi-Hitler-loving-skin-head White broad or a broad that liked the nappy dug out, I wouldn't have a problem—as if I had a choice in that matter too. It was hard for me to register in my head that for the next five years, I was done making my own choices. From now until my release, someone else would tell me when to eat, sleep and shit.

I placed my toiletries on the shelf mounted to the wall above the thinly padded, twin size bed that I would be spending the majority of my time on.

"Shar?"

I looked up and saw Keisha standing in the doorway of my cell.

"Oh my God." I jumped up and hugged her. "I'm sorry," I said, letting her go. "It's just good to see a familiar face."

I stepped back. Her pants were sagging and her mannerisms were more masculine than I had remembered. She introduced me to her cellmate who she also stated was her girlfriend.

"As in girlfriend-girlfriend?" I asked to clarify what she had said and what I had heard.

She whispered something to the girl, who was reluctant to leave her alone with me. "It ain't like that with me and Shar," Keisha assured her.

People said that prison changed people. *They ain't ever lied,* I thought to myself. Keisha sat on my cellmate's bunk.

"You don't owe me an explanation," I said.

"You won't judge me?" She asked.

"There's only one Judge, Jury and Executor and it's not me," I said. "Really…what you do is your business."

Keisha was on death row. Any love that she received from any person whether it was a broad or a male prison guard; I couldn't find it in my heart to fault her for accepting it. After all the shit Wayne took her through, she deserved to be loved by someone.

"Lil' Wayne's doin' good," she said, smiling. "He was adopted by a good family. I wrote my old social worker and begged her to find out where he was. They sent me some pictures of him. He looks happy and that's all I prayed to God for…for him to be happy and be in a good home." Keisha had tears in her eyes.

"That's good to hear."

"You cut your hair off."

"Yeah…I had a little breakdown."

"It's for the best. In here…like out there," Keisha pointed to the window in the cell. "The prettier you appear the harder they go after you but don't worry…I got your back."

"Thanks, Keisha."

"Okay, well, I'll see you in the dinin' hall."

Out walked Keisha and moments later, in walked my cellmate. *Ain't this some shit.* I shook my head and rolled my eyes. "Ummmph...guess mama got left behind too."

Aleesha ignored me. We had both given so much of ourselves to a man that abandoned and betrayed us—the same man at that. She turned around and faced me. Her eyes were puffy and swollen. Her hair was slicked back into a nob of a ponytail. Her eyebrows were bushy as hell. Unfortunately, we weren't at a day spa or salon. I suppose I didn't look my best either.

"I waited...waited for him to come and bail me out of jail. He promised that if anything ever happened...like me gettin' arrested that he would come for me...hire the best lawyers. I waited and he didn't come."

"Maybe he didn't know you were in jail." *Why the fuck am I tryin' to console her ass?*

"They showed me gettin' arrested on the news. Believe me, he knew."

"He promised," her voice cracked. "He promised," she cried.

"I know," I moved from my bunk to hers and wrapped my arms around her. "He promised me too."

"He's incapable of lovin' any woman," Aleesha said.

"I know," I said, knowing the reason why. A man who hated his own mother could never truly respect and love any other woman.

"I stole from him."

"Huh?"

Aleesha raised her head up. "Half-a-million dollars. When I get the fuck up outta here...I'mma be set." She dried her eyes.

"What about you?"

"Nothin'...I ain't got nothin'."

Now, I was crying and Aleesha was consoling me. "You still breathin' and when you get out of this motherfucker…you still gonna be young…able to get your paper up. Me, I'mma be over forty when I get out this bitch."

Slay was wrong about me being more mature than Aleesha. Having book sense was useless on the streets. Aleesha had the one thing that I lacked, street sense and enough of it to hustle half-a-millon dollars right from under a nigga's nose.

Chapter 30

UNFINISHED BUSINESS

"Ain't that Mike?" Keisha asked. "Your high school beau?"

"Huh?" I looked up at the 19" television mounted up high in the corner of the prison's common area. "Yeah, that's him."

Mike, my old beau from high school, was going in for a lay up. He had left Duke his sophmore year and was making a name for himself in the NBA. The camera panned to a White broad with some bleach blonde extensions in her hair. She flashed a smile and then the rock on her ring finger in front of the camera. It was bigger than the fake ass, cubic zirconia, engagement ring that Slay had given me. I was sure that hers was real. Mike had signed a multimillion-dollar contract with the Clippers. *They need a star player.* I was proud of him.

"Congratulations to Mike Massey and his fiance Amber. The pair got engaged this weekend and plan to marry this summer," the announcer said.

"He is fine as hell," Keisha said. "What?" She asked, reading the expression on my face. "I still know a fine nigga when I see one."

We laughed and I averted my attention back to the book that I was reading, *Continuous Fire: A Collection of Poetry* by Sonya Sanchez. It had mysteriously come in the mail for me, postmarked in Atlanta, Georgia. In fact, there wasn't a month that went by without me receiving a new book in the mail. Someone out there was thinking about me as much as I was thinking about him. *One day,* I thought to myself. *We'll cross paths again.*

I put the poetry book aside and picked up my English Composition book. Through the prison and its' partnership with the University of Kansas to help inmates interested in pursuing a higher education, I was finally enrolled in college. We had class twice a week with an instructor via satillite and communicated with him through our prison email accounts. Mr. Roth, our English instructor, encouraged us to start keeping a journal and making daily entries. I found myself writing continuously, honing my writing skills and releasing pent-up anger. I suppose it was all a part of the rehabilitation process.

Doing time wasn't easy. It was more of a mental struggle than a physcial one. That is if you could escape being raped or assaulted or both. And, being confined to a cell twenty-three hours out of the day could drive a nigga or a broad insane. But, I had made up my mind that I was going to do my time and not let it do me.

Every now and then, I received a letter from Ms. Trina, letting me know that she was still alive. "I ain't overdosed yet," she said in her last letter. *Ms. Trina knows she's crazy.* And in each letter, she promised to check herself into rehab. I always looked at the return address on the envelope her letters arrived in just to see if she'd kept her promise. She hadn't; not yet.

"Reid," the prision guard assigned to my block yelled my name. "You have a visitor."

"Really?"

Once a month, Khalilah visited me. Carlo even came on occasion. They were happily married and expecting their first child. Khalilah had received her Associate's Degree in Business

Administration. The Tap Room had closed down but was reopened with a new name, Lilah's.

"Do you know who it is?" I asked. Khalilah had been up earlier in the month and Niecy, who made the drive up to see me when she could, usually let me know in advance when she was coming.

"Nah."

As I followed the prison guard to the designated visitor's area, my heart pounded. I had no idea who was waiting to see me. At one of the round tables sat my father. I recognized the back of his head. His hair was balding in the front but he still had that familiar Baptist-preacher shag in the back. He looked like he had lost weight, more fragile than I ever remembered seeing him. His watch looked like it could slide right off his wrist. He was on his death bed and the only reason he had come to see me was to seek my forgiveness. I wanted to turn away and go back to my cell.

Things had changed between my father and I. I didn't race and jump into his arms as I did so many times as a child. We didn't even embrace. I pulled out the chair in front of him and took a seat.

"How's Shanelle?" I asked. She was the only person I cared about—not my mother or my father. My disdain for them ran as deep as my hatred for Slay.

"She's good…growing. You know, she'll be twelve soon."

"I know. Have you let her see the birthday cards I've sent her over the years?" My father didn't answer. "I was your daughter…your daughter got damn it!" I hit the table with my fist.

"I'm sorry, Shar." My father's eyes watered.

"You let me go without fightin' for me…for me and my future. You should have fought for me," I cried. "I was still a child…you said it yourself."

"You're right...I...I just thought that I was doing what God wanted me to do."

"God wanted you to abandon your own daughter. What kind of shit is that?" I had never cursed at my father but our relationship had changed. Shit, we didn't have a relationship.

"Forgive me, Shar, please forgive me."

"Why?"

"I'm sick...got pancreatic cancer. There's nothin' the doctors can do."

"And here, all along, I thought you were a man of faith. Where's your faith, Daddy? All the sermons you preached in the pulpit about God being a lawyer in the courtroom and a doctor in the ER."

"I don't want to die with you hatin' me."

"It doesn't matter...you've been dead to me for years." I left my father sitting at the table just as he, my mother and Slay had left me—alone.

* * *

Aleesha and I cleaned our cell in anger. Our shit was scattered everywhere, from prison guards conducting a search looking for any items that they considered to be contraband. It reminded us both of how the police had trashed the mansion. The prison guards had done the same to our cell in one of the prison's surprise cell shake downs. *They on that bullshit.* I picked up all of my books from off the floor. One of them had landed in the toilet. *Motherfuckers.* It was soaked in piss water. The toilet barely flushed properly. I closed my eyes and reached in to fetch it out. They had also yanked the sheets off of our mattresses and thrown them and the mattresses themselves in the middle of the floor. And they had ripped the notebook papers that we had taped to our cell walls with Bible scriptures written on them. *They don't even give a fuck about the Lord.* I picked up my toothbrush. It was covered in dust and lint. *Fuck!* They had even opened up never-before-opened bags of Roman Noodles and emptied them on the floor.

"They some dirty ass motherfuckers," Aleesha said.

"What the fuck…they think we opened up a bag of noodles…hid some shit in there and then glued that shit back together. What kind of shit is that?"

Down the corridor, we heard scuffling and an inmate cursing the guards out. "Fuck y'all motherfuckers…don't got no got damn respect for a broad's shit. Fuck y'all." We heard her spit.

"Bitch," we heard the guard say. "You fuckin' spit in my face."

"Yeah, I did it. Now, what." We heard her scream that her eyes were burning and suspected that the guard had maced her.

"Tomorrow…you go in there and tell that motherfuckin' parole board what the fuck they want to hear," Aleesha said. "Say what the fuck you need to say to get the fuck up outta here."

After almost serving three years of my sentence, I was up for parole.

* * *

A single chair had been placed directly in front of the parole board. The prison guard led me to it. He left me handcuffed and shackled at the ankles. I wasn't a violent offender but it was customary for all inmates who appeared before the parole board to be constrained at the hands and feet. In the past, an inmate had viciously attacked a parole board member, slashing her throat with a handmade knife with a blade made out of plastic from straws. It was reason enough for the constraints and even the cell checks, but it was the way in which shit was done. The inmates didn't respect the prison guards because the prison guards didn't show any respect towards the inmates. *Shiesty Asses.*

"Ms. Reid," a Black lady that reminded me of Congresswoman Maxine Waters started the hearing. She adjusted her glasses on top of her shiny nose. "Do you acknowledge that you committed a crime when you failed to report that your boyfriend was involved in illegal activity?"

Bitch, you have my file in your hands. You know I plead guilty. I bit my tongue. "Yes, Mam, I acknowledge that."

"You acknowledge what?"

This bitch right here gonna make me... "I acknowledge that I committed a crime by failin' to report that my boyfriend was a drug dealer."

"Good enough," she said.

"Ms. Reid, do you regret not reporting to the authorities that your boyfriend was a major druglord?" Another board member asked. It sounded like the same damn question I had just been asked, just rephrased.

"Yes, Sir, I do."

"Who do you blame for your circumstances?" The third board member posed his question to me. It was the hardest for me to answer. I had been blaming everyone but myself—my parents and Slay mainly—for the choices I had made.

"Sir, I blame no one for my circumstances but myself. I was raised to know right from wrong, but I was blinded by the love that I had for my boyfriend."

"Ms. Reid," the Maxine Waters look-a-like said. "Do you believe in forgiveness?" She removed her glasses and leaned her head forward, waiting intently for my response.

"Mam, I spent most of my entire life in church, listening to my father preach about such topics as forgiveness, faith, hope and love. I know that I'm only twenty-two, but I have been through some things in my life that I believe gives me the right to be bitter and angry. But, since I have been here…in prison…I learned that before I could move on with my life I had to first forgive those people who I believed had betrayed, abandoned and turned their backs on me. So, yes, I believe in forgiveness."

The board members consulted with each other and then rendered their decision. "Ms. Reid, congratulations…you have been granted parole."

"Thank you."

The prison guard led me outside to the yard where the rest of the inmates on my block were congregated. I spotted Aleesha sitting at a picnic table.

"How'd it go?"

"Parole granted!"

We hugged and jumped up and down. Aleesha, once my archnemesis, wasn't just my cellmate. She had become my bestfriend, my sister and my mother. *Ain't that some shit?*

"Here this bitch come." Aleesha rolled her eyes and smacked her lips.

We watched as a broad named Cynthia made her way over to where we were. She and Aleesha had gotten into a knock-down-drag-out fight earlier in the month that had added an extra year to both of their sentences—all over a Honey Bun.

"Don't bring no shit, won't be no shit," Aleesha said.

"I know, bitch."

Before I had realized what happened, Aleesha folded over, holding her side. She collapsed to the ground.

"No…no!" I screamed, holding her in my arms. Flashbacks of the day TaNaysha died flashed in my head. I applied as much pressure to the wound as I could. Blood started draining from the corner of Aleesha's mouth.

"The…the…"

"Don't talk...don't talk...save your energy. Help!" I screamed. "Some fuckin' body help!"

"The money...buried..."

"Ssshhhh..."

"Back...yard...man...man..mansion."

"Huh?"

"You...can have...the money."

"No...you gonna need all that money when you get out of this motherfucker. Just hold on, okay. Hold on."

Aleesha closed her eyes and took her last breath.

* * *

"Thanks...Cheez." I hung up the pay phone.

It's funny how the people we thought we hated ended up turning into the best friends we never had and the people we thought we loved ended up becoming our biggest enemies. The entire time I was locked up, Cheez made sure that my books stayed stacked. Even in prison, I didn't want for anything. Then again, I didn't need much—just to know that a nigga cared. There was no love connection or no shit like that between Cheez and me. It was all business. I actually hooked him up with Niecy. She not only liked the nursing-home types but also the overweight lovers.

I hadn't seen or heard from Slay since our abrupt split, but I knew exactly where he was—in New York, where the cashier's check had been cashed. According to the connections Cheez had in the city, Slay was trying to make a name for himself as a hardcore, rap producer. *The tape of him and Bop would surely do his reputation good,* I thought and smiled wickedly. I had some unfinished business to take care of. But first, I wanted to have a little fun. I had forgiven him for all the shit he had put me through, but I hadn't forgot.

I walked out of the Topeka Correctional Facility with a black trash bag—filled with my belongings—flung over my shoulder. I had several stops to make: the bank to cop the tape, the mansion to cop the half-a-million dollars buried in the backyard and then to Ms. Trina's house to cop the .40 I had stashed in her bathroom vent. There were two bullets left in the chamber with Ernie Pain and Slay's names written on them. And this time, I wouldn't miss my intended targets.

The End